HARROW ROAD

A Novel

By Margie Taylor

Mediscript may be contacted at mediscript30@yahoo.ca

www.mediscript.net

ISBN # 978-1-896616-15-5

First Edition

Printed in Canada

The author gratefully acknowledges the support of the Canada Council for the Arts, the Ontario Arts Council, and the BC Arts Council in writing and researching *Harrow Road*.

As always, for Ken

TAYLOR-MORGAN GENEALOGY

Joshua Taylor m. Elizabeth (Betsy) Huxtable   Edward Morgan m. Anne Maria Davies
(1827-1915)   (1828-1899)   (1821-1874)   (1821-1900)

Mary Taylor   James Taylor   William Huxtable Taylor   m.   Annie Elizabeth Morgan   Edward Morgan   Maude Morgan   Arthur Morgan
(1847-1896)   (1854-1898)   (1849-1926)   (1851-1937)   (1849-1862)   (1853-1941)   (1855-1904)

Victoria Mary Taylor   Annie Edith Taylor   William Huxtable Taylor   Edward Morgan Taylor
(1872-1968)   (1874-1930)   (1876-1879)   (1879-1972)

"And the Union workhouses?" demanded Scrooge. "Are they still in operation?"

Part One: Admission

1.

The child couldn't be buried while the ground was frozen.

It was bitterly cold – the papers said it was the coldest November since they started keeping records – and it followed on the heels of a wet dismal summer when the sun never shone. Fruit refused to ripen, potatoes rotted in the ground. What vegetables made it to market were weak and tasteless, priced out of reach for all but the rich. Day after day the wretched gloomy skies endured, banishing the song-birds and dragonflies to other, more congenial, parts of the earth.

The yellow fog settled over the city, crept through the cracks in the doors and window frames, wormed itself into their very bones and blood. They kept their coats on indoors, stopped the crack under the door with bits of rag, pasted sheets of newsprint over the windows which darkened the rooms and did nothing to keep out the biting cold. In the end they tore them down.

They said the French and Dutch were having the worst of it. People were dying of the cold in those countries but it was wretched in England, too. The River Exe was covered in ice and parts of the Thames were frozen.

And Bill out of work for almost three months, unable to find a single print shop or weekly paper in want of a journeyman printer. Too many men out of work, too many shops closing down.

Comes home after a day spent tramping the pavements in the cold and refuses the meager supper she'd kept warm in the kettle.

"Give it to the children – I had something at the pub."

But he didn't.

"You have to eat. You can't go looking for work on an empty stomach."

By November he's pale and haggard in the face – has lost a stone in weight. Lies about it: "Mind over matter is what. I feel better now than I ever did. My head is clear. I can think."

Her own clothes hang on her; she sleeps in them to keep warm. Also to avoid seeing the way her body is changing for lack of food. Whatever they have goes to the children – to the boy, of course, he gets the lion's share, but the girls, too – can't let them starve.

And so she joins the midnight line-up outside the butcher's shop, waiting in the cold for a free soup bone. Humiliating – women she never thought to have to speak to, now she's one of them. Tightens her cloak around her, tries to keep apart but it's useless – she needs that meat bone as much as any of them and they know it.

***

The doctor is all sympathy and kindness at first.

Can you afford to pay for the funeral?

Yes, we have burial insurance for the boy. We bought it in May.

Really? Just a few months ago? And now your child is dead.

He won't sign the certificate.

Bill says it's because of the stories that have come out, people killing their children for the insurance money.

This will have to go to inquest.

Gives them a piece of paper, tells them to get down

to the Coroner's Court on the South Wharf Road on Saturday morning. And aren't they treated like criminals when they get there:

When did you first notice your son was unwell? Did you not think to take him to St. Mary's? Have all your children been insured or only the boy?

Bill does all the talking: We thought it was from falling in the canal, thought he'd caught a chill. Didn't think he was as sick as he was until it was too late. No, we didn't insure all the children. We might have done, but we couldn't afford it.

In the end the jury confirms what they already know: scarlet fever. Death from natural causes. He has not been smothered, strangled, poisoned or drowned. The doctor signs the certificate and they're given back the body of their son. But no apology. No one says sorry for your troubles. Sorry for the death of your boy.

***

It was a proper funeral with nothing spared. The men in mourning suits, the women in borrowed black from head to toe – crape gowns, long black veils, black gloves, handkerchiefs edged in black. The girls too must have their dresses suitably dyed; owning only one dress apiece means they'll be dressed in black long after the obligatory year. But it must be done properly for this their oldest boy.

What does it cost to bury a three-year-old? Hearse, with one horse; mourning coach, with one horse; stout elm coffin, covered with fine black, plate of inscription, lid ornaments, three pairs of handles, mattress, pillow, a pair of side sheets; use of velvet pall, mourners' fittings, coachmen with hat-bands and gloves; bearers; attendant with silk hat-band. Total cost: £5.

Bill says they'll need to give the pallbearers extra gin to make up for standing out in the cold.

Don't, she says. It'll go to their heads, make them rowdy.

He doesn't listen and gives it them anyway but thankfully they don't make a scene.

And God shall wipe away all tears from their eyes; and there shall be no more death, neither sorrow, nor crying, neither shall there be any more pain: for the former things are passed away.

They stand on opposite sides of the coffin, hats and bonnets sodden and flat, coat-tails and overskirts whipping in the wind. She thinks she might faint; her mother, guessing, puts out a protective arm to steady her. Bill keeps apart, taking no comfort in any of this. There is no Heaven for him, no hope of reunion in the hereafter. She can't bear the thought. Frightening to think of there being nothing when you die. Just closing your eyes and letting go into – what? Nothing.

In my Father's house are many mansions: if it were not so, I would have told you. I go to prepare a place for you. And if I go and prepare a place for you, I will come again, and receive you unto myself; that where I am, there ye may be also.

When the vicar's done they lift the box and place it with the others in the stone vault, waiting for the spring. Waiting for the ground to thaw so they can bury the dead. Don't! She wants to say they mustn't go, mustn't leave the child – *her* child – alone in this place, away from his mother. He'll be afraid – he's never liked the dark.

Bill and the other men head to the pub. The women from the neighbourhood gather in the parlour, sharing bits of food and gossip. Unable to eat, she paces from room to room, picking up bits of William and setting them down again: a tinplate soldier preparing to shoot, three clay marbles in a jam jar. The wooden sword his father carved. A football made of rags.

Her mother makes tea with laudanum. Drink this, she says, all of it. It will do you good.

It tastes bitter in spite of the sugar.

"His toys, Mama. Won't he need them? He should have them with him."

"Go to sleep, now. It'll be better in the morning, you'll see."

Her eyes close but she can't stop seeing – William laid out in his little wooden box, lost in that terrible sleep.

***

Early morning, still dark. He stands in the middle of the room, holding his printer's stick, his case on the floor beside him. He hasn't changed from the day before but he has shaved.

"I'm leaving now. For good. I won't be back."

"You can't."

"I said good-bye to the girls last night. They'll be all right. You will too."

"You have a family – you have a wife and children – "

"My son's dead and I'm leaving."

She wants to say he has another son. She wants to remind him there's another boy, not six months old, who needs his father.

"Where are you going? You can't just leave. Come to bed, Bill. Talk to me."

"I'm done talking. We have nothing to say to each other."

"She's a fool." She throws the words out from her corner of the room, not caring if the girls, asleep just inches away, hear or not. Not caring if she wakes the baby. "She's a fool and you're a coward. You deserve each other."

He says nothing, picks up his case and leaves, shutting the door softly behind him. Somebody calls out to him, but she doesn't hear him reply.

***

Two days later: Brydges stands in the doorway, cap in hand, not wanting to look her in the eye.

"He's gone, Annie. He shipped out this morning on a steamer to Cape Town. I thought I should let you know."

Emigrated. He did what he said he would – Bill always did what he said he would. He left as easy as if he never had a wife or children, never owned a single reason to stay.

The money. He would have needed papers, money for his passage and the woman she believes he took with him.

Brydges says it was the union that gave Bill the money – the London Society of Compositors. Emigration relief, they call it, glad to be rid of men who aren't working. Let it be another country's problem.

It takes a moment for it to settle, what Brydges is saying. He *planned* this – he would have made application weeks – maybe months – ago. It wasn't because of William, it wasn't because their son died. While she was standing in line at the butcher's … while she was haggling with the rag-and-bone man for a decent price for their bedding … all the while he was planning his escape.

Was he alone – was *she* with him? Would he have had the cheek to bring his mistress to the house of his friend? They share everything, he and Brydges – always have. If Bill has run off with that girl from the bindery, Brydges would know. She's aching to ask but her pride prevents her.

Brydges fumbles in his coat pocket, pulls out two ten bob notes and gives them to her. "I wish it was more, Annie, I really do."

It's generous – times are hard in the newspaper trade. She thanks him, asks if he'll stay for supper. But he says he must be off, Clara's expecting him home. In reality, he's being kind. He's not about to eat what little she has.

She sits at the table nursing the baby and tries to work out how far she can stretch a pound. If she avoids the landlord and doesn't pay the greengrocer she can give the butcher 8*s* on account and have enough left to keep food on the table for a month. Or she can pay the coal dealer and keep them warm but starving.

Food or firewood. Shoes or shelter. The poor man's choice. Which of course is no choice at all.

2.

Her hair has always been her vanity. When she was a girl complete strangers used to compliment her on it – well, compliment her mother, which was the same thing. It was lighter then and had more red in it. She wore it in ringlets down to her waist and it was natural, Mama never had to put it in rags to get the curl. She still remembers the disappointment she felt when she went into service and had to start wearing it up.

Bill used to come to her at night as she brushed it out, taking it in his hands, holding it up to the lamp to catch the light. He called her Ophelia. *Leave it down, Ophelia.* His way of saying he wanted her.

You're not supposed to like it, are you, if you're a decent sort of woman? The ones on the street – strumpets … whores … whatever you call them – they can take pleasure in it but if you're a good woman and you choose marriage and family and all that goes with it – well, you can't say you like that part of it. You're supposed to "get through it". Close your eyes and get through it. Is she the only one? How would she know? You can't ask anyone. You can't bring it up and you can't talk about it and so you'll never know.

The advertisement read, "HAIR – If you want to Buy or Sell HUMAN HAIR try 46, Praed Street (over Tobacconist's)."

This is it, then – number 46. She stands in front of the shop window, hesitating. Wedged between a tailor and a fruiterer and set back from the pavement, Number 46 might be overlooked altogether were it not for a sandwich board urging passers-by to "Come in for the Best Smoke in London".

A side door leads up a flight of stairs to the first floor landing. Two doors to choose from: one is boarded up, the other displays a hand-written notice. "Bernstein & Meir, Practical Wig Making & Ladies' Hair Dressing. Please Knock."

She knocks. In a moment the door opens to reveal a middle-aged gentleman, stout rather than fat, sporting a moustache in the style of the Emperor Franz Joseph. She must have caught him in the middle of dinner – one hand clutches a half-eaten roll while the other fumbles in his coat pocket for a handkerchief.

"Yes, can I help you?"

"Do you buy hair?"

"Well, that all depends. Are you selling?"

"Yes."

"Come in and stand by the window. And please remove your bonnet."

Free of hat, hairnet and pins, she feels like a girl again as he lifts a lock of her hair, tests the weight, the texture, presses it between his thumb and forefinger. So odd to have a stranger touch her like this but he must do it every day – it means nothing to him. He holds it up to the light to get a better look.

"Will you buy it?"

"Is in good condition, but is not the fashionable colour. They all want yellow these days. But brown is good, too, when it has red in it, like yours. Yes, I will buy."

Now that she's here, now that she's set herself to do this thing, she's determined to get a good price. "What will you give me for it?"

"Ten shillings."

It isn't enough. She needs at least a pound. "Can't you give more than that?"

He shrugs. "I am in business – ten shillings a head is what I am paying. Sometimes if the quality is good I pay more."

He picks up a large fine-toothed comb from a tray near the window. "Let me look again."

She stands still, head bent, while he combs through her hair. Searching for nits, most likely. Well, he won't find any. Not on *this* head, thank you very much.

"Is better than it looks – very clean and strong. You brush every night, yes? I can tell. Twenty shillings and you aren't getting better than that anywhere in London."

"I'll take it."

Taking a piece of coloured twine from a nearby drawer, he gathers her hair with one hand, twists it into a loose braid, then ties it at the nape of her neck. The cold metal of his scissors presses against her skin. She wants to put up her hand to stop him: I've changed my mind – don't cut. Too late … the blades open and shut. Twice.

"Done."

He stands there holding what used to be her hair. It looks like a horse's tail but worse – like something that used to be alive. She shouldn't have done it … it was a mistake.

He smiles. So often this happens. They all feel sorry afterwards, no matter how much they need the money. The ones who need it most feel the worst.

"Is only hair, yes? It will grow back."

She has an urgent desire to be gone. She takes the money, puts on her hat and hurries out of the shop, down the stairs, into the street. Feeling faint, she leans against the wall of the fruit shop for support. For a moment she thinks she'll fall – her hands are trembling and her legs won't support her. Tentatively, she reaches under her bonnet and touches the soft, naked skin at the back of her neck.

It's only hair. It will grow back.

3.

The letter from the Board of Guardians arrives on a Friday in the middle of a blizzard: "Application for Out Relief denied." She leaves the baby with the girls and makes her way from the house on Park Road to her mother's flat. Reluctantly, over a cup of tea, warming herself by the kitchen stove, she reveals the awful truth: she and the children have been ordered into the Paddington Union workhouse on Harrow Road. She has three weeks to get her things in order.

Not that she has anything – not anymore. Everything she treasured has been sold. Or pawned. Or traded for food. A small work-table lined with silk. A fireplace screen with a painting of Warwick Castle under a full moon. A pair of Japanese fans that once decorated the mantelpiece. An imitation Turkish rug that covered the warped floor boards in the parlour. A pair of muslin curtains her mother made to hide the view of the street.

Oh, and the blue-and-white porcelain bowl she found in a shop in Westbourne Grove. She filled it with artificial flowers and set it in the fireplace, the way they show in the illustrated papers. Bill called it a bourgeois affectation; when Edith came down with the whooping cough he pawned it to pay the chemist. Even the curtains were eventually taken down and sold to the ragman. They put up roller blinds instead – Bill said they were more effective and they were. But they were ugly.

Her mother is shocked, which Annie knew she would be. She's refused to believe things were as bad as they were. Even after Bill left and Annie sold her hair, nothing could make her mother believe her daughter – *her* daughter, a respectable printer's wife – could sink so low.

"You can't! You cannot bring my grandchildren into that place. I won't allow it." She slaps her hand on the table for emphasis: "I won't allow it, Annie, do you hear me? Are you listening?"

"And what do you suggest? Are you offering to take us in – me and the baby and the girls? Are we to move in with you and Arthur?"

"I've had the girls to spend the night. We can fit another

12

mattress on the floor."

"And food? And clothes to wear? Victoria's supposed to be in school but I don't have the miserable penny a week to send her. She needs shoes, and stockings – she hasn't had new boots in almost two years. Are *you* going to buy them for her?"

"Your brother will give you what he can."

Again not to be taken seriously. Her brother, the Commercial Traveler. Spending his weeks in and out of wayside inns and music halls, dressed like the gentleman he strives to be, charming the local barmaids, treating his clients to whisky and porter ("Part of the job, Ma, you've got to keep the clients happy"). Back to the hotel to gossip with his comrades about the shopkeepers: who's "safe", meaning credit-worthy, and who's not … whose business is flourishing and who's about to be revealed as a bankrupt in *The Commercial Service Gazette*. A knight of the road, that's how he sees himself, free from the ties of office or factory, with a wealth of experience of the "outside" world that gives him the right to comment unceasingly on any and every topic under the sun.

The girls love him though. He comes home with funny stories about life on the road – cleaned up of course for their delicate ears. She could just about bear him for the sake of the girls if only he weren't so damnably, incessantly cheerful.

"I don't suppose …"

"If you're about to tell me to go to his parents you can forget it. They wouldn't lift a finger to help me when we were together and they're certainly not going to do it now."

"Even to feed their own grandchildren?"

"Betsy Taylor carries a grudge like it has handles. You know that as well as I. She never even came to the funeral."

"Then you must find a wet nurse and go out to work. You worked before you were married – you were good at your job. Mrs. Bellwether always liked you. And her husband, remember? He gave you that book for Christmas."

Annie says nothing. She'd rather not remember the Bellwethers, thank you very much.

"It was a good position. You never should have left – I said that at the time, didn't I? Of course, you'll have to wait till your hair grows out. Nobody's going to hire you looking like that."

"Nobody's going to hire me anyway. I'm a married woman with three children and I haven't worked in eight years. I can*not* go back into service. And it's all I'm fit for."

Thanks to you, she wants to add. But she doesn't. There's no point … it was too long ago.

"You've none to blame but yourself. That tongue of yours is what's done it. Everyone who might have helped –"

"Oh please, spare me your lectures! Do you think it helps to be told my troubles are my own fault? You've been telling me that since I was 16 – I don't need to hear it now."

"Perhaps it was meant to be. Perhaps it's part of God's plan."

"Really? You think God planned all this? Planned for Bill to leave me and the children to starve?"

"You must have faith, child. *Trust in the Lord with all your heart, and lean not on your own understanding.*"

"And He'll pay the bloody coal dealer will he? Very well. I'll just drop Mr. Halliday a note and say charge our account to God."

"Hush, girl. I won't have *language* under my roof." She lifts her spectacles and studies the wall calendar. "When did you say it was?"

"Three weeks."

"But that's Christmas!"

"The day after. The 26th is what it says in the letter."

"Thank God your father didn't live to see this. And your hair – he would have hated that."

Pansy, he called her, because he said she had a face like a flower. Thinking of him now … his unfailing kindness, his faith in her ability to do what was needed in any given situation …

Her mother slumps in her chair. She's spent, like a houseplant left too long in the sun. And now she's to be shamed in front of her neighbours. The widow next door will tell her daughter the barmaid and *she'll* tell the publican's wife and by tomorrow the whole street will know: Proud Mrs. Morgan in Number 64, that's her daughter's been left by her husband, that's her oldest girl off to the Union.

There are old men and women who, if given the choice, would prefer to die from starvation and the cold rather than go to "the house". When she was seven a woman two streets over tried to kill herself when the order came from the Board of Guardians. Threw herself off the roof, landing spread-eagled in the back courtyard next to the water pump. She survived but in the end it was all for nothing: they took the children into the workhouse and she followed, once she left the hospital.

It's getting late. The baby will need to be fed.

"I won't be able to visit you. You know that don't you? I can't manage it, not with my bad knees."

"It's all right, Mama. I wouldn't expect it."

Slowly, counting the steps as she descends, she feels her way down the narrow flight of stairs leading to the street. It's disgraceful, really, the state of this stairway. Her brother is always threatening to write to the parish about the missing and broken steps, no light of any kind, or handrail to prevent you from falling. A man could fall and break his neck.

Out on the street the snow has stopped falling, the lamps are being lit. An omnibus displaying an advertisement for Goodall's Yorkshire Relish skids to the side and narrowly misses colliding with a hackney cab; an old horse pulling a milk float clomps by, weary after a day of making its rounds. Papa was a dairyman … he had a horse just like that. Dear old Bluebell who knew the rounds so well she could have done them on her own. Whatever happened to her? Was she sold when Papa died? Why doesn't she know that – she *should* know. Mama should have told her. She pauses to unfurl her umbrella, steeling herself for the walk back home.

A familiar figure steps down from the ominibus and lifts his hat in greeting.

"Hullo, Annie, been to see our Mam have you? Where are the kiddies?"

There are but three years between her and her brother and yet he looks younger by a decade – single, tolerably well-dressed, with nothing more urgent on his mind than a bowl of Mama's lamb stew. At that moment she hates him for all that freedom.

She pushes by without speaking and hears him respond

cheerfully to her back:

"Never mind then love, in a hurry are we? Cheerio darlin', lovely to see you again!"

4.

She was born in 1851, the summer of the Great Exhibition. Her parents went on One Shilling Day taking her older brother, Ted, who was just a toddler at the time, leaving four-week-old Annie in the care of a neighbor.

Along with thousands of others they joined the queues in the galleries to view the wonders of the modern world: the public conveniences you could use for a penny, the expanding hearse, the printing machine that could produce 5000 copies of the Illustrated News in an hour! Not to mention the 27-foot-tall Crystal Fountain. The stuffed elephant in the Indian section was so life-like Mama stood well back, shading her son's eyes from the beast.

The Koh-i-Noor diamond however was a disappointment; it had arrived from India with a curse on it but when her father saw it he was not impressed.

"All that fuss for a lump of old glass. I've seen milk bottles that shine better than that. Makes you wonder what the world has come to."

As a souvenir of that marvelous event Mama kept a framed poster depicting the Crystal Palace. There were great feathery plants with huge leaves and flowers that looked like no kind that ever grew in London. You could live in those flowers, Annie thought: curl up and hide in their soft petals like a fairy. It quite broke her heart that she had missed all of this simply by being born too late.

***

Her father was a forelock-tugger, devoted to Queen and country, touching his hat to any gentleman that crossed his path. While others strove to better themselves, Edward Morgan was content to make his rounds delivering milk, butter and cheese to his neighbours. He was gentle-spirited, kind-hearted, and had less ambition than a slug. But he was never out of work. People would always need milk. Sometimes it was all they could afford – milk and toast for breakfast, dinner, and supper with the odd potato thrown in for good measure.

As the wife of a dairyman, Annie's mother milked cows, churned cream into butter, and made the excess milk into hard Caerphilly cheese. That was her daytime work; in the evenings she was a seamstress. Although she'd say that was a fancy word for what she did: she sewed collars and cuffs for a shirt-maker on Church Street. It was piece-work and it paid very little. The hours were long – eight hours of steady sewing to earn sixpence. At first she sewed by hand but they made her switch to a machine and she hated it. It hurt her eyes – she had to be watching every single stitch as the slightest flick of a finger could make it all go wrong and she'd have to rip it out and start over again. After a while the constant vibration gave her the trembles. In the end she went back to hand-work; it paid less but was easier on the nerves.

Annie adored her father but she was her mother's daughter in every way that mattered. Unlike her older brother who was shy and soft-spoken like Papa, she had her mother's steely spirit. When the butcher short-changed her on a cut of meat or the greengrocer tried to fob off old potatoes to her, Maria Morgan stared them down like the Welsh aristocrat she believed herself to be till they stammered and blushed and apologized, offering a nice bit of lamb or fresh spring carrots in exchange, blaming the "mix-up" on the new girl in the shop who was useless really.

Her mother was born on a farm in Cardiganshire near a village with a name Annie could never quite pronounce: Llanbadarn-Fawr. From the stories Mama told, Annie believed Wales to be a country of saints and poets and brave warriors who fought the English. The fact that they ultimately lost didn't make them any less heroic. Her mother claimed kin with Llywelyn the Great, the King of Wales, and his daughter, Gwladus the Dark. She had been to see the empty stone coffin in the parish church of Llanrwst which once held the King's body. Once when she was a youg girl, before she came to England, she climbed to the top of the old square tower on the banks of the River Rheidol where Owain Glyndwr held court after defeating the English. She shut her eyes and in the distance she could hear the sound of the battles fought long ago in the Rising.

"Battles, Mama? Like ghosts? Miss Purdy says there's no such thing."

Miss Purdy was in charge of the Sunday school – she was very firm on the subject of ghosts.

"Miss Purdy is English," Mama sniffed. "The Welsh are more respectful of ghosts. All the old families have a spirit or two haunting their bed chambers. And proud of it they are as well."

It occurred to Annie that if Wales was as wonderful as Mama described it, why did she leave? When asked, though, her mother was tight-lipped.

"Ask no questions and you'll hear no lies."

***

They lived in the parish of St. Marylebone in a small terraced house off the old Portman Market. Their neighbours were cab men, paper hangers, fruit vendors, carpenters, shoemakers, plumbers, nursemaids. There was little sense of stability or security … families moved frequently, harried by rising housing costs, pushed west and north by the railway, by new roads, by a multitude of gentrification projects that involved pulling down the cheap old buildings and putting up newer ones no one could afford.

Bounded on the north by Regent's Canal and the Stone Yard and on the south by Paddington Basin, Marylebone was noisy, congested, and dirty. And dark – the gas lamps that brightened the streets of the West End were nonexistent in these parts. The narrow courts and alleys smelled of fried fish and cabbage-stalk, trademark aromas of the back slums.

The old parish workhouse marked the eastern boundary, spreading itself over an entire city block like a giant barnacle. It was familiar and terrifying, a kind of medieval keep, and was known by various names: the Union, the Spike, the Bastille. Many of the families who fled the famine in Ireland ended up in there. Often it was merely a matter of hours between disembarking at the London docks and knocking on the door of the spike as if an invisible cord led from the blighted Irish countryside to the wretched shelter on offer at the workhouse.

It was generally thought that the Irish didn't mind – they were used to living in poverty and at least the Union fed them.

Maggie Boyle had lived in the workhouse – practically born there, she said. The Boyles lived next door but one, above the Devil's Arms. There were five of them in two small rooms and they took in lodgers as needed. At various times they had staying with them a needlewoman, a laundress, a railway porter, and an omnibus conductor, none of whom stayed very long.

Mr. Boyle worked infrequently as a "flying dustman", trundling from door to door with his horse and cart, shovel and baskets, wheedling tips from those who could afford it and sometimes those who could not. Collecting dust was thirsty work, after all; the ashes and cinders caught in his throat and required impressive amounts of beer to quench the dryness. If the householder refused the tip, or gave less than expected, Mr. Boyle would be sure to track mud on the carpet or smear the wallpaper with slime the next time he came to collect. On very wet days, he chose to stay home and attend to his pigeons, or joined his colleagues at the local tap-room, returning home in the small hours drunk and looking for a fight.

Mrs. Boyle was the mainstay of the household: she cleaned houses, took in washing, and made hat boxes in her spare time. While she worked, Maggie took care of the children. She was never in school – needed at home, her mother told the truant officer when he came knocking. Did you ever go to school? Annie wanted to know. Once, when we was in the workhouse in Belfast, she said. Before we come to England.

Maggie was six at the height of the famine; Irish workhouses were bursting at the seams and the government offered free passage to England or the colonies. Her vote was for Australia where her two older sisters had gone to work as maids but she was too young to count. England won out in the end. Some of the family had resettled in Liverpool and it was thought they'd be willing to take in the new emigrants and offer them shelter till they got on their feet. According to Maggie the offer was rescinded after only a week.

"It was Pa's drinking – he drank 'cause he had no work and Auntie said he had no work 'cause he drank. So they kicked us out and Pa said we should come to London but we didn't know nobody here and Pa drunk up all the emigration money so we went to live in the Union. And the Union was better than back home in Ireland and not so crowded."

The stories she told about what went on there – like the time the workhouse staff got in trouble for beating several young pauper girls so badly one of them almost died.

"They beat those girls bad," Maggie said, "with whips and sticks. The master too, he done it, we all knows he done it. I saw the blood. They showed us the marks on their backs and their arms, like. It was terrible bad, Annie. My Pa said he wouldn't whip a dog like they done them girls."

Maggie's parents were Orangemen which meant they hated the Pope. If you believed their stories – and Annie half did, in spite of herself – the clerics of the Roman faith were demons of perversion, always ready to pounce on unwary children and perform unspeakable rites upon them. The details of those rites were vague but no less horrible for their lack of clarity. Maggie was particularly well-informed on nuns, whom she feared as much as she hated.

"It's when they makes the sign of the cross," she said, switching baby Donal from her left hip to her right and grabbing John the Third before he fell into the street. (There'd been two other Johns before him, both dead before they reached their first birthday. Annie thought it unlucky naming this one John, too, but the Boyles appeared to favour the name. Or maybe they were simply lacking in imagination.) "When they crosses themself they're making a promise with the Divil. They're promising to catch you and give you up to him is what."

"If they caught *me* I wouldn't go."

"You'd *have* to. They'd take hold of you with their bony fingers and put poisoned wine in yer gob and make you swallow it. And when you fell asleep, that's when they'd take you to the Divil."

Annie had some familiarity with nuns: the Sisters of Mercy in Blandford Square took in young girls and trained them to work in service. They were generally regarded as pious and hardworking women with unblemished reputations. They didn't *seem* to be in league with the Devil. Still, Annie was intrigued. "Where do they keep the poison?"

"In the sleeves of their dresses. That's why they wear them big black smocks with the long sleeves, so they can hide the poison."

"Where do they get it from?"

"It's communion wine, right? They steal it from the church and take it outside, and once it's outside it turns to poison, right? And if you drink it you'll die."

Technically Maggie was contradicting herself on this point – she'd already claimed that the poisoned wine merely made you fall asleep. However, when Annie rather smugly pointed this out, Maggie gazed on her with the pity reserved for the gravely misinformed.

"Well, acourse it makes you fall asleep – and then you die, right? How else d'you think you gets to the Divil? You has to die before you goes to the Divil – everyone knows that."

Everyone except Annie, apparently. Her parents were Church of England but the finer points of the Christian faith were not discussed in her home. She and her siblings attended Sunday School and had been baptized in Christ Church Marylebone by the great Reverend Llewellyn Davies, so they were not heathens. Her mother made a point of attending church on the important religious holidays – Christmas, Good Friday, Easter Sunday, New Year's Day and St. David's Day – but it would have been considered strange and even indecent to talk about any of it outside the church. People who did were Holy Joes and thought to be wildly eccentric. Religion was for church and school, not for everyday life.

The family Bible was only opened to record births, baptisms, marriages and deaths. Annie leafed through it once, hoping for some pictures, and was rewarded immediately with a black and white engraving of a man and a woman in a garden looking at a snake. The snake was wrapped around a tree and the man and woman were naked. You knew that not so much from the picture itself, which had a lot of leaves and plants strategically placed, but from the caption underneath: *And the*

*eyes of them both were opened, and they knew that they were
naked.*

This was a promising start. She turned the pages
eagerly, hoping for more of the same, but there were no more
pictures. Only page after page of words that made no sense.
Who were the couple in the picture? Why were they naked?
Weren't they cold? She turned back to the frontispiece and
looked at it for a long time and in the end she worked it out:
Mama had a poster of the Crystal Palace pinned to the wall.
In large flowing letters it said, *Come and see the largest
greenhouse in the world.* There were great feathery plants
with huge leaves and flowers that looked like no kind that ever
grew in London. You could live in them, those flowers, curl
up and hide in their soft petals, like a fairy. To Annie, it was
obvious: the naked man and woman were in Hyde Park, in the
greenhouse.

As for the Devil, she knew there was little point in
asking her parents for their thoughts on the matter. Mama
would say it was stuff and nonsense, the kind of tomfoolery
created by ignorant, idle minds. Maggie, she said, was a poor,
uneducated immigrant. You don't want to be taking her word
for anything. Her father would say he didn't much hold with
religious doings but he knew the world ran best when people
kept themselves in their place. So there was really no point in
asking.

***

For a poor, uneducated immigrant Maggie knew a great deal
about a great many things. She had the kind of knowledge that
gave you the heebies at night and made it hard to fall asleep,
even with Mama in the room and two warm little bodies curled
next to you. Maggie knew about the gypsies who followed the
circus at Whitsun and would linger after the tents had folded
and come find you and snatch you from your bed while you
were sleeping and take you back to their caravans to be a tinker
and a thief. Or sell you to a coster and he'd make you sell
herring and whitefish from a barrow in the street.

"An' if the coster don't want you, he sells you to a

beggarman and he cuts your leg off and puts you in flitters so's you can go out an' beg."

The babies, though – it was the thought of the babies that haunted you as you ran past the forbidding walls of the Union, eager to get home before the gray soup of a London afternoon turned dark as the coal dust that made it. Maggie was particularly knowledgeable about babies. She'd had the care and feeding of five younger brothers and sisters, two of whom had actually lived. She knew of babies born dead like her little brother Christy and babies born with cauls covering their heads bringing good luck to the family. It was Maggie who told Annie about the baby farmers who would take your unwanted newborn and kill it for money. According to Maggie, the corridors of Marylebone Union were haunted by the ghosts of dead babies, born in the workhouse infirmary and smuggled away to be chloroformed or strangled.

Back then Annie was a literalist. "Why do they haunt the workhouse? If they took them away and killed them, shouldn't the babies haunt where they were killed?"

"To teach them a lesson. They haunts the Union 'cause it's the Union's fault they're dead."

When she tried to continue the argument Maggie knew how to shut her up.

"Was it you what lived there, Annie Morgan? Or was it me?"

Annie had to concede that it was Maggie, after all, who had lived there.

"All right then. And if it was me what lived there then it's me what knows what goes on there. Right?"

Right.

Was it easy to strangle a newborn? It seemed that if they weren't born dead babies developed a remarkably tenacious grip on life considering how puny and generally unwanted they often were. They might eventually give up after a few months of neglect but in the beginning they appeared to be determined that now they were in this world they planned to stay. It would take more than a simple flick of the wrist to strangle them – you'd really have to mean to do it.

She often thought how much easier life would have

been if some thoughtful midwife had strangled her siblings after delivering them. It wasn't that she hated them – she was mostly indifferent. It was the noise and mess they created and the work involved in lugging them around. Not that life would be any less noisy or messy without them: it just wouldn't be her responsibility. If Annie had any kind of a fantasy life as a child, it was in her heartfelt longing to be an only child.

Only children were rare. Most families in the area had five or more skinny, scrappy youngsters who survived, and another two or three who died in infancy. The younger ones were cared for by their older siblings; in Annie's case, she was in charge of her sister Maude and her brother, Arthur. From the time she was five she never went anywhere without one or both of them attached to her pinafore. And not just her own brother and sister; she developed a reputation for being good with babies so other mothers often left their little ones in her care.

By the time she was seven she'd become adept at calming a crying baby: a few drops of gin did the trick. Gin was cheap and plentiful and everyone kept some on hand, especially during the cholera years when it was safer to drink than water. Annie's parents kept a bottle of Booth's Gin for medicinal purposes on a shelf in the pantry, along with turpentine oil, Angostura Bitters, the Bible, and her mother's prized possession, *The Memoirs of Owen Glendower (Owain Glyndwr)* by the Rev. Thomas Thomas. This was significant for having belonged originally to her mother's brother who succumbed to dysentery when he was away at school. He was a scholar, Mama said, the only one in the family. He would have gone on to *be* someone had he not died of the flux.

Annie's first experiment with gin was not a success. She poured some into a spoon but in the end she wasted the lot – she couldn't get the baby to swallow it at all. It was Maggie who showed her the proper way.

"You've got to mix it with water, right? Otherwise the babby'll hate the taste and spit it up. If you've got a bit of sugar that works even better. Babbies'll take anything if you make it sweet. And don't use a spoon. Dip a bit of rag into it and let the babby suck on the rag. It'll work a treat."

The next time she followed Maggie's instructions

and the child closed its eyes and slept sweetly for a good two hours. There was one time, however, when she came close to poisoning one of her charges: being out of gin she used the turpentine oil. Thankfully, she was cautious and used half the usual amount and stopped the baby from sucking when he fell asleep. He slept for a very long time and just when Annie was beginning to worry that he might not wake up at all, he did. His mother commented that he was "terrible fretful" for the next day or so.

***

Four years older than Annie, Maggie got the curse early – when she was only thirteen – and showed her the red-brown stain it had made on her shift.

"It'll never come out," she said, and it was one more thing that Maggie knew and Annie didn't. "It cannot come out because it's the stain of a virgin, and it means I'm a woman now, not a babby like you. Any day now I'll be having a babby of my own."

"Will you give it up?" She was thinking of the baby farmers.

"I will not! And if they try to take it from me, I'll wrap it up in a cloak and hide it in the privy and when it's dark I'll sneak away to the docks and get on a boat to Australia. And by the time they find me they won't 'cause I'll be far away across the ocean and they'll never catch me – never!"

After that Annie checked regularly to see if Maggie was having the baby yet.

"Not yet, but soon."

After a while she got tired of asking but every now and then she glanced at her stomach to see if it had started to grow. She knew that much – you had to grow the baby in your stomach before you had it.

***

The winter of '61 her brother Ted came down with typhus and was taken to the Fever Hospital in Islington. There he was bled by leeches and given mercury mixed with chalk to clean out his bowels. After five days of treatment he was pronounced cured. Her father fetched him home in the milk float and he died the following day.

Her mother blamed his death, as she did everything, on the *Saeson*. The English had been responsible for every evil since King Edward I and what she couldn't blame on the English she laid on the backs of the Irish – dirty, ignorant people who couldn't help but spread their filth and contagion to respectable families. "I will not lose another child to this place," she said, and announced that they were moving.

"To Wales?"

Mama was always saying she wanted to be buried in Wales; wouldn't it be a good idea to go there now, while she was still alive?

But no, they were not moving to Wales. They were relocating to Notting Hill on the northern outskirts of Kensington. There were plans to expand the railway and houses were going up all over that part of London. Her father said where there were houses there were people needing milk. He found an opening for a dairyman and within a month they were ready to leave.

Maggie of course had something to say about this. "Notting Hill is where the Gypsies camp. On the Dale. Gypsies and pigs, that's what you got in that place. *I* wouldn't live there. Not if you paid me I wouldn't."

The morning of the move what little they owned was loaded onto the float; Annie and her parents would walk the distance leading Bluebell, while the cows, Daisy and Dill, brought up the rear. Maude and Arthur would ride, perched precariously amongst the milk cans and cooking pots and their few sticks of furniture. Each was assigned something to carry and as the oldest now that Ted was gone Annie had the honour of bearing the chamber pot. She felt important; several families had come out onto the street to say good-bye and there were tears and promises to keep in touch. Notting Hill was less than three miles from Princess Street but it felt much further.

It was beginning to rain and her mother was fretting that the feather bed would be soaked if it kept up. Maggie came out to see her off, the newest Boyle asleep in her arms.

"Are you goin' now, then?"

Annie nodded.

"Swear by the Divil you won't forget me!"

Annie swore and waved goodbye; the cart rolled down the street and turned west on Church Street. She heard her name being called and looked back to see Maggie running towards her, skirt hiked up around her knees.

"Annie! Wait!"

"What is it? I have to go."

"I'll name her after you! The *babby* – I'll call her Annie!"

5.

26th December, 1879: Boxing Day. When she was in service, this was the day the tradesmen came round to collect their tips. She and the cook would package up the Christmas Day leftovers and give them to the chimney sweep, the men who delivered the coal, the grocer's boy and the milk man. Papa got tips as well, even from the poorest customers. If they couldn't afford money, they gave a handful of eggs or a jar of pickled beets from the garden. Once a very poor but attractive woman gave him a kiss. Papa said it was the best present he got that year and Mama said she'd make her sorry if she ever did it again. But she was laughing when she said it.

There will be no tips for the tradesmen who come to *her* door – not this morning. The fire in the grate has gone out. Wrapping herself in a shawl against the cold, she gathers up their belongings while the children sleep. There's little enough; they're down to a single bowl between them … what clothes they own they're wearing.

Vic outgrew her old boots and ran around barefoot all summer. When it got too cold for that Bill came home with a pair of Balmorals courtesy of the Printers' Benevolent Fund; they were too big and missing some of their buttons. Bill said it didn't matter: "She'll catch fewer colds that way." Edith has been wearing Vic's old boots stuffed with newspaper and the baby is too young to need shoes at all.

Her own shoes are full of holes; she's taken to cutting out pieces of cardboard and fitting them inside to keep her feet dry. They're close to falling apart but they'll make the journey to the workhouse; after that they'll most likely give her something more serviceable.

Speaking of falling apart, if she didn't need to cover her head she wouldn't be caught dead in this old bonnet: a wedding present from Mama, dark green velvet with a high spoon brim. Quite fashionable at the time but her mother had used cheap velveteen and the pile was flat and worn in places, the ribbon faded and torn. Still, it hides the worst of what's left of her hair. It was a mistake to sell it. The money didn't keep them out of the workhouse, it only prolonged the inevitable. Standing in front of the looking-glass, she runs a tentative hand across the top of her head, feels the shock of bare skin at the back of her neck. *It's only hair. It will grow back.*

The parish church bell begins to ring. She wakes the girls, hurries them into their clothes, gathers up the baby and wraps him snugly in his blanket. When they're ready to leave she takes one final look around the place, looking for – nothing, there's nothing here for any of them anymore. She shuts the door quietly, and follows the girls down the back staircase, through the courtyard and out into the alley.

If any of the neighbours are up at this hour they'll know where she's headed. Everyone knows everyone's business in this place – there are no secrets. It will be no surprise to anyone, not even the landlord most likely, to find she's taken the children and left leaving no forwarding address, owing two months' rent. The word will spread quickly: by mid-morning half the street will know that Annie Taylor's done a flit.

***

The snow that fell on Christmas Eve layers the doorsteps and hedgerows in a creamy blanket that sparkles in the places where the gas lamps shine. The view from the top of the street is dramatically unfamiliar: roofs and chimney-pots, tree branches and lamp posts – everything is frosted in silver. Even the pavement is immaculate, not yet blackened by soot and churned into mud and slush by the cabs and carriages and all manner of pedestrians.

Infected with the novelty of it all – nobody else around and the snow so lovely and soft – the girls are in high spirits. In spite of her forebodings, Annie experiences a flicker of hope; it is, after all, a relief to be doing something. To have somewhere to go. An adventure, she says. Aren't we lucky?

"How long will we stay there?" Vic wants to know.

"Not long. A week or two."

"And then what?"

"And then I'll be working and we'll find somewhere nice to live – much nicer than where we were."

Edith is satisfied with this but Victoria as always wants

to know more. "Will you get a job?"

"Yes. I said I would, didn't I?"

"What will you do? You can't sew like Gran. Will you make flowers like Mrs. Griggs?"

"Oh, I think I can do better than that."

"What then? What will you do?"

"For the love of God, child, I don't know!"

"Then why did you say it? You shouldn't say it if you don't know."

Classic Vic. She has a way of getting under Annie's skin. Always prodding, pushing. She's like Bill that way – never satisfied with an easy answer.

Their route takes them south and west toward Lisson Grove, once a fashionable shopping centre. It might be again if the developers have their way. They're tearing down all the dirty old buildings and putting up new ones in their place, ploughing under the old footpaths. So many of the trees are gone: the tall elms that screened the shops and public houses, drawing landscape painters from all across London, they've all been felled. They rebuilt the old narrow bridge over the Great Western Railway – the new one is safer but not as romantic. Further north they're replacing the stone bridge over the canal with a modern one of iron. No doubt it will be ugly, too.

At Paddington Green they stop for a drink at the fountain. Vic's boots won't stay on properly ... they make her look like a "guy", she says. Annie's tempted to tell her that's the least of her worries. Instead she hands the baby to Edith and stoops to re-tie them.

"I'm hungry," Edith says. "Will they give us something to eat when we get there?"

"I don't know. Maybe."

Edith's lower lip juts forward in a pout. As a rule, "maybe" means "no".

There's a bit of bread and cheese in Annie's coat pocket – she was planning to wait till they got to the Union in case there's a line-up but they'll have it now. Picking a bench just inside the gate to St. Mary's Church, they brush away the snow and Annie divides the food between the girls, reserving a small piece of cheddar for herself.

While her daughters eat, she nurses the baby, shielding him from the cold with the fringe of her scarf. None of them have eaten since supper the night before: a boiled potato and the last of the sausages which she suspects were off – the butcher gave them to her half price and she couldn't complain as she owed him 17/6. There are some who won't be pleased they've left – the butcher, the landlord, the coal dealer. Her cheeks burn at the thought of it – being the talk of the neighbourhood, her failed marriage exposed.

Her neighbours were eager to let her know, once Bill was gone, that they weren't all that surprised that he left. There was the time he was seen just two streets over holding hands with a girl young enough to be his daughter – well, she looked it, anyway. Though there was nothing daughterly about the way she was leaning into him, practically cuddling him there in broad daylight.

"Why didn't you tell me?" Annie said. "It would have been nice to know."

Oh, they couldn't – well, it wasn't their business really, was it? They all thought she knew, the way he was carrying on. It wasn't as if he was keeping it a secret.

***

Revived after their little lunch, which Edith happily calls a picnic, they continue on their journey, past the housing developments that have displaced the farmland, the building sites where cows and horses once grazed. A parlour-maid appears in the doorway of a brand-new brownstone, preparing to sweep the snow from the front steps. In a moment of sympathy Annie catches her eye and smiles: How many mornings had she done that when she was in service? The girl sees only a poor woman who might be a gypsy and turns away. Feeling foolish, Annie urges the girls to hurry, in a sharper voice than she intends.

By the time they reach the wooden footbridge the morning sky has clouded over threatening flurries. Her arms ache from the weight of the child in her arms, her feet and cheeks are numb. She worries about the girls being so long in the cold – Edith, especially, who is the frailer of the two. She survived a bout of pleurisy when she was a toddler; when she developed whooping cough last spring the doctor warned that her lungs were most likely damaged. Don't let your daughter get a chill, he said – keep her out of the damp. What would he say now if he could see her out here with bare legs and no mittens?

Hurry, she says. Hurry hurry hurry.

They cross the bridge and now they can see it, the Paddington Union Workhouse, dominating Harrow Road like some medieval keep. She stops to adjust her hold on the baby, her insides churning with dread and anticipation. Until now she's been fixed on the task of getting here. Now that they're within sight of the place she wishes to God Almighty they weren't. Taking that step – walking up those stairs and under the stone archway, entering that great gray gloomy building – it's the final humiliation. Once inside there'll be no going back. For the rest of her life she'll be marked as a pauper.

Edith tugs at her coat. "Come on, Mama – I'm cold."

A small stone building fronts the pavement – the workhouse lodge, as forbidding in miniature as the great house itself. "Pull Cord for Attendant". An old man sticks his head through the window.

"Casual or permanent?"

She's not sure. Does he mean is she planning to stay here for good? Or just a night or two. He asks to see the letter, scans it briefly, then tells her she's permanent. And early.

"Any spiritous liquors on you?"

"No! Of course not."

"Go 'round the back and wait."

A long gravel path leads around the main entrance to the Reception Block at the back. Thirty or so are ahead of her already, waiting in line. Most of them are old. There's a scattering of very young children and a few women around her age, widowed or deserted most likely.

Doors won't open till noon, someone says. Make yourself comfortable. It is meant as a joke: There is nowhere to sit, nowhere to shelter from the wind. She gathers the girls next to her, one on either side, and they stand with their backs pressed against the stone wall, in the shadow of the eaves.

"Maybe the butler don't know we're here." This from the wag who told her to make herself comfortable. "Should we knock?"

"There's a thought," says another. "They're probably busy making our dinner and can't hear over the steaming of the pudding."

"Oh, aye, that'll be it. I've heard they lay on a right good tea – chalk bread and all the canal water you can drink."

Encouraged by the laughter this generates, the two continue in this vein until the joke, such as it is, has been well-milked. Annie laughs, too, not because their remarks are witty but because it's good on such a morning to be able to do so.

After a while it begins to snow, a few light flakes at first, then turning to sleet, the ice pellets bouncing off the flagstones, creating a hazard for new arrivals crossing the courtyard. One of these, a pretty young thing who might even be beautiful if she were better dressed and coiffed, minces delicately from stone to stone, her protruding belly threatening to throw her off balance with every step.

"Up the pole," Vic says, and Edith snickers.

"Hush," Annie says. Not that it matters. The girl, confident in her youth, takes no notice. She sashays through the passel of old men like a latter-day Helen of Troy, nodding and smiling her way to the front of the queue.

"Blind me," says one of them, "if that ain't the prettiest little gal I've seen in a month of Sundays."

"Looks ain't all," says his friend. "She's barmy, that one." And he taps the side of his head.

"No! You don't say."

"I do. Deaf and dumb to boot."

"She don't look it. How d'you know, anyway?"

"She's a flower-seller. I seen her in the streets – oh, many times. She's a regular up in Covent Garden. Comes up to you with her baskets of violets or whatsomever and taps you on the elbow and nods and points and holds out her hand, like she's trying to say, 'Buy my flowers, mister. Penny a bunch.' Does pretty well, I think, being so handsome and all. But make no mistake – she's deaf as a post and feeble-minded, too."

***

Midday. No more joking. Even the wags have relapsed into grim silence, waiting for the door to open. The workhouse bell tolls twelve and Edith begins to chant: "Ding dong bell, pussy's in the well. Who put her in? Little Tommy Flynn. Who's Tommy Flynn, Mama? Do we know him?"

"It's just a song," Vic says. "Don't you know anything? You're so stupid."

"I'm not stupid. I can count to a hunnerd and everything. I'm not stupid, am I, Mama?"

"No, Edith, you're not stupid. Vicky, say you're sorry."

"All right. Edith, I'm really sorry you're stupid."

Five more minutes. Ten. The *door*, open the door for the love of God. Someone makes the daring suggestion of knocking for admittance. Somebody else suggests kicking the door open. "Go ahead, then, *do* it." "I've a mind to do it, I'm telling you." "All right, *do* it, man. You *said* you would so go ahead and *do* it." "I *will* if they take much longer."

The door to the Reception Block opens, revealing a tall, strapping young man whose badge identifies him as the porter. He smiles and nods at those with whom he's acquainted, picking his teeth with a metal toothpick.

"'Bout time, Stoker," says one of the crowd. "Havin' your dinner, was you?"

"Just a little mutton stew," Stoker says. Slapping his belly he adds, "Got to keep me strength up, don't I?"

"Come on, guv, we're freezin' out here. Are you lettin' us in or not?"

"All right, all right, keep your hair on. Get in line, you lot. Women and children on the right, you mugs on the left. And be quick about it. I don't have all day."

And so the separation begins: women on one side, men on the other. A couple of old dears hold on to each other until the last moment. Edith wants to know why they are crying.

Vic says, "Because they want to stay together, stupid."

"Why can't they?"

Why can't they indeed? Instructing the girls to keep

close by her side, she follows the women into the female receiving ward, a long narrow room with a stone-flagged floor and lime-washed walls so painfully white it hurts your eyes. A single desk at the far end is occupied by a sour-faced woman in a somber, high-collar dress and apron, filling out paperwork.

Once everyone's inside, the porter shuts the door and tells them to line up against the far wall. "No pushing and shoving, you hear? You'll all get seen to soon enough."

"Soon enough" means another hour in line, moving up incrementally, painfully slowly. Step forward, stop. Wait. Step forward, stop. Wait. She would kill for a cup of tea. The baby wakes and she gives him over to the girls to keep him amused for a while. He doesn't seem hungry, which is a blessing as she can see no alcove anywhere to slip in and nurse him.

When they finally arrive at the front of the line the woman doesn't bother looking up. "Name."

"Mrs. Taylor."

"First name."

"Annie. Elizabeth."

"Well, which is it? Annie or Elizabeth?"

"Both. Annie Elizabeth Taylor."

The woman sighs. "Have you been here before?"

Annie shakes her head. "No, I haven't. I mean, I came here last month to meet the Guardians … but if you mean have I been *in* here before?"

"Never here before. Nearest relative."

"That would be my mother, I guess."

"Name and address."

"Of my mother?"

The woman lifts her head and glares. "Of course *of your mother*. Who else are we talking about?"

She's given offence. She hasn't wanted to give offence. She assumed she'd be able to get through her time here in a civilized fashion. She's not like some of them, is she? She may be poor but she's respectable. She's the wife of a printer, after all – correction: *was* the wife of a printer. She reads the paper every day … well, skims the headlines while Bill eats his supper, kept warm for him after the children are in bed.

The best time of the day – *their* time, just the two of

them in that small cramped kitchen, talking in low voices so as
not to wake the girls. And William asleep between them … the
roof could blow off and he wouldn't wake up. Whizzing like
a fireball all day long, hurtling through the alleyways with his
infant army, terrorizing the muffin man and the organ-grinder
and chasing the neighbourhood cats … kicking an old canvas
football discarded by the bigger boys … abandoning the game
when, and only when, it's too dark – or too foggy – or too cold
to continue. No wonder he sleeps so soundly.

Slept.

She gives the woman her mother's information: Anne
Maria Morgan. Number 64, Chippenham Road.

The list continues: Age. Creed. Occupation. Single,
married, or widowed. Cause of admission.

"I don't understand the question."

"*Cause of admission*. Lord, woman, are you simple?
Why are you here?"

Somehow she thought the woman would know all that.
From the interview with the Guardians. They were given all
that information – must she say it, in front of all these people?

"My husband left us."

"Desertion." It gets written down along with everything
else. Then she must give the names and ages of all three
children, and have the girls been to school, and can they read or
write, and are any of them deaf mutes, cripples, or imbeciles?

"Sign this," the woman says, "or make your mark."

Annie signs the piece of paper; the woman adds her
own signature and signals for an attendant. "Follow her. Next!"

An old pauper in a faded nurse's uniform steps forward.
"This way, dearie."

Annie turns to see that the girls are following her but
Stoker is blocking the way. Before she can intervene, he hands
them off to someone else and they're hustled out of the room.

"Wait – they're with me – we're together…"

"Here now, where do you think you're going?"

"My girls – they're taking my daughters."

A heavy hand grips her shoulder.

"Leave them be. Do what you're told and follow her."

Turning away from him, Annie appeals to the woman at

the desk.

"Excuse me, ma'am, there's been a mistake."

The woman looks up. It was quiet enough in the room before this – now the silence is charged with a sense of danger. Every head is turned toward her, waiting to see what will happen.

"A mistake?"

"My girls are very young. I mean them to stay with me."

"You *mean* them to stay with you – is that what you said?"

"Yes." It comes out as little more than a whisper. Perhaps it's from standing so long … she feels light-headed. As if she might faint.

"Do you know where you are?"

Annie nods and tries to catch her breath.

"You know you're in the Paddington Union Workhouse?"

Again, a nod. Yes, she knows.

"Oh, good. I thought maybe you thought you were at the circus. Or at the Zoo. Feeding the lions, yes?"

It's a joke but no one dares to laugh. Glancing down at her book she reads out the girls' names and ages: Victoria Mary, seven. Edith Annie, five. Both of them old enough to be separated from their mother and housed in the children's ward.

"I just – at the interview – they told me my girls would stay with me. Seven and under, they said."

"I'm afraid you were misinformed. Now move along."

"If I could just speak to the matron …"

"*I* am the matron of this house and you've taken up more than your share of my time. I caution you not to waste any more of it."

There is no more to be said. The pauper nurse takes her by the elbow and steers her out the door. They descend a set of wide stone steps and through an open door into a large windowless room.

"All right, dearie. I'll leave you to have your wash and come back for you when you're done."

This, then, is the bath-house, a damp cellar furnished

with a stove, a bath-tub filled with water, and a table supporting a stack of linen. A dozen women have already been bathed this afternoon; the water may have been clean, once, but it's now so murky you'd come out dirtier than when you went in. No alcoves in which to undress – she must strip in front of strangers.

There are two bath-house attendants – a pregnant young woman who relieves her of the child, and an elderly crone in need of a good wash herself. When Annie removes her bonnet the older woman grins, revealing a mouth of blackened teeth. "Sold yer hair, did you? I hope you got a few bob for it. Did that myself before I come here but I wish I hadn't. Never grows back the same after that."

When she's been scrubbed and her scalp combed for lice, she's allowed to get out, pat herself dry and don her pauper uniform: a thin cotton shift, a blue-and-white striped dress to be worn under a drab grey smock, dark blue fustian stockings, and a pair of ill-fitting hobnailed boots with iron tips. The whole dismal outfit is topped off with a checkered muslin cap which at least serves to hide her ragged head.

When she asks about her own clothes, she's told they'll be inspected for fleas, then folded and ticketed and put in storage to be returned to her upon discharge. The baby is bathed separately, in a smaller tub set aside for that purpose. To the attendant's surprise, he laughs and slaps the water in delight as she runs a cloth over his body.

"They generally hate it," she tells Annie. "Most of 'em scream blue murder."

"He loves his bath," Annie says. "I wash him every night."

The old woman is astonished. "No – really? We never washed when we was little. Ma said it would make us sick."

Annie offers the suggestion that it works the other way around – that *not* washing is more likely to make you ill – but the attendant is unconvinced.

"All I know is our Ma never had a bath in her life and she lived to a good old age. Is he creepin' yet?"

"No, not yet."

Pawing through a pile of infants' wear, she comes up

with a long slip and undershirt, a pair of socks, a nightgown and cap, and a handful of thin grey flannels. "These'll do for now. When he starts gettin' about you can ask for a shorter dress."

"Might you give me back my crape armband? My little boy died last month – I'm in mourning."

"Sorry for your loss, dearie, but we only give 'em to widders. Everybody's mournin' someone and if we give 'em out to one of you we has to give 'em to everyone. Crape's not cheap neither. There'd be a dreadful how-do when the Guardians found out. But I can give you this for the baby."

She hands Annie a sugar-tit – a piece of linen wrapped around a lump of sugar.

"I don't like to use these …"

"You say that, but you'll find it comes in handy. In here, you can't always feed the baby when he needs it. I had it made up for a young thing who come in here last week with her newborn. The baby died so I took it back. Right, then, you both been badged and ticketed. Go along with Nurse and she'll show you where to sleep. And don't you be worrying about that sugar-tit. He didn't have anything ketching."

***

The women's casual ward is located at the western end of the workhouse next to the sick ward. It doesn't officially open until six o'clock so the room is less than half full. She hesitates in the doorway. The nurse advises her to choose a bed near the door and not at the back of the room adjacent to "the facilities". The smell, she says, can be "fair nasty" especially at this time of year.

"Strickly speaking, they ain't allowed in here if they bin drinkin' but a-course with women you can't always tell. Men like their beer and porter and the smell stays with 'em but with women it's gin and a coupla peppermint drops hides the smell so's you got no idea what they bin up to till they start rowin'. Mrs. Chancer – she's the Super here – she handles 'em just fine, they knows better'n to act up around her, but I tell you, I wouldn't be Super in this here ward for all the tea in China."

The beds, if you can call them that, consist of straw-tick mattresses set in coffin-like troughs three or four inches apart. She picks one near the door and settles down to nurse the baby. Lately it takes forever to fill him up; is she running out of milk? Perhaps she should ask for a wet-nurse. Surely with all the young women coming here to have their babies there must be some with milk to spare. She'll ask the doctor about it when she sees him.

The baby stops sucking at last and falls asleep. Such a long day. It's hard to believe it was only this morning they left the house … only four hours since they were admitted. She could fall apart with exhaustion. This bed, too, may have been a poor choice being so near the door; the draft is considerable. Too tired to do anything about it, she curls up next to her son and subsides into an uneasy sleep.

6.

If Annie's parents cherished the hope that life would be more healthful in a part of the city which had been rural countryside not so long ago, they were mistaken. This after all was Notting Hill, the scene of the terrible cholera outbreak in 1849 and another one five years later. They could not have thought it ideal, having lost one child already, to bring the rest of their children to this place. The move to the suburbs likely had more to do with the evictions caused by the ongoing slum clearances than any deliberate forethought on their part.

They rented a house on St. George's Road just south of the site of the new Hammersmith and City Line. It was what you would call a mixed neighbourhood. There were the "decent" poor – a grocer's assistant, a laundress, the owner of a second-hand furniture store – and the "rough" poor – hawkers, costermongers, horse-keepers, flower-sellers, cab-runners, rag and bone men, pickpockets.

Many of the women supported their families by taking in laundry – the water there had been famous for hundreds of years. Coarse and hard-working, the laundresses were respectable enough but their husbands were looked down on as idle good-for-nothings who relied on their wives' earnings to keep them in beer money. "To marry an ironer is as good as a fortune" was what they said. They could sit back and loaf and be set for life, as long as their wives could work.

The flat, low-lying area to the west was known as the Piggeries and Potteries, infamous for the poverty of the place and the stench that went with it. Brick-makers had settled there first, attracted by the heavy clay; the pig-keeping "Islanders", as they called themselves, followed when the developers pushed them out of Tyburnia. Making bricks required digging huge holes in the clay and keeping pigs meant collecting "refuge" and offal from the houses of gentle-folks, feeding most of it to the pigs and boiling down the fat.

It was a deadly combination: the slurry and sewage from the pigs filled the holes dug by the brick-makers, creating stagnant open ditches, breeding grounds for filth and disease. An especially notorious ditch occupied an entire acre; the locals called it "The Ocean".

The Islanders kept emaciated horses and donkeys and shared their tumbledown shacks with scrappy chickens and starveling dogs – at one time, so the story goes, the animals outnumbered the people three to one. The stink was overwhelming when the wind was from the west.

The worst area was the Special District: Bangor Street, Crescent Street, St. Clement's Road, St. Katherine's Road, and William Street. Children born here didn't live long; most died before their fifth birthday. Half-starved women begged in the streets and the pot houses advertised "Rat matches every Monday night". Common lodging houses with overflowing privies and windows patched with rags and brown paper accommodated families of ten and eleven children in single rooms rented by the week.

And the rents were always going up. What rented for 3s one week cost 5s a week later. Rooms were sublet and then let again so it was common to see a sign in a window advertising "A part of a room to let". Beds, too, were let in eight-hour shifts – sometimes even the space under the bed was rented out. The neighbourhood had long been a law unto itself; for years the only way into it was from the fields along a narrow mud road called Cut-throat which later became Pottery Lane. If you had no reason to enter the Special District, you didn't.

***

As Maggie foretold there were indeed gypsies in Notting Hill but not as many as there used to be. The old encampments were disappearing. Housing estates had replaced the open fields and pastures, and the Romany folk exchanged their tents and caravans for scrappy little flats and run-down tenement cottages. In the winter they made their living selling horses and mending pots and pans and when the weather warmed they disappeared into the country-side. Some got married and took the oath – no drinking, no gambling, no telling fortunes – and others didn't.

Gypsy women in wide-brimmed hats and headscarves, trailing silent dark-eyed children, came to the door with buttons and thread for sale. Her mother always bought; the thread was good quality and you could always use a button. Sometimes they brought bunches of lavender – sixteen for a penny – and she'd buy those too when she could. Mama steeped the leaves in oil and used it for making soap and an ointment to heal cuts and sores. The flowers were hung to dry and used to make lavender tea … leftover bits were added to the bath water on Saturday night.

It was one thing to buy from the gypsies; it was quite another to venture into their territory. Mothers warned their children to steer clear of the places the gypsies frequented lest they catch something. "Catching something" was a very real danger when you lived in the Dale. All mothers worried about it but mothers like Annie's who'd lost a child to typhus worried more than others. She set strict limits on her children's wanderings. They were never to step foot in the Brick Yards and were forbidden to venture along the canal towpath where rival Irish and English gangs regularly engaged in drunken free-for-alls.

Still, even given those restrictions, there was plenty to see. A half dozen taverns dotted the route that led to school and it was not unusual to witness a brawl on the way home. It was good entertainment, all this fighting, but they knew not to tell Mama: one mention that they'd stopped to take in a bust-up in the beer-garden on Pottery Lane and they'd be in for a hard knock on the head from a thimble or darning egg – whichever was closest at hand.

The Sunday market on Norland Road was a weekly treat, a chance to duck away from Mama in her shawl and market basket and escape into the crowded road to take in the sights: organ grinders, brass bands, conjurers, men and women on stilts, Highland bagpipe players, vendors of patent medicine. It was there she saw her first *Punch and Judy* show and there she witnessed a fight between two fishwives that resulted in one being carried off for dead. The woman recovered and was back the following Sunday looking a little worse for wear but plying her trade as rudely and cheerfully as before.

Annie and her siblings generally managed to avoid detection for an hour or two before being found by Mama and brought home. The market, though, went on all day and half the night. At eleven o'clock, with the toll of the church bells, the shop-owners finally put up their shutters, the policemen swept away the last of the street-sellers, and the market was brought to a close.

Just to the east was Portobello Lane where an amiable Frenchman with sad dark eyes walked his small dog each afternoon. Little Banjo, who owned a variety of colourful silk jackets, could do all kinds of things – shake hands, play dead, roll over on command. And he could count: "Un, deux, trois!" the Frenchman would say, and Banjo would bark three times.

Annie longed for a dog of her own but knew not to ask her mother. Maria Morgan had a farmer's distaste for domestic pets and wouldn't have an animal that couldn't earn its keep. Had Annie asked for a chicken or even a goose she might have won her over but dogs – especially a useless little Pug like Banjo – were out of the question. Cats were allowed in the cow shed as they kept away the rats. But never in the house. Annie had to content herself with patting Banjo when she saw him and marveling at his wardrobe.

The Franciscan nuns had come to Portobello Lane and Mama, who was out of work now that they lived so far from the shirt factory, went to them and persuaded them to let her mend their undergarments. It was Annie's task each day after school to pick up the discrete brown paper package tied with string that was always left just inside the main gate. When the Frenchman saw her he would say, "Ah, it is Ariadne, my little seamstress!" She didn't like to tell him it was her mother who did the sewing – she liked being called Ariadne, whoever she was.

Besides giving her a chance to indulge her love of small dogs, this daily chore allowed her a certain status among her classmates; when discussing what exactly nuns wore "under there" she could tell them: black stockings, a simple linen shift and drawers. Which was pretty much what their mothers wore and disappointed those who were hoping to hear about chastity belts and such.

***

It was while they were living in Notting Hill that a gypsy told Annie's fortune. She came to the door on a bad day for selling buttons … Mama had been laid up all week and there was no sewing money. Her rheumatism was acting up and she'd put Annie to work churning the cream into butter – a twice-weekly task Annie dreaded. The metal crank was stiff and awkward; Mama could turn it with one hand and have butter in thirty minutes while Annie, using both hands, never managed it in under an hour.

When the knock came, she rushed to open the door, glad to have an excuse to leave off churning. The woman who stood on the doorstep was not one of the regulars, and she was on her own – usually they came in twos and threes. Mama came to the door, drying her hands on her apron. When she saw the gypsy she was about to send her away when she noticed that one of her hands … the one not holding the buttons … was deformed: the fingers were bent into a kind of claw. She kept it close to her chest, as if she would hide it from sight. Most peddlers would consider a hand like that an asset and would keep it well on display. The fact that this woman did not was unusual. And so Mama stood in the doorway hesitating.

The woman saw her chance. "I'll tell your future for a penny."

"There's no point in it. My future is here and it's not about to change."

"Hers then." She indicated Annie, hovering just behind her mother. "The girl is young, she has all her life to live. A ha'penny and you won't regret it."

Annie was sure her mother would say no; she called it mumbo-jumbo, a waste of time and money. But to her surprise Mama agreed. The gypsy took Annie's hand in her good hand, the one that wasn't crippled, and studied it for a moment.

"Give me the other," she said, and Annie obeyed. After a moment she nodded as if something she saw there confirmed what she thought.

"Your right hand is what you're born with, it is the hand God gave you – your left hand is what you have done with it. That's the way it is with women but with men it goes the other way around. Look at your hands. See how they are different?"

Annie peered at her hands as if looking at them for the first time. The gypsy was right. The lines were similar but they went in different directions. Mama stood by watching; she was starting to regret that she'd agreed to this but she was not one to go back on a bargain.

The woman began tracing Annie's right palm with her index finger. Her nails were long and it tickled a little. Annie tried to keep still.

"This top line that goes straight across – that is your heart line. You keep your feelings close to your heart, you don't give them away. You will have love but it will disappoint you. You don't trust easily but when you do you will demand loyalty. I see no sickness – you'll be healthy till you die. Give me the other hand."

Wishing her mother would go back inside, Annie did as she was told. She wanted to ask more about her heart line.

"You see this line? These are things you must decide about. Sometimes you will be right and sometimes you will be wrong. It is the way of all things. This line is your line of destiny. It shows your fate."

"What does it show? Am I going to be rich?"

The gypsy bent her head and studied the palm before responding. "I see something better than money."

What could be better than money? Annie waited, but the gypsy was waiting, too, her hand outstretched.

Mama wasn't buying it.

"If you're done, then - "

"Hope," the woman said. "You will always have hope."

Mama sniffed her disapproval: such foolishness, she should never have agreed. She retrieved a half-penny from her apron and handed it to the gypsy.

"Here you go now. Good-day to you."

She shut the door.

Annie was disappointed. What good was hope? She felt cheated – wasn't a gypsy supposed to see something exciting in your future? Lizzie Burch had *her* fortune told at the Norland market by the Amazing Fortune-telling Poodle; *she*, it turned out, was going to marry a tall, dark, handsome stranger and ride to church in a carriage.

"Do you think she's right, Mama? Do you think she really knows what's going to happen?"

"Get on with your work," Mama said. "The butter will not come at all if you don't keep at it."

7.

The sound of women's voices drags her awake. She has slept for an hour, maybe more. It must be after six: the overhead lamps are lit and the ward is almost completely full. Many of the women are old and infirm – come here to die, most likely. There's a scattering of pale, scrawny children and a few tough older girls, swearing like navvies. *Language* – her mother would be appalled. The youngsters hide behind their mother's skirts and steal fearful, admiring glances at their older comrades. Once they're back on the streets they'll have substantially increased their vocabulary for the worst.

They're not all strangers here – several of the women know each other from previous stints in here or places like it; they discuss the various "spikes" comparing this workhouse with others they've stayed in. St. Giles the Leper is the most crowded and the food is the worst: the bread is puffy and full of holes and gruel left over from the night before is boiled up and served for the next day's breakfast. Notting Dale, where paupers are forced to break stones for up to 60 hours a week, is the cruelest. The general consensus appears to be that this is one of the better ones.

"Still and all," one woman says, "it's bloody filthy. They don't ever stove them blankets, like they do up north."

A pale blonde girl sporting an enormous bruise under one eye says she was in Whitechapel Road before Christmas. "This 'ere's a bleedin' palace compared with the Chapel. You'd think you died and gone to 'ell in that place. Got the Itch and look what it done to me. Near got eaten alive."

She lifts her shift, exposing her naked legs, bleeding from bites and scratches all the way up to her thighs.

"That's nothing." This from the dark-haired, heavy-set woman in the bed next to Annie. She speaks with authority – you get the impression she's been through more than a few of these places in her time. "You think the Whitechapel spike's bad, you want to go to Clerkenwell. Bare straw to lie on and the room's so close you can't breathe. Can't roll over without smashing into the gal next to you. Right next to the dead-house, too, and the smell is fierce. Still, they don't make you wash so it ain't all bad."

Having said her piece she settles down to have a smoke. The others warn her to put her pipe away before the Super sees and turns her out but she simply shrugs it off.

"Let her try. They got to keep me for a night now I'm here. I know my rights."

Turning towards Annie she nods in a friendly manner and smiles at the baby. "You're new. Don't believe I seen you here before."

"They put us here till the doctor sees us."

"Ah, could be a while this being Christmas and all. Did you get your toke?"

"They gave me clothes to wear – is that what you mean?"

"No, no. Your *toke*. Did they give you anythin' to eat when you come in tonight? Did you get some supper?"

"No, I haven't eaten since this morning."

With everything else going on, she hasn't thought about food. Have the girls been fed? Surely they wouldn't put them to bed hungry.

"Hang on."

Heaving herself out of bed, Pipe Lady stomps over to the door and bangs on it with her fist. After a moment the key turns in the lock and the attendant pokes her head in.

"What is it?"

"This here new girl didn't get her toke. Get her somethin', will you?"

The woman disappears, returning in a few minutes with an apology for the lapse. "It's because you're not casual. I just figured you ate already."

When she leaves, Pipe Lady explains that the Super had to oblige them. "There's very strict rules about what you get when you come in here. She could get herself written up for not giving you your toke."

The "toke" is an inedible hunk of bread so hard it must have been made a week ago; black bits that might be rat's dropping are speckled throughout. As hungry as she is she can't bring herself to gnaw her way through it. She sets it aside and an emaciated old woman a few beds down limps over, wincing with each step.

"Are you not going to eat your bread, my dear?"

"No, I'm not hungry."

It's a lie but she'd starve before she'd eat such garbage.

"Will I take it off your hands then?"

The woman is surprisingly well-spoken, given the circumstances. The kind thing would be to pretend it's she who is doing Annie a favour, rather than the other way around.

"Please do. I wouldn't like them to think I wasn't grateful."

"Very well, then, dear, if you're quite certain."

She has the bread firmly in her grip. Had Annie suddenly had a change of heart no amount of pleading would have induced her to return it. Hiding it under her smock, she smiles and hobbles back to her bed. There's not a tooth in her head, from what Annie can see. How on earth she will manage to eat that lump of rock is a mystery.

One of the younger girls, the one they call Saucy Sal, is watching this play out. It seems to amuse her no end. "That's Old Lady Dribble. Ain't she somethin'? She's in 'ere all the time and she always talks like that. Half the time she don't even know she's in 'ere – thinks she's visitin' her sister or somethin'. Crazy old bat."

Most likely the old woman *is* a little crazy but who wouldn't be, spending your old age in places like this?

"I think she was brought up to expect something better."

"What're you in for, then? Lemme guess – desertion, right?"

There's no point in denying it. "Yes, my husband left us."

"I knew it! Maisie said you been in the asylum 'cause of your hair but I said it was desertion and you sold yer hair for the money."

She turns to the girl next to her, the one with the bruises who was bitten in Whitechapel Road. "See, Maisie, 'er old man scarpered. I was right."

"Bully for you. Anyways, she ain't a reg'lar. She didn't even know to get 'er toke, did she?"

At the risk of encouraging them Annie asks if that's what they are – regulars. The question sends Sal into a fit of laughter. "Reg'lars! I'll say we're reg'lars! We're in-and-outers, ain't we, Maisie?"

"Well, why not? Ain't nothin' wrong with it. We check ourselfs out when we're bored and 'ave a night of fun. We're young, after all, why shouldn't we enjoy ourselves? When the money's gone, we pitch the blokes and come back in time for tea."

Sal lets out another screech – the girl is easily amused. "Ooh, Maisie, yer awful, you are! She'll think we're a coupla doxies the way you carry on!"

"Don't care what she thinks, do I? If she don't like it, she can go to blazes. Nobody tells me what to do. I do what I please when I please. It's like I said to that Charley cove down in the Chapel. 'Listen,' I says, 'you think 'cause yer buyin' me drinks you got some rights over me. Well you don't so let go me arm or you'll be sorry.' That's where I got this eye, didn't I? But I don't care – I give 'im a good kick in the tallywags and that took 'im down a peg or two."

By the end of this speech Sal has dissolved into fits of appreciative laughter. She snorts, hoots, and almost chokes and when she does manage to recover herself enough to speak, she confirms what Maisie has said: "It's true! It's bleedin' true! She didn't half tip 'im a walloper!"

Up to this point, Pipe Lady has said nothing. Now she takes her pipe out of her mouth, spits on the floor and tells Sal and Maisie to "give over" with their "flash" talk. "Nobody's impressed so you might as well shut your gob."

But Annie is curious. "Isn't it horrible spending so much time in this place? Wouldn't you rather be home with your family?"

"Family!" Maisie makes it sound like a dirty word. "Don't talk to me about family! This place is a hundred times better'n my family."

Sal agrees. "She ain't got no Ma an' her Pa put her on the street when she was only ten. *My* ol' man walked out on us an' my Ma kicked me and my brothers out when she went on the game. I got sent to prison and then the 'Formatory and

I never seen my brothers again. Dunno what happened to 'em and I don't care."

Annie starts to say something about being sorry but Sal cuts her off. "Don't you go bein' sorry for me! I'm doin' just fine. And anyway, it ain't a bad life in 'ere, if you can put up with the do-gooders and gospel grinders what come 'round tryin' to reform you. Ain't that right, Maisie?"

"Creepin' round 'ere 'andin' out tracks and askin' if you're ready to meet your Maker. I tell 'em if my Maker wants to meet me 'e better have a few bob in 'is pocket. I don't come cheap!"

Another screech from Sal. "Oooh, Maisie, you're a scream! No, you don't come cheap and I know it better'n anyone!"

Pipe Lady shakes her head. "You don't want to be paying attention to those two hussies. They're full of blather and nonsense – half what they say is a lie and the rest is pure shite. Look at the blinker on that one. You think she was having her jollies when she copped that? I don't think so."

It's true. Maisie's left eye is swollen shut and her arms are covered in bruises. Someone has treated her roughly and fairly recently too.

"You ain't one to talk, Mrs. Clarke. We all know about you – yer no better'n the rest of us."

"Shut your mouth and mind your manners. And if you don't, I'll mind 'em for you."

"You ain't in charge 'ere. You can't tell us what to do."

"No?" Pipe Lady sets her pipe on the floor, gets to her feet and begins to roll up her sleeves. Her forearms are tattooed like a docker's and just as thick. "You want to take me on, girl, and we'll find out who's in charge?"

This appears to have the desired effect. Sal and Maisie settle down for a bit and Pipe Lady returns to her bed.

"So how're you finding it? In here, I mean. It can be strange at first, but you'll get used to it. The fleas are the worst. They don't bother me now but when I first went on the road I thought they'd eat me alive."

"On the road? When was that?"

"Forty years ago. We were circus performers, Mr.

Clarke and me, so we were on the road all year round. He was a contortionist. That man could twist himself into a knot so small you could lift him up and put him inside a drum. Called himself 'The Amazing Fernando'. Wasn't his real name of course but the Italians were in favour back then and we thought it sounded better than Fred."

"What about you? What did you do?"

"Oh, I guess I did a bit of everything. Jack of all trades, I was. Worked as a knife-thrower's girl for a time … lovely gentleman he was, very polite. Taught me to juggle knives. So I did that, and when things were slow I did some fortune-telling. Palms and tea leaves mainly. Never went in for the crystal ball – too hocus-pocus for my taste. When we was with Batty's circus I did a little riding. Mr. Clarke used to say, 'The great thing about my missus is she can turn her hand to anything.'"

"It sounds exciting."

"Well, I reckon it was. Up and down the country we were, all year 'round following the circuit. One week we'd be in Epsom, next week Moulsey, then Ascot – oh, my it was a time. And when the racing season was done we come back to London and down to Brighton. All over the place. It was a great life if you liked the outdoors, and we did. We had our own little caravan, it was ever so homely. 'Course that was before Mr. Clarke fell and broke his backside. After that he could only do the odd bit of clowning – back end of a horse and such. It broke his heart."

Setting her pipe on the floor between them, Pipe Lady hoists herself out of bed and stretches.

"You'll have to excuse me – I got to use the facilities. Nice talkin' to you. It does make the time pass when you have someone to chat with, don't you think? Ah, there's the bell. Eight o'clock – they'll be shuttin' us in now."

As if on cue, the door opens and the Super enters, wheeling a trolley.

"All right you lot, the ward is closed. 'Ere's your night shirts. Put 'em on and get into bed. An' if yer thinkin' you need to use the facilities best do it now before I turn off them lights."

The appearance of the so-called night shirts causes something of a revolt in the ward. Looking nothing like women's garments, they are in reality shapeless grey calico tents with armholes; PROPERTY OF PADDINGTON UNION is stamped across the front.

"I ain't wearin' that. It looks like a tater sack."

"Can't we just sleep in our clothes?"

"Quit yer snivelin'," the Super says. "Put 'em on and don't make me have to come in 'ere and tell you again."

With that, she extinguishes the overhead lights, wheels the trolley out the door and turns the key in the lock.

Shivering, Annie strips down to her chemise, pulls the tent over her head, and gets into bed. Within moments she's under attack by an army of creeping things – it's the blanket … filthy and crawling with bugs. She throws it aside and sits up. A child a few beds down has been crying since he got here. His mother finally tells him to shut up or she'll give him a "thick ear". He continues to howl so she slaps him which seems to do the trick. The crying stops, although he continues to snuffle a little from time to time.

"Missin' his pa," his mother explains.

"In the men's ward, is he?"

"Lord, no," she says. "Died a week ago. He wasn't up to much, our Frank, but he was awful good with the children."

An hour passes. Eventually, she nods off, only to be jolted awake by a crashing sound and someone swearing in the dark. One of the women saw a rat and threw her boot at it.

"How do you know it was a rat?"

"I knows rats. I seen enough of 'em in my life to tell a rat from a dormouse."

"Did you get it?"

"No, dammit, the bloody creature got away."

That's the end of sleep for Annie. She sits up, clutches the baby to her breast, and waits for morning.

8.

Aside from gypsies and the attractions of Pottery Lane, Notting Hill was the scene of Annie's education – the only time, in fact, that she formally and consistently went to school. In Marylebone she had attended a local charity school but disliked it so intensely she was in the habit of feigning illness to escape the tedium. Sometimes she didn't need to pretend; Mama often needed her at home to help with the chores so that, too, kept her out of the classroom.

By the time they left Marylebone she could read and write well enough but did not excel at anything and had no desire to do so. She was ten years old, after all, and might be out working, contributing to the family income.

But it was 1861. London, like the rest of the country, was in the middle of a building boom, and a recently published Education Report was promoting the building of schools as a way to rescue poor children from a life of delinquency and crime.

Parish officials combed the neighbourhood in search of parents who could be encouraged to enroll their children at the newly-built Church school on Walmer Street. In spite of Annie's protests that she had all the education she needed, her mother enrolled all three children for the grand sum of sixpence a week. And because she was paying for the privilege of educating them, she threatened dire consequences if they played truant.

"Sixpence a week is money that could go for food or a new pair of shoes. You keep that in mind if you get to thinking about spending that money on sweets. And don't think I won't find out because I will. Miss a day without telling me and you'll be well and truly sorry."

Erected next to a pig farm, the school was a substantial brick building with separate rooms for boys and girls according to their age, and separate play areas at the back, each with its own toilet. The school day was divided evenly between academic studies in the morning and "useful learning" in the afternoon. Which, for the girls, meant needlework.

The morning mistress was Emmeline Hodge, a

Scottish-born patriot with ginger hair and blue eyes that flashed with intelligence. She taught them penmanship and reading, arithmetic and grammar, and just enough geography to instill within them a proper sense of England's place in the world. Miss Hodge kept a large map of the world pinned to the wall behind her desk; for ten minutes every day she used that map and a long wooden pointer to illustrate a short but informative history lesson.

The method of instruction was this: Miss Hodge would point out something on the map and make a brief statement about it. She would then walk between the desks, stopping at random to put a question to one of the girls. If the unfortunate student had not been listening carefully or did not answer immediately, she would have to stay in at midday and write out the answer in her copy book one hundred times. There was no dozing in Miss Hodge's classroom.

"Now girls, pay attention. This is Britannia. She is the emblem of British power and unity and the personification of everything that is good and fair and strong and supreme. She is everything that you should be and should strive to be. In everything you do and say, let God and Britannia direct your path. Sykes!"

"Yes, Miss!"

"Who should direct your path?"

"Miss, God and Britannia, Miss."

Directing her pointer to the images on either side of Britannia – Red Indians and American cowboys, half-naked Africans and Australian Aborigines – she continued: "These are the people of the Empire. We see them paying tribute to Britain for bringing justice, freedom and democracy to their countries. Morgan!"

"Yes, Miss!"

"What has Britain brought to their countries?"

"Miss, justice, freedom and democracy, Miss."

"This –" the pointer moved to a pie-shaped piece of the map – "is India. India is rich in spices and gold and silk and copper. The British have educated the Hindoos and the Mussulmans who now eagerly await the benefits of Christianity. Nichols!"

"Yes, Miss!"

"Who have the British educated?"

"Miss, the Hindoos and the Mussulmans, Miss."

"Chapman!"

"Yes, Miss!"

"What do they now eagerly await?"

"Miss, the benefits of Christianity, Miss."

And so it went. Gazing at that map it was hard not to be impressed with all those swatches of red and pink smeared across the globe. Britain may have lost the American colonies but she had India and South Africa and Australia and the Province of Canada. She had produced the greatest writers, soldiers, sailors and explorers the world had ever seen and her people currently served under the greatest Queen. Britain had defeated Napoleon at Waterloo and sorted out Russia in the Crimea. Her Royal Navy ruled the seas and her Army, while smaller than some, boasted the most confident and professional officers in the world. Everywhere you looked you saw proof of the superiority of the British race. Who wouldn't want to be British?

Annie's mother was skeptical of these tributes to Empire. "You may have been born in England and you may live in England but before any of that you are Welsh and the Welsh owe allegiance to no one. It is not for nothing that the heir to the English throne is called the Prince of Wales. Don't you be kneeling down to all things English, my girl, or you'll answer to me."

It was useless for Annie to explain that she was proud of being British not English as such for her mother saw no distinction between the two and had little use for either.

As for her classmates, not all of them shared her imperialist pride. The Irish girls made fun of the Queen and her German husband and told naughty stories about the making of all those baby princes and princesses, one after another. Several of them went so far as to suggest England should not rule over Ireland – that the Irish were capable of ruling themselves. These were Fenian sentiments and they had no place in an English schoolroom. But there was nothing to stop them spouting their republican views once they were outside on the streets. It came to fisticuffs sometimes among the boys and hair-pulling among the girls. There were times when it was simply better to find a different route home.

***

In a very short time, Annie became devoted to Miss Hodge. She demanded a great deal of her students but was quick to praise their efforts, and she was the only woman Annie had ever known to speak out against marriage.

"Girls," she said, "there is more to life than being a housewife. You may not be allowed to vote or stand for political office but if you stay single you will answer to no one but yourself. Do not let the burden of domesticity oppress you. Speak your mind and find your own way in the world. The day may come when a man comes to you and says, 'Marry me and be my wife, and give up your work and your books and devote yourself to me and me alone.' If that day comes, be strong, girls. Look him directly in the face and say, 'No, thank you. I was not born to be a slave.' O'Byrne!"

"Yes, Miss!"

"How should you look at that man?"

"Directly in the face, Miss!"

"And what should you say to him?"

"No thank you, Miss. I wasn't born to be a slave!"

Fine words, indeed. But not to be repeated outside the classroom. Mama would have removed her from the school if she knew Annie was being exposed to such unorthodox views. It was one thing to have her daughter educated – quite another to encourage her to reject her natural role as wife and mother.

The Sewing Mistress was as do. Where Miss Hodge was tall and fiery, Miss Titch was all curves and dimples, and her opinions were much more conventional. She was engaged to be married and once that great event took place her contract with the Board would be terminated. Men were allowed to teach after marriage; women were not.

It was thought that Miss Titch felt sorry for Miss Hodge because she was single and too old to ever find a husband. She liked to remind the girls that while a smattering of history and mathematics was all well and good it was here, in the sewing room, they were acquiring the skills that mattered.

Under Miss Titch, the students were divided into classes according to their levels of skill. Annie already knew how to hem and stitch collars and wristbands, so she was put directly into the Fourth Class where she learned to gather waistbands. After three months of gathering waistbands she was allowed to move up to the Fifth Class – buttonholes – and then to the herringbone stitch and so on through necklines, darts and seams. By the time she reached the Finishing Class she was twelve, which made her one of the older girls although she was never made a Monitor. That coveted position was given to Georgina Kelly whose samplers were regularly held up as examples of perfection.

There was a test at the end of the Finishing Class; you had to answer a series of questions one girl at a time:

Q. On which side do you sew a patch?

A. On the right side, Miss.

Q. How do you finish it?

A. Turn the garment and cut out the worn part, leaving enough material to form the fell, then nick it a little at the four corners and turn it in flat and smooth.

Q. In cutting out all flannel garments, what should you allow for?

A. Shrinking, Miss, unless it be first washed.

Most girls left school once they passed the final test in needle-work. It was understood that, having learnt to sew, knit, and cut out garments, their education was at an end.

***

Reluctantly, Annie quit school two weeks short of her thirteenth birthday. As Mama said, she had no reason to stay. She could read and write and she'd passed her sewing class. It would have been useless to argue that she enjoyed school – that she was eager to learn even more. Mama would have called that "getting above" herself. Remember your place, is what she always said. Don't be thinking you're better than you are.

To Annie, it always seemed an odd thing to say, coming

from someone who knew in her bones she was better than most of her neighbours. Being Welsh, and being descended from the great Llywelyn Fawr who fought for a free and united Wales – this was not a woman who took second place to anyone.

And yet. She had married a dairyman – married for love, she once confessed to her daughter: "I made my bed and must lie on it." The girl who stood on the banks of the River Rheidol and heard the cries of soldiers long dead had become a seamstress and a dairyman's wife. Perhaps she just wanted to protect her daughter from dreams.

Having made the decision to leave school, Annie thought she would stay home and help with the sewing but in spite of getting through all eleven sewing classes she made a botch of it. Mama said she was worse than useless and took it upon herself to find her a job. Through a neighbour she got her taken on at the steam laundry on Silchester Road. It would be good practice, she said, for when Annie was married and had her own family's washing to take care of.

She was put on as a plain ironer at 2/6*d* a day. There were 200 of them, women and girls, working underground from six in the morning till nine at night. Apart from an hour for dinner and a half-hour break for tea, they were on their feet the whole time, arms and faces bathed in sweat. The ceiling fans arranged in the centre of the room did little more than waft the heat back and forth, stirring it up but not cooling things in any noticeable way. Little girls in short petticoats – much younger than Annie – handed the ironers their work and fed the soiled linen into the big machines. These were the "learners" and would graduate eventually from earning a shilling a day to fully paid washers, ironers, packers and sorterd – assuming they lasted that long.

The older women drank beer and ale to keep "moistened" but the young ones had the worst of it. At least once a day a girl would fall to the ground in a faint from the stifling, steamy swelter of it all.

Laundresses were reputed to be rude, abrasive women who swore and drank like sailors but why wouldn't they be, working in those conditions? The women Annie saw worked hard – harder than any of their husbands, if they had them

– and they kept their families out of the workhouse. People criticized them for putting their infants in crèches so they could go back to work but wasn't that better than giving them up to baby farmers? Or staying at home with them so they might all starve together?

She hated the job after the very first day and wanted to quit. Mama wouldn't let her – she said she had to stay on till she found something else. All right then, Annie said, let me be a maid. She'd seen a picture on a cigarette card … a woman dressed in a crisp black uniform with a white cap and apron, holding a feather duster in one hand and a bunch of keys in the other. It looked like easy work compared with the steam laundry.

Mama tried to dissuade her. She'd been a domestic herself before marrying Papa. She said it was hard work and it was lonely.

"They don't want girls who live near their families," she said. "I had to come all the way to London to find work. I cried myself to sleep for a year and you'll do the same. You'll be homesick."

But Annie could be stubborn. With that image in front of her – the smart black uniform, the white cap and apron – she held her ground and eventually her mother gave in. She might leave the laundry if she found a good, respectable place. And by respectable, she meant a household in a decent neighbourhood with no riff-raff. In other words, a better neighbourhood than their own.

Papa made enquiries on his rounds and found a woman whose sister-in-law was looking for a girl to live in. They lived in Ealing and had three children, all in school, plus a cook and a gardener. He was a banker; she was from good Yorkshire farming stock. Mama gave it some consideration and in the end gave her consent. In return for her room and board, Annie would be taught what she needed to know in order to one day move on to a paying position at a better sort of house.

Of course this was never said. The fiction was maintained that once taken on a servant would remain loyal to her employer until her dying day. But both parties knew it to be an arrangement of convenience; when it no longer served one or the other it would come to an end.

The Saturday before she was due to leave the household bustled with activity. While Annie washed her underthings and hung them in the kitchen to dry, Maude polished Annie's boots and Mama put the final touches on her uniform. What bliss it was to have a mother who sewed! Three changes of clothes she'd made her: a cotton print dress and pinafore for morning service, a black dress with a muslin cap and apron for afternoons and evenings, plus a second apron to change into, and a decent shirtwaist to wear on her monthly half-day off. She adored the black uniform with its long puffed sleeves and had begged Mama to replace the white cotton collar and cuffs with ones made of lace – an extravagance she refused to consider.

"That, Annie Morgan, would be butter on bacon. You don't want them thinking you don't know your place."

When a knock came at the front door, Mama sent Arthur to answer it. "We want nothing, mind. I'm too busy to be looking at buttons this morning."

In a moment, her brother ran back into the kitchen in a state of excitement:

"It's *Miss*, Mama – Annie's teacher!"

Her mother was alarmed. What on earth did the teacher want with coming around to the house like this? Such a visit was unprecedented – the neighbours would be sure to be fluttering around once the word got out.

"Put on the kettle, Annie, and take off your apron. Arthur, bring her into the front room. For heaven's sake don't keep her standing in the street. Have you gone deaf, girl? Don't be standing there – do as you're told. When you've made the tea, bring it in. And use the good cups, will you, not the chipped ones. Oh my dear God, will you look at the state of this place – well, it can't be helped. She's given us no notice, she'll have to take us as she finds us."

Smoothing her skirt and tucking several stray wisps of hair into her bun, Mama left the kitchen and Annie hurried to make the tea. Miss Hodge or Miss Titch, she wondered? She adored Miss Hodge and loathed the sewing mistress, but she couldn't imagine either of them coming to see her like this. Had she left something behind in the classroom? If that were the case, it would have been delivered by one of her classmates. She rinsed out the good cups and saucers and set them on the tea tray, and fretted over whether to fetch the milk from the scullery. Papa liked his tea with milk, her mother did not. In any case, a dairyman's family did not waste milk.

Deciding to be safe rather than sorry, she poured a small amount into a jug, and placed it on the tray. There were no biscuits; she could make buttered toast but Mama might see that as excessive, having asked her only to make tea. And it was not even midday ... the teacher would probably not be hungry.

Arthur and Maude were hanging about in the hallway, as curious as she was to know what was going on. Her brother hurried to open the door for her; as she entered the room she saw the familiar figure of Miss Hodge sitting primly on the edge of her father's armchair. She didn't know whether to feel relieved or intimidated.

There is something incongruous about seeing a teacher out of the classroom. Meeting up with one in a shop or at a summer fete is strange enough – you find yourself tongue-tied and hope not to be detained very long. But to walk into the parlour, as Annie did, and see one perched between your mother's sewing table and her work-basket, discussing the weather – well, it felt strange. For a moment, Annie saw the room through the eyes of her teacher: the old-fashioned flock wall-paper, the weathered carpet ... everything looked timeworn and bleak. Even Mama's poster of the Crystal Palace, which had always lent the room an air of gentility, seemed shabby and foolish.

She set the tea tray down on the occasional table, praying the one rickety leg wouldn't give way, made a small curtsey in her teacher's direction and turned to leave.

"Stay where you are, Annie," her mother said. "This is about you."

Heart pounding, Annie tried to think what she'd done – or said – to give Miss Hodge reason to approach her mother. She'd been out of school for almost a month; she could think of nothing she'd done in that time to offend the teacher. They'd parted on good terms … or so she thought.

She could tell by the way her mother was sitting, perfectly still, hands folded in her lap, that she, too, was concerned. Miss Hodge had told her only that she was here about Annie, and preferred to discuss it in her daughter's presence.

The teacher smiled. "I've been making enquiries on Annie's behalf and I think I have some good news. I've had a letter from the Bluecoat School in Bishop's Tawton. They would be happy to have Annie as a pupil."

"But Annie is finished school."

"Yes, I understand that, Mrs. Morgan. The thing is, I believe Annie could be a teacher, if she put her mind to it. She's bright and has a curious mind, and I will tell you that is a rare quality today. If she finished out her schooling in Devon she could be trained as a teacher by the time she's eighteen. And it wouldn't cost you anything – Bluecoat scholars are taken on charity."

Mama's face closed tight, like a drum. "We don't want charity, Miss. Thank you but it's not how we do things."

Miss Hodge saw her mistake. "I'm sorry, I put that badly. I didn't mean charity, as such. I simply meant that these schools are very good, and they welcome bright scholars whatever their circumstances. It would be a wonderful opportunity for Annie, don't you think? It would – well, it would give her a future."

Instead of replying, Mama indicated that Annie should pour the tea.

"Do you take milk in your tea, Miss?"

"Yes, thank you, Annie."

There was silence while the tea was poured out. Annie's hands were shaking … the novelty of it all: her teacher and her mother, sitting here talking about *her*. Talking about her *future*.

Miss Hodge took a sip of her tea and began again. "I can understand that you'd be concerned, Mrs. Morgan, about Annie being so far from home. Let me assure you – the school is located in a very respectable area, and the girls are well chaperoned. The headmaster is a friend of mine, which is why I approached him about Annie. I can show you his letter, if you like. I have it in my purse."

"That won't be necessary."

"Very good. Shall I let him know you accept? On behalf of Annie, that is?"

"You can let him know what you like, Miss Hodge, but Annie won't be going."

"But – I don't understand."

"It seems you don't think my daughter has a future, is that it?"

"I'm sorry, I didn't mean –"

"The truth is, she does. She has been hired as a domestic with a family in Ealing and she starts work on Monday. So you see, she really has no need of any more schooling."

"But as a *domestic*, Mrs. Morgan!"

"Yes, as a domestic. It's what many young girls do all over this country and there is nothing at all shameful in it. I was a domestic myself before I was married and I don't regret a minute of it."

"But you *do* believe in education. You sent your daughter to school – both your daughters, in fact, as well as your son. And Annie has told me about her uncle who was at Rugby. Wouldn't you like to see her follow his example?"

Another misstep. Mama didn't believe in sharing family stories with outsiders.

"I take it, Miss Hodge, that you think more schooling will improve my daughter. Is that it?"

"Well, I suppose that's one way of looking at it. I do think it's a pity not to give her the opportunity to continue learning while she can."

"And what will she do with all that learning? When she's married and can't teach any more, and she has a husband and children to care for? What good will it do her then?"

For a moment Annie thought her teacher might be about to reveal the scandalous truth: she didn't believe in marriage. Instead, she simply asked, "What harm will it do her, Mrs. Morgan?"

"It will make her unfit for the life she's meant to lead."

The teacher tried another tack. "Perhaps we might hear

from Annie on the subject. What do you think, Annie? Would you like to continue in school?"

Before Annie could reply, Mama interjected. "My daughter has nothing to say in the matter. She will do as we've decided and take the position she's been offered. As I said, Miss Hodge, *this* family does not take charity."

Mama stood up – the meeting was over. Miss Hodge stood now, too, her cheeks glowing pink as the flower in her button-hole.

"I'm sorry you feel that way, Mrs. Morgan. I only have Annie's interests at heart."

"As do I. Good day to you. Annie, you may see Miss Hodge to the door."

It had begun to rain. Annie waited while Miss Hodge put up her umbrella, a sturdy, sensible affair, the kind a doctor might carry. Neighbourhood women didn't own umbrellas – when it rained you pulled your cloak over your head, and walked faster. She felt she should say something but what? The teacher was just that – a teacher. She was not her mother – she couldn't make decisions for her any more.

"Good luck, Annie," Miss Hodge said. "I wish you all the best. Are you looking forward to your new position?"

"Oh yes, Miss, I am. I have a proper uniform and all."

"Well, I'm sure you'll succeed, whatever you do."

"Yes, Miss. Thank you, Miss."

"Who should direct your path?"

"God and Britannia, Miss."

The teacher smiled. "If your mother should change her mind …"

"She won't, Miss."

"No, I don't suppose she will. Good-bye, Annie."

"Good-bye, Miss."

Back in the kitchen, Mama handed Annie the muslin cap, ready for pressing.

"Mind you don't scorch it now. And be sure to wet it first."

Nothing was said about the teacher's visit – at least, not to Annie directly. But that night she heard her mother speak to her father about it.

"The *nerve* of the woman, coming here with no warning – no invitation of any kind. Seating herself in *my* parlour telling *me* what's best for my daughter. If that's the kind of teacher they're turning out these days, I hope never to meet another."

"Well, now, I suppose she meant well."

Mama refused to be appeased. "And the hem of her coat was unraveling. There she sits, giving out orders like the Queen of Sheba, and her hemline is dragging on the floor. I was embarrassed for her, if you want to know the truth. I truly was."

9.

For ye have the poor with you always.

There are Bible verses all over this place, but that's the one you see first thing in the morning, the minute you open your eyes. It's printed in three-foot letters on the wall – faded, but visible.

The poor. With you. Always. Forever.

Separates us out, she thinks. We, the poor, are always with you, the gentry. That was Bill's word for them – gentry. He said it the way you'd say shit or bollocks or weasel, and he didn't mean just the landed gentry, he meant anyone with pretensions. All that hate for his "betters". He said he came by it naturally – drank it in with his mother's milk, he said.

The Super unlocks the door and calls them awake … those who were lucky enough to sleep in the first place.

"Up you get, now. 'Ave a wash, get dressed. Breakfast at seven-thirty."

Fifteen minutes later she returns to take attendance. Stand at the end of your bed, wait to be counted, answer when your name is called. It's like being in school. But when she says as much to her friend the Pipe Lady, Sal, overhearing, sniffs in disgust.

"Really? Well, ain't you the proper scholar, then."

Pipe Lady shakes her head.

"Don't you mind her. That one never saw the inside of a schoolroom in her life. I'd be surprised if she can write her own name, let alone add two and two."

"Don't need to, do I? I was in the 'Formatory for two years and I learnt more from them other girls than I would've got from any book. None of 'em could read or write but they knew plenty about gettin' along in the world."

At seven-thirty they file into the workhouse dining room, a long, high-ceilinged room furnished with narrow wooden tables. Each table is fitted with a wooden bench along one side, so that everyone sits facing the front. The back wall is taken up almost entirely by a three-part window in the Palladian style, reaching from floor to ceiling and looking out on the courtyard. Gas lanterns hang from the roof and the whitewashed walls are decorated with Scriptural messages in letters three feet high: "GOD IS GOOD", "GOD IS LOVE", "GOD IS JUST".

The Ten Commandments, the Lord's Prayer, and the ubiquitous Workhouse Rules are posted at eye-level. Playing cards, speaking when told to be silent, using obscene language, refusing to work – all of these and more come under the heading "Disorderly Behaviour". Punishments are varied: one might miss out on breakfast or be locked up for twenty-four hours on bread and water. More serious offences are termed "Refractory". Break a window or attempt to escape and you'll find yourself up before the Magistrate and perhaps sent to prison.

Plenty of reading material, anyway, for those who can read.

The women occupy the tables on one side of the room, while the men, entering silently through another door, are seated on the far side of the hall well away from their wives and daughters. Nursing mothers, like Annie, are herded together into a section at the back.

Now the matron enters, leaning heavily on her stick and walking with a noticeable limp. Her lips are compressed as if each step causes her pain. When she reaches her place at the front of the room, she instructs them to bow their heads in prayer.

"Merciful God, make us well and truly thankful for these Thy blessings. Amen."

With the grace out of the way the women are allowed to begin their breakfast: tea with milk but no sugar and a pint of skilly, which is a thin gruel made without salt or sugar. Its one redeeming factor is that they serve it hot. Baskets of bread are passed from table to table by the female officers of the house, who remind the women they risk a severe reprimand if they take more than one. No danger of that, she thinks. She'll be lucky to choke down what she's given – like her toke last night, the bread is barely edible.

The baby is awake and restless. She fed him during the night but he's likely still hungry. *Babbies'll take anything if you make it sweet*. Deciding it's worth a try, she digs the sugar-tit

out of a pocket and puts it to his lips. His blue eyes widen –
this is something new. He accepts the treat and sucks it eagerly,
entirely satisfied with the substitute.

They eat in silence. Were it not for the raising of
spoons to mouths and fingers pulling at crusts of bread these
drab figures could be mistaken for ghosts, spectres from some
ghastly penny-dreadful.

It's a relief when the bell rings, signaling the end of the
meal. Once again they bow their heads and give thanks. It feels
strange to be praying at mealtime again. At home Papa always
said grace before the evening meal, but after she was married
Bill wouldn't allow it. Prayer, he said, was for serfs. He would
bow his head to no one.

As it is still the Christmas holiday they are assigned
no work – a very mixed blessing, as Annie soon discovers. By
mid-morning she's longing for some task to take her mind off
the mind-numbing boredom of the place. Nothing to do but sit
in the Women's Day Room and stare at the walls. Nothing to
read but the Workhouse Rules. Nothing to look at but the sad
faces of lonely women, punished for being poor.

She finds a quiet corner and settles down to nurse the
baby while the woman-chatter undulates around her. A young
girl has Sal and Maisie in hysterics with her impression of
Matron, strutting around the room barking out orders and
dragging one leg behind her.

One old lady objects, saying the matron is to be
respected for doing a difficult job and doing it well in spite of
being crippled. "I've seen her be hard and I've seen her be fair.
And I should know 'cause I been coming here longer'n any of
you."

"Really? Well maybe you have. When was it you come
in, do you remember?"

She has to think for a minute. "It was the week they
hanged that butler – you know, the one that killed Lord
Russell."

"That was forty years ago – you ain't been in here all
that time!"

"In and out," the woman concedes. "But the first time
was back then – I remember them talking about it here in the

Union."

A tiny old woman with a swayback says she remembers it like it was yesterday. "He was foreign, that butler. A bleedin' murderous foreigner. Hangin' was too good for him."

"You're right there, Mrs. Higgins. I knew his housemaid. She said he was quiet and nicely mannered. His Lordship, I mean, not the murderer. I said to her, 'What did you think when you found him in bed with his throat slit?' and *she* said, 'You could knock me over with a feather.' With a feather, she said, and I believe her!"

A young slip of a thing, silent up to now, says, "I met him once, the man who did the hanging. Mr. Calcraft. When I was only little."

If she intended to provoke a reaction, she's succeeded. Several women make the sign of the cross as if the name of the Devil has been mentioned. And in a way it has. If ever there was an executioner with a worse reputation than Jack Ketch it's William Calcraft. There are those who say he would have done it for nothing. At the end of his career he sat for Madame Tussaud; Bill took the girls to see his figure at the Waxworks.

"Well, go on then, girl," says Pipe Lady. "What was he like? You'd best tell us now you've brung it up."

"He had a white beard all bushy and his hair was long and dirty. He was coming down from Smithfield market with a big goose under his arm. Pa said it was him and not to say nothing but I looked and he saw me looking and he said did I want a sweet but my Pa wouldn't let me take it. I think of him sometimes and all them people he killed. I don't hope to see him again, never as long as I live."

"Well you're safe there," Pipe Lady says. "He's dead now, ain't he? Died just before Christmas."

"I never saw him up close," another woman says, "but I went to one of his hangings."

"Which one? There were a few."

"It was when they hanged the Mannings. I wanted to see it – you don't get that a lot, do you, a man and wife hanged together? I was interested."

Several women nod. Oh, yes, they remember the Mannings.

"Well, I don't," Sal says. "Never heard of 'em."

"You wasn't born yet is why. But it was a terrible thing."

"She was French, wasn't she? Bloody foreigner."

"Swiss, Mrs. Higgins."

"Same thing."

"Well, come on then," says Sal, "what did she do?"

"She and her husband killed her lover and buried him under the kitchen. I walked all the way to Surrey to see it but it put me off hanging for good. It was terrible, all the laughing and screeching – people were fighting to get a good view, making up songs about them. I was ashamed to be there. I thought to myself, 'We're just like them Romans back in the day lookin' to put them Christians in the arena and kill 'em for sport.' We ain't changed much over the years."

This leads to a lengthy philosophical discussion of Calcraft's soul now that he is dead: is it burning in eternal torment for the hundreds of people he killed or is he singing with the angels for doing God's work here on Earth? Pipe Lady, as usual, has the final word.

"The man is in Hell and it ain't because of the hangings. It's because of how he treated his mother. She was living in Essex somewhere and they said she was terribly poor and they ordered him to pay something towards her keep. Three shillings a week is what I heard. And he refused. Told 'em to put her in the workhouse. A man who'd treat his mother like has no place sittin' next to God."

***

This, the longest day in her life so far, drags on, punctuated by the workhouse bell. It tolls at twelve o'clock, two o'clock, six o'clock, and eight. Pipe Lady, who has taken it upon herself to act as Annie's guide, says the clanging of the bell regulates everything that happens – rising, working, eating, sleeping, praying.

"You get used to it but it takes a while. It can get right under your skin if you let it. I once knew an old gal who said it drove her mad. She tried to murder the porter. They sent her away to the asylum and when she got out she was fine but she said she'd happily go back if it meant not having to hear that bloody bell ever again."

That evening, with the temperature falling yet again, the ward is more crowded than ever. Pipe Lady gives up her bed to an elderly woman with dirty yellow skin and a constant hacking cough.

"But where will you sleep?" Annie wants to know.

"Oh, don't you mind about me. I've got a friend in permanent who'll sneak me in once the lights go off. I won't be sleeping on the floor."

As the night progresses the old woman appears to be struggling to breathe; Annie gets a wet rag and places it on her forehead but she shrugs it off and continues to cough.

Pneumonia. This from Mrs. Higgins, whose bed is across from Annie's. "I seen it before. She won't last the night."

"What shall we do? We must call someone."

"Won't do no good. She's past helping, that one."

She knows what Pipe Lady would do if she were here: she's bang on the door for the Super. The night wears on and still the woman struggles for breath – sharp, painful gasps punctuated by spells of coughing that seem to go on forever. Unable to stand it any longer Annie gets out of bed and pounds on the door, ignoring the shouts of the others to pipe down and get back into bed. To her relief she hears the sound of the key in the lock … the door opens and Mrs. Chancer is standing there in her nightcap and dressing gown looking extremely annoyed.

"*You* again! What is it this time? If you didn't get your toke it's too bad. Kitchen's closed."

"There's a sick woman here. Very sick. I think she may be dying."

"Is it ketchin'? I ain't comin' in if she's got somethin' ketchin'. I got me 'ealth to think of."

"I have no idea if it's catching or not. But you must see to her – she needs care."

With extreme reluctance the Super enters the room and advances towards the woman, expecting at any moment to "ketch" something. The elderly woman, in spite of the cold, is bathed in sweat; in the eerie glow of the gaslight her skin has changed from yellow to pale blue and the front of her nightdress is spattered with blood and sputum.

"What's up with you then? Are you sick? Did you say you was sick when you come in?"

The woman makes an effort to sit up, then falls back again with a groan.

"The sick ward's closed. We'll see to you in the mornin'. Now quit snivellin' and go to sleep."

"I think she needs to see the doctor."

"Nobody asked what you think! Hold your tongue. And don't be bangin' on the door again or I'll have you written up for bein' fractious."

With that she leaves, locking the door behind her.

The next morning the door is unlocked early, before the seven o'clock bell. Annie, who's been awake all night, sees the Super standing in the doorway, her bell in one hand and a handkerchief in the other. "'Ow is she, then? Still snivellin'?"

"You'd best come in and see for yourself."

Handkerchief pressed against her mouth, the Super edges toward the bed where the woman lies completely still, her eyes open, staring at nothing. She nudges her gingerly once or twice but there's no response. After a few more unsuccessful pokes the Super leaves, returning shortly with Matron in tow. Without saying a word Matron limps over to the woman, bends down to listen for any breathing, then feels her neck and wrist for a heartbeat. After a moment she stands and shakes her head. The woman is indeed dead.

The Super is indignant. "They ain't supposed to be let in if they're sick. Stoker knows that – it's 'is responsibility to send 'em to the sick ward if they look like they got somethin' fatal. 'Ow'm I supposed to know? I ain't a nurse, am I? I ain't a doctor. It could be somethin' ketchin', couldn't it, and 'ere I am with me bad lungs and 'e's lettin' in all sorts of sick old women, puttin' us all at risk. It shouldn't be allowed. I've a mind to get me son to write to the Board about it. It's a disgrace is what it is."

"All right, Mrs. Chancer, calm down. I'll speak to Mr.

Stoker. We'll see it doesn't happen again. There's no need to bring the Board into it, we can take care of these things ourselves. Go ring for the attendant and tell him we need a couple of men to carry the body to the Mortuary. Tell them to bring a box. And send someone for the doctor – we'll need a death certificate."

The Super leaves the room and Matron turns to the women, calling for silence. It's unnecessary to do so – everyone is awake now and no one is saying a word. A woman has died … passed from this Earth in their very midst, with none of the usual sacraments. It sends a chill through the room – even the children sense it.

Leaning heavily on her stick, Matron says, "Hear me now, all of you – Mrs. Chancer is upset but she's right. This woman should not have come here if she knew she was ill. She should have applied at the Infirmary. Instead she put the rest of you in danger by coming here and lying among you. People like her don't think about the consequences. They go about getting sick and making other people sick and then they die. This woman's death is the result of improvidence. Let it be a lesson to you all."

"It was the Super's fault she died."

Annie doesn't know what made her say it but she has the matron's attention. She has, in fact, the attention of everyone in the room – girl, woman and child. It doesn't matter – she's not sorry. It needed to be said.

Matron glares at her. "What did you say?"

"I said the Supervisor's at fault. If she had called the doctor last night this woman might still be alive."

"I know you, don't I? You're the one who kicked up a fuss in the receiving ward."

"I didn't – it wasn't a fuss, exactly …"

"What's your name?"

"Mrs. Taylor."

"And you are a nurse, is that it?"

"Oh no, I'm not."

"No? But you do have some training in that line, am I right?"

"No, not really. When I was in service I had an

employer – she'd get these terrible headaches and I, you know, I'd give her medicine for them …"

Her voice trails off. The matron is watching her in a way that says, Stop talking. You've already said more than enough.

"So you're not a nurse but you think you have a right to judge how things are done here. That *is* what you said isn't it? You said this woman would've lived if Mrs. Chancer had called the doctor."

"Well, yes. I did say that. But ..."

"The fact is you really don't know what you're talking about, do you?"

Annie says nothing. It's clear the matron doesn't expect a response.

"And Mrs. Chancer, who's been the Supervisor of this ward for six years and has had to deal with all manner of sickness and depravity – you're saying *she's* to blame. That's what you said, right? That Mrs. Chancer let this woman die?"

"I said …"

"I *heard* what you said, Mrs. Taylor. I suggest you don't say anything more. If you ever speak to me like that again I'll write you up as Refractory. And if I hear that you've spoken against any Officer of this House, anyone at all, I'll have you sent before the Board. Do you understand?"

"Yes."

"Beg pardon?"

"Yes, *Ma'am.*"

"Good. Now get dressed before I change my mind."

There's a brief lull directly after she leaves; soon enough though the grousing and complaining resume. No one speaks about what just happened. What is there to say? She gets dressed and gathers up the baby, avoiding the looks directed her way. Stupid woman, they're thinking. She's put Matron against her and her children, too, perhaps. And for what? Speaking up did nothing – there was no good to be gained by it.

Mrs. Dribble comes up to her and pats her gently on the arm. "I was saving this but I want you to have it."

She holds out a desiccated lump that looks as if it

started life as an Eccles cake a very long time ago.
"It has raisins, my dear. Raisins!"

10.

Bluebell was uneasy – this was not the usual route. With every corner she turned her head to look back at them: Here? You want to turn here? Are you sure?

Papa was driving her to the station in the milk dray. There'd been a thunderstorm the night before and the stink was worse than usual. The sweepers were out brushing away the puddles into gutters already overfull of sewage and garbage; she was glad not to be walking. Turning down a side street, they passed a garden gate with crimson flowers overhanging. Papa stopped the horse and got down from the cart to pluck a poppy for her buttonhole. She told him he must have one too and so he picked another for himself and said they were like gentry now, weren't they, with proper buttonholes and all?

Once they reached Paddington station, it was hard to say good-bye. He couldn't come in with her as there was nowhere to leave the horse and cart and they had to be quick as the cab men were dropping off passengers and waiting to pick up others. At the last minute her courage failed her.

"I've changed my mind, Papa. I don't think I want to go."

Her father never argued with his children. He never said "You must do this" or "You must never do that". And yet as long as she could remember, she wanted only to please him.

"Well now, Pansy, I can see as you might feel that way. It's hard for me to think about you going off, like, and being so grown up and all. But there it is, isn't it? You're a big girl now and you have these fine clothes your Mama made you and where would you wear them if you didn't go and do this? And what would your Mama say if I brought you back to the house now? She'd give me a good scolding and send you right back to the station. So it's probably best you just go off now and we'll both get it over with."

It was probably the longest speech he'd ever made. She wiped her tears and blew her nose, gave him a quick hug and hurried inside. By the time she reached the ticket window she'd recovered her composure. Papa was right: she was a grown-up now. And she was British. God and Britannia would direct her path.

***

The Thomas Bellwethers of Myrtle Cottage, Ealing, were what you might call "hankering" middle-class. They were resolved to rise in the world, and Annie, unpaid though she was, was a step in that direction.

Cordelia Bellwether was a Yorkshire farmer's daughter who had married above her station – her husband worked for one of the commercial banks in the City. His father had kept a shop and had the good fortune to secure a contract during the Crimean War providing salt and sugar to England's troops. He came out of it a wealthy man and managed to send his only son to a decent public school. There young Tom made the friendships that eventually led to his job at the bank.

The fact that his father had been in trade would always be a handicap to Mr. B.'s social ambitions, but it need not be so for his children. His son, now away at preparatory school, would attend a better public school than his father and find himself further up the social ladder. His daughters, given their advantages, would marry well and produce children who would in turn keep climbing. They were being trained for just that at a small establishment school run by a gentlewoman who taught them ladylike accomplishments like painting, drawing, and dancing. All this might someday result in the ultimate reward: a peerage for his only son and marriage into minor aristocracy for his grandchildren.

Until then, Mr. B. took the bus into the City and Mrs. B. worked diligently to gain favour with the local gentry. While her grandchildren might someday take their status in society for granted, she could not do so. She must constantly strive to better herself, to mind her P's and Q's when she was in company, and ensure that the world was aware – the world in her case being the parish of Ealing and its civic leaders in particular – that the Thomas Bellwethers were worth knowing.

They hired Annie because they weren't yet wealthy enough to afford a proper maid and because she was young enough to be molded. It helped as well that she was from

Notting Hill and not Ealing. Mama was right: families did not like to take on local girls; they feared they would gossip about their employers and run back home at the first sign of trouble.

The house, a two-storey, red brick villa, was favourably situated on one of the better streets in Ealing, meaning it was tucked well back from the bustle of the High Street and enjoyed that sense of privacy and seclusion so important to suburbanites. The position was a good one, as far as these things went. Because there were just three of them in service, a certain amount of juggling was required. Hitchens, the gardener, was also in charge of cleaning the silver; occasionally he was called on to double as butler if anyone grand was invited to dinner. As he did this very seldom, it often had disastrous results and by the time Annie left their employ the Bellwethers had found a suitable manservant who did not live in but could be relied on to come in and wait at table when needed.

Hitchens occupied a small shed in the back garden. He may have had a first name but Annie never knew it or heard him called anything but Hitchens. Cook was always called Cook unless you were talking to her directly in which case you called her Mrs. Drew. As far as anyone knew she'd never been married; it was a form of respect. All cooks went by "Mrs." and all housekeepers, too.

So there was Cook and Hitchens and Annie. Cook prepared the meals and cleaned the kitchen and in the morning she answered the bell. Annie was grateful for that because there were interruptions all day long. Tradesmen called at the back door, visitors dropped in for tea, and the penny post arrived several times a day – although it was only when the postman rang the bell twice that one was expected to stop work and go to the door to greet him. A double ring meant something important – a telegram most likely. Anything else was left in the basket to be looked at when there was time.

Being taken on as a general domestic servant meant she was chambermaid, laundry maid, lady's maid, and scullery maid. Up at six to rake out the ashes and clean the flues, she lit the stove, put the kettle on, and polished up the cutlery. After bringing Cook her tea – nothing was done in the kitchen until after Cook had her morning tea – it was time to clean the grate, shake out the hearthrug, light the fire in the dining room, dust the furniture, and whiten the front steps.

All of this had to be done before the family came down to breakfast, which was the one time of day when they didn't expect to be waited on at table. Mrs. B. served out breakfast from a large chafing dish on the sideboard and while they ate Annie emptied and rinsed the chamber pots, stripped the beds, turned the mattresses, swept the floors, brushed the bedroom carpets, and tidied up the nursery. If the weather was fine, she opened the windows to air out the rooms and ran a cloth along the sill to wipe away the worst of the soot.

Then there was just time to eat the breakfast Cook set aside for her, clear the table, sweep up the crumbs and help the girls dress for school. With them out the door, Mrs. B. was her main priority. She helped her get dressed and did her hair and then together they made up the beds and prepared the rooms for cleaning.

Each room was "turned out" on a different day of the week, which meant moving some of the furniture, hiding the bigger pieces under dust covers, pinning up the curtains, and taking the candlesticks downstairs for Hitchens to clean.

At midday the girls came home from school. They ate luncheon in the dining room with their mother while Annie waited on table. (This was something she learned the first day she was there: the midday meal was luncheon, or lunch, and the meal at the end of the day was not supper, as she was used to calling it, but dinner. It was confusing at first but she soon became accustomed to announcing that luncheon was served and inquiring about Cook's plans for dinner.) Afterwards she cleared the table, swept the carpet, and tidied the dining room before changing into her afternoon uniform. If Mrs. B. was receiving visitors, she helped her dress and prepared the drawing room for company; if her mistress was going visiting herself, Annie helped her get ready to go out, after which she had two hours in which to dust, polish, and wash and wax the floors.

At four o'clock she changed into a clean apron in order to lay the table for dinner and wait on the family. When the evening meal was done, she cleared away the dishes, swept the carpet, and tidied the dining room before joining Cook and Hitchens in the kitchen for her tea.

It was a rule of the house that dinner should be served at five o'clock precisely – at the very moment that Mr. Bellwether walked through the door. Mrs. B. had confided that this was a new development for them. Until recently they'd had their dinner in the middle of the day, but it was out of fashion now she said – the *best* people ate their dinner at night.

"And so we made the change, Annie, but I don't mind telling you – I do get peckish by the time dinner comes round."

Officially Annie's workday ended at ten although she generally spent at least another hour setting the table for the next day's breakfast, laying the fire in the kitchen, and cleaning the family's boots before getting undressed and collapsing into bed. In some ways this wasn't such a bad thing – had she not been exhausted she might have had time to be homesick, like Mama said, and cry herself to sleep.

Sometimes there were house-guests which meant more beds to turn out, more boots to clean, more people to feed and wash up after. But the people weren't the worst of it: about three months after she came to work there the children were given a puppy. It was a darling, playful little creature; the girls named it "Rompers" and at first Annie, who'd always wanted a pet, was as charmed as they were. Unfortunately, no one, least of all Mrs. B. and certainly not the children, saw any need to attempt to house-train it – it was allowed to run riot, pissing and shitting where it liked, chewing curtains and shoes with impunity, tramping mud across Annie's freshly-scrubbed floors. Cleaning up after it, brushing away the hair it shed, and mopping up puppy tracks day after day created an agonizing amount of work. Annie thought seriously about giving her notice.

One afternoon when the family was away Rompers found his way into Mr. B.'s dressing room – how he got in, the door always being shut, was a mystery to everyone but Hitchens and the cook. While he was in there he destroyed one pair of Mr. B.'s brogues and did his business in another. That did it. The children protested loudly but were overruled.

Rompers was removed from the household.

***

Apart from the dog, her most burdensome chore was the
weekly wash. Her own family had fewer things to wash in a
year than the Bellwethers went through in a month.

Annie came from a long line of women who never
owned more than two dresses at a time: one for ordinary wear
and one for good. Each year you sewed a new dress; this
became your good dress while last year's good dress was used
for everyday. Previous everyday dresses were cut up to make
frocks for the children or, if they were beyond saving, were cut
into squares and used for quilts, towels, and cleaning rags.

Things in the Bellwether household were different. Mrs.
B. began the day in her wrapper and morning cap in which
she served and ate breakfast. Once Mr. B. and the children
were out of the house, she went upstairs and changed into a
housedress and apron in order to help Annie with the morning
chores. The apron was removed at luncheon as it was important
to keep up appearances even if one was dining alone – or with
the girls which was essentially the same thing. After lunch,
the housedress was discarded in favour of shopping clothes: a
walking suit usually, worn with a shawl or lined coat depending
on the weather. By three o'clock Mrs. B. was home with just
enough time to change into an elaborate silk dress and cap for
paying or receiving her afternoon calls. After dinner, if she and
her husband had no engagements, she removed the cap and
changed back into her wrapper. Four changes of clothes in a
single day – is it any wonder the washing piled up?

Monday was wash-day, but the work began Sunday
night when everything was collected, sorted and soaked.
Monday morning she rose two hours earlier than usual in
order to get the water heated to boiling. Once the clothes
were washed, rinsed, and wrung out, they were hung to dry
in the back garden, or in wet weather in the kitchen, which
never pleased Cook as she had to duck damp, dripping
linen as she worked. Then came the ironing the following

morning, followed by folding and putting away – only to have everything dirtied again and the entire process begun all over.

Still, her workload was no more than any girl did in such a family. Up at dawn, in bed well after everyone else, and a half-day off once a month. When it rained or was too cold to go anywhere she spent that afternoon up in her room, writing to her mother and mending her clothes. On fine days she left the house and walked up the Uxbridge Road to Haven Green, the site of the annual fair – for three days in June nobody in the village went to work or did much of anything else but crowd the gingerbread stalls, visit the tents of the Fat Lady and the Giant and the Dwarf, and get their fortunes told.

Shortly after she arrived that first summer the local board erected a huge tent on the Green in honour of the marriage of the Prince of Wales to Princess Alexandra. They had sports and fireworks on Ealing Common and all the important men of the parish and their wives came for a celebration dinner, including the former Home Secretary, Horace Walpole. Annie didn't attend, of course, but she heard all about it from Mrs. B. who got the details from a woman who'd actually been there. It was a pity, said Mrs. B., not to have been invited but no doubt similar festivities would be held when Prince Alfred married and by then they were sure to be included on the list. After all, His Highness was only second in line to the throne and surely the invitation list would be a little … broader.

Tuesday was Mrs. B.'s at home day – from three to five she was officially "in" and receiving visitors. Dinner was pushed back to six and Mr. B., not wanting to run the risk of encountering any of the lady callers, took the later train home. As a rule a half dozen ladies dropped in during that time. No one ever stayed more than fifteen or twenty minutes – it would have been terribly rude to linger when a new person appeared – and they kept their shawls and bonnets on in order to make a smooth departure.

On a few dreadful occasions, Mrs. B. sat alone in the parlour for the entire two hours. Thankfully that didn't happen often and generally there was an excuse to be found such as the weather or some afternoon entertainment to which she had not been invited. While this was disappointing it was to be expected; she comforted herself in the knowledge that these slights were fewer now than they had been when she was first married and the time would come when they would be absolutely a thing of the past.

***

Through Mrs. B's visiting days, Annie came to know several other domestics and soon learned the order of importance. At the very bottom you had the poor little waifs from the workhouse, sent out at the age of seven or eight to drudge for families too poor to afford proper help. Available for a few pounds a year, they were more slaves than servants. Like Annie, they received their board in the place of wages; unlike her, they had little hope of ever rising to anything better. Most of them were broken by the time they came to the job and made terrible servants being unused to living and working in a regular household and unaware of the niceties of dealing with glass and silverware. Many ran away or were let go and ended up as prostitutes or drunks. Some just went back to the workhouse and stayed there.

As pitiful as they were, they were not in the majority. Most domestics were like Annie, children of working-class parents whose choices were few: they could go to work on factory assembly lines, sell watercress or flowers in the street, or take in laundry or needlework at home. None of these situations provided any kind of security and if you were foolish enough to lose a finger on the factory line or get hit by a cab in the street – well, there goes the job! You might be lucky and meet a decent man and get married but that didn't mean you wouldn't still be working in the factory or taking in laundry, only this time you'd be doing so with a baby on the way.

Being in service meant long hours and hard work but it also meant respectability and a roof over your head. You might, if you were clever and kept your wits about you, move slowly but steadily up the ladder and become a ladies' maid or even housekeeper in a big house, rubbing shoulders (not literally) with the gentry. It would be a very long time before Mr. and

Mrs. B. would be in a position to hire servants of this sort.

Even though by Annie's standards the Bellwethers were wealthy people, there was never quite enough money to fulfil their hopes and aspirations.

Cook's half-day holiday, for instance, had long been a bone of contention. Officially, her time was her own from two o'clock Sunday afternoon until the following morning. This meant the Bellwethers were without a cook for dinner. Some of their friends managed this inconvenience by having a cold dinner on Sundays consisting of leftovers from the day before, but Mr. B. rejected this idea out of hand.

"Am I to be expected to go to work Monday morning on the strength of a gammon sandwich and a morsel of cheese?"

Many Englishmen went to work every day on far less, but his wife knew better than to say it. Mr. B. had many fine qualities but he did not care to be challenged. His home was his castle and while he might have to bend his neck in submission during the workday he not prepared to do so in the domestic realm.

It was a difficult time. Mrs. B. found herself pleading with Cook to stay after luncheon and "throw together something" for the evening meal. Cook responded, with some asperity, that she wasn't in the habit of *throwing* things together and if they didn't sort things out soon she'd be forced to give notice. For her part, Mrs. B. shrank at the thought of the work involved in advertising for a new cook and then training her in the delicate complexities of Mr. B.'s digestive system. It had taken almost a full year for Mrs. Drew to get it right and *she* was relatively experienced in such things, having spent the previous ten years as a cook at the Lunatic Asylum in York. If Cook stayed on and they hired someone part-time just for Sunday dinner it would cost them at least 3*s* a week and there would still be all the trouble of teaching her about her husband's stomach.

In the end, Mrs. B. came to the conclusion that it would be easier and cheaper to cook the Sunday dinner herself. She'd grown up on a farm and was no stranger to the kitchen. In fact she rather prided herself on her cooking. It had certainly been good enough for Mr. B. in the early months of their marriage before they had servants. And if it would save a few shillings – well, so much the better.

"You must keep me company, Annie. I like to cook, but I must have someone to talk to. It'll be your job to stir the soup and keep the fire going."

Years later Annie would say she had Mrs. B. to thank for teaching her to cook in the modern way. When she was growing up, meals were cooked in a kettle or frying pan over a small open grate. Mama had described in great detail the marvelous cast-iron kitchen ranges on display at the Great Exhibition but until Annie went to work for the Bellwethers she'd only seen them in the illustrated papers and had never even lit one before.

Preparations for Sunday dinner began immediately after the luncheon dishes were cleared away. Donning an apron to protect the dress she'd worn to church, Mrs. B. sat at the kitchen table and leafed through Mrs. Beeton's *Book of Household Management*. When she found a receipt that appealed to her she read out the list of ingredients and Annie searched the pantry to see whether or not they were on hand. This could be a lengthy process.

If, for instance, Mrs. B. decided on apple soup, she would be confounded to discover they were out of cloves. Rather than move on to another receipt she would spend several minutes discussing the possibility of replacing cloves with something else, such as cinnamon, for instance, or aniseed. Frequently she set her heart on something rather unusual and was disappointed to learn that the main ingredient was not only not on hand but was out of season as well. When this happened with Mrs. Beeton's receipt for Curried Cod, Annie suggested it might be a good idea to plan these meals a day or two ahead of time as Cook did in order to ensure a well-stocked larder. That, however, would mean getting in the way of Cook's business in the kitchen and Cook would never stand for that.

No, it must be done on Sunday.

Once the menu was settled and the ingredients found, Mrs. B. went to work with a will. She never seemed to hurry but her pace never slackened. And she could carry on a conversation – one-sided though it was – while rolling out the pastry for the rabbit pie that was her husband's favourite and never miss a stroke.

"It has rained now for eight days straight, Annie – which is a good three days more than Mrs. Prickett promised when she delivered the milk last Saturday. She's a terrible one for the rheumatism, my heart goes out to her. (Pass me that fork, there's a good girl.) She tells the weather by the aches in her hands – she knows when it's going to rain and she knows when it's going to stop. Last week she said to me, 'Mrs. Bellwether, we're in for a bad week of it – Sunday to Sunday, it'll rain cats and dogs.' And didn't we wake up to it last Sunday, just as she said, and here it is Sunday again and we're not seeing an end of it. Ah, but she's had a terrible hard life. All those children and a husband who drinks – well, he did so when he was alive, God rest his soul. I don't expect he's doing much drinking these days, having been dead these past eighteen months. When he was alive Mr. Bellwether used to see him staggering along the High Street roaring drunk and kicking up a row. (I'll take those slices of ham now, Annie.) I suppose it's a blessing he's gone – at least he can't be beating her about with a stick. She's getting too old to carry them milk pails and her boys have gone off to work in the mills up in Manchester and she never hears from them. And her daughters! The oldest girl's moved into a lodging house in London and they say she's working on the *stage*! I can only imagine the kind of life she's leading. I'll tell you, Annie, I pray every night that neither of my girls take it into their heads to go off and live like a Bohemian. The shame of it would fair kill me. (Those eggs should be hard-boiled now, I think. Peel and slice them for me, and then you can pound the mace.) Mr. Bellwether always says the world can be a harsh and unforgiving place for a young woman alone. And he knows, he does, working in the City. He sees downfallen women every day and his heart bleeds for them. There are those what pass them by and think nothing of it but not Mr. Bellwether – he passes them by, too, of course, but he thinks on them often. (I'll need that grater for the nutmeg.) You want to be grateful, Annie, that you've landed here in a good home with decent folk who won't take liberties. You hear stories all the time – I heard one only the other day. Up in Gloucestershire, it was, an old vicar was brought up in court for 'aiding and abetting a suicide'. That's what they called it, aiding and abetting. He seduced his kitchen maid and the shame of it drove the poor girl to drown herself in the river. A *clergyman*, if you can believe it! Did you ever hear anything so terrible? The Women of Caritas are writing a letter about it – it'll be in the paper next week, we must look out for it."

Mrs. B. was very proud about the Women of Caritas. It was an exclusive organization, and she'd only recently been voted a member. Their motto was "Helping the Deserving Poor to Help Themselves", with emphasis on the word "deserving": the Women of Caritas had no truck with those lazy and shiftless souls who simply refused to work.

With membership came certain responsibilities, among them a seemingly endless number of charitable events, each requiring a new frock. Or alterations to ones she already owned. She kept a running account with Madame Aurore, the Kensington dressmaker whose advertisements proudly proclaimed, "From Paris". Annie's job was to accompany her on these forays into town and to stand close by in order to help pinch, squeeze and prod her into Madame Aurore's creations.

It was from the dressmaker, chatting away in an accent that sounded artificial even to Annie's ears, that she learned the importance of flattery when dealing with one's betters.

"It feels a bit snug in the waist," Mrs. B. would say, peering into the looking glass and straining to see the way the material came together at the back. "Do you think I'm putting on weight?"

"You, Madame? Oh, *non, non, c'est impossible*," the seamstress would reply, cocking her head to one side with just the right amount of Gallic cheekiness. "You are – how do you say? *Comme un sylph, n'est-ce pas? Tres, tres slendair*."

"Really? You think so?"

"I know so." Then a wink in Annie's direction and a comforting pat on her customer's fleshy upper arm. "We will take it out, just a *soupçon, oui*? To give Madame extra movement, if she wishes. But there is no need, you understand?

No need whatsoever."

And Mrs. B. would leave the shop feeling once again that Madame Aurore might charge more than the seamstress in the High Street but she was worth every shilling.

11.

It's been a long time since she was in church for anything other than a wedding, a funeral or a baptism. She attended when she was in service – domestic staff were always required to attend church, unless the head of the household conducted Sunday morning prayers in the servants' hall. She didn't mind – it was interesting to sit and look about the congregation and think about who they were and what they did when they weren't sitting in their Sunday-best clothes, all pious and perfect.

There was old Mrs. Switcher, who sat across from the Bellwethers and generally fell asleep during the sermon. She lived alone with her companion, Miss Trevelyan, in a falling-down house at the top of the street. While her mistress snored, Miss Trevelyan gazed with something close to adoration as the vicar read the lesson and led the congregation in prayer. Was she in love with him? And, if so, did he know it?

Three rows down, on the other side of the aisle, Mr. and Mrs. Buller and their children took up an entire pew. There were seven children, if you counted the baby, and they were upstanding members of the congregation. But she'd seen Mr. Buller whisper something in the ear of Miss Wilmot who taught the infants' class, and Miss Wilmot had blushed and raised her fan and if Mrs. Buller hadn't stepped forward just then to steer him away might Mr. Buller have said something more?

It was delightful to think about these things. It made an otherwise tedious two hours pass more quickly. One could sit and daydream during the sermon and the Scripture readings, but you couldn't do that with the singing of hymns. You had to stand and sing along and they weren't the popular street songs that everyone knew but old-fashioned and dreary, like "Go Worship at Immanuel's Feet". It had eighteen verses and by the time you arrived at the final stanza the glory and power of the message was lost through sheer mind-numbing exhaustion:

> Not earth, nor seas, nor sun, nor stars,
> Nor heaven His full resemblance bears:
> His beauties we can never trace
> Till we behold Him face to face.

After the service the family, dressed in sombre Sunday black, returned home, marching sedately up the street, while Annie and the cook hurried on ahead to get dinner ready. Hitchens, for some reason, was never made to attend church – Annie envied him for it.

Once she was married, she got out of the habit. It was because of Bill, really; he thought church-goers were fools. It was rather shocking when he said it. She asked if he was an atheist and he said he believed in the gods of social progress and individual freedom.

"Whatever crushes individuality is despotism – and that holds for any man or any God. John Stuart Mill said that and I have more respect for him than for any priest or pastor, living or dead."

What would Mr. Mill, if he were still alive, make of Bill abandoning his family? Is it individuality or selfishness to leave the house one morning and never return? Is it social progress to get on a ship bound for South Africa with another woman, leaving behind a wife and three children and no money, not even enough to pay the landlord?

***

"Stand for prayer!"

A clean-shaven young man in clerical dress steps forward, raises his arms to the heavens, and launches into his petition with remarkable gusto. If God is listening He will not fail to be impressed:

"Our Heavenly Father, we beseech Thee on this great and glorious morning – this morning which Thou hast made – this morning created by Thine own hands for the good of mankind on every part of the Earth – we beseech Thee O Lord to look with favour on these poor sinners. Behold these wretched men and women gathered here in this house of shelter, this temporary home for those who have none – for those with no place to lay their weary heads – for those with no succour in times of distress but the charity of their fellow men. Forgive them, O Lord! For though their sins be as scarlet yet they shall be as white as snow. Look with favour upon them as You did the adulteress and the cripple, as You forgave even those who nailed You to the cross, as You will forgive the lowest of the low should they but ask for Thy forgiveness. Bless the Officers of this house, O Lord, who provide the food and clothing and comfort for these Thy children. Give them the strength to carry out their duties. For did not the Apostle say, 'I can do all things through Christ which strengtheneth me'? Let the food of the Spirit, like manna from heaven, nourish these Your humble servants and look with favour on this blessed house. And so we ask it in the name of the Father and the Son and the Holy Spirit. Amen."

Murmurs of "amen" and the rustling of cloth as the captive congregation is allowed to be seated. The chaplain announces the text of his sermon for the morning: Luke 15, verses 11 to 32. The parable of the prodigal son.

It's a familiar story, even to Annie who's had little to do with Scripture since leaving school. Hearing it now in these surroundings it occurs to her that this is not a story about forgiveness, as she was taught. It is about food. Think, the chaplain says, of the young man starving in the fields, living off the husks thrown to the pigs. He remembers how in the house of his father there is plenty of food. Even the servants have bread enough to eat. And when he returns his father orders them to kill the fatted calf that they may feast and make merry.

For this my son was dead, and is alive again; he was lost, and is found.

All that food – roast beef and bread and potatoes and wine – wasted on an ungrateful son. And here she sits with a pint of skilly and a lump of hard bread in her stomach. Because she has, finally, given in to her hunger and eaten her breakfast toke.

And why must they be forgiven anyway? What sins have they committed, any of them here, except for growing old and poor and unable to care for themselves? When her mother was a girl, things were different – people pitched in and helped each other. And when your neighbours couldn't help, you'd apply to the Parish and they'd come up with enough to pay the rent, buy a little meat and milk, a bit of bread. Sometimes they paid for medical treatment, where it was needed, or a decent frock to wear when knocking on the doors of respectable houses, looking for work.

But that was before the new Poor Law, back when it was no sin to be poor. Now, if you're to be helped, you must be made to feel the full disgrace of your situation, preferably amid surroundings as dismal as they can make them. You must to be made to feel that your poverty is of your own making. You must be punished.

***

The sermon ends, the final Benediction is given, and they are dismissed. Now the time is their own. They may leave the building for a few hours, with permission, if they have anywhere to go. Most don't and others, like Annie, want to be here for their weekly visit with their children.

Sal and Maisie scamper out; Annie watches them leave, envying them a little even though she knows, without being told, they'll be up to no good. The dormitory is off-limits during the day-time and it's too cold to sit outside, so she heads to the women's day-room, a long, airy room with low windows overlooking the courtyard – a grand name for an uninviting square of paving stones with a water pump in the centre, surrounded by a half dozen benches. It's also known as the exercise yard, although the only exercise that takes place here is the constant sweeping of brooms and beating of carpets.

Her friend the Pipe Lady is there already, holding court in a corner of the room, surrounded by a handful of her comrades. Seeing Annie, she beckons to her from across the room.

"We've just been talking about you," she says, once Annie and the baby are settled. "I hear you were quite the hero this morning."

It's difficult to tell if she's teasing or not, but before Annie can reply, another woman interjects.

"That was a fine thing you did, speaking your mind like that. There's not many would dare to do it, but you did and we all saw you do it. Good for you."

"I probably shouldn't have. She's going to hate me now

– I should have kept quiet."

"Don't be so sure," Pipe Lady says. "She won't love you for it, that's for certain. But she'll see you as someone with a bit of backbone and that may come in handy some day. You did the right thing."

All the women are agreed on this point; it's as if Annie's been granted a kind of seal of approval among them. Pipe Lady, it seems, is a member of a kind of pauper sisterhood. There's old Mrs. Higgins, bent almost double with curvature of the spine; Mrs. Fitzgerald, whom everyone just calls Fitz, a large, dour woman who never seems to smile; Mrs. Hatchett, the youngest, although she's at least ten years older than Annie, and Mrs. Knight, the one who first came in the year Lord Russell was murdered.

"Sunday Knight," she says, "that's my name and you can laugh, most folks do when they hear it. I was born on a Sunday and Knight's my married name. If my poor ma, God rest her soul, knew what I been through living with that name she'd've called me Sally and be done with it."

They've known each other for decades and are obviously friends, but it's Mrs. Clarke – who will always be Pipe Lady to Annie – who wields the most authority.

As Mrs. Hatchett explains, "We been around a while, you see, and we look out for each other. We don't travel together, exactly, but we come across each other and give each other the news. Like if there's a new master at one of the unions and he's changed the dietary. That kind of thing."

Attention turns to the baby, who fell asleep halfway through the sermon this morning and has been sleeping ever since.

"He's a lovely thing," says Mrs. Knight. "How old is he now?"

"Six months – six and a half, really."

"Keep him on the diddies as long as you can. As long as the babby's sucking they won't take him away."

Mrs. Hatchett agrees. "I had my Jimmy with me when I first come, and I kept him on the diddy for three years. He was a big boy by then, and he didn't want it so much but I made him take it. Told him it was so he could stay with his mama.

They took him anyway, in the end, but I made it that long."

When Annie asks where they took her boy, the woman's eyes fill with tears.

"That I don't know. My sister says they sent him to Canada. They handed me a paper and said to sign it, didn't they? But I can't read, I don't know what it said. I made my mark and they took him away."

"I'm so sorry."

"Ah, dear me," says Fitz, "but it's a wicked world when they can take your boy away just like that."

The women all nod in agreement. It's a wicked, wicked world.

***

Just before two o'clock Matron appears at the door of the day-room and rings her bell for attention.

"Those of you expecting visitors will make your way to the receiving ward. You will go there directly, mind – no dawdling or talking along the way."

As Annie and Fitz prepare to leave, the others observe them with envy. To have a visitor is a rare thing for most. Mrs. Hatchett hasn't had one in more than a year – Mrs. Higgins says her son came to see her once a few years ago but they argued and he hasn't been back.

She finds a chair next to the far wall, settles the baby on her lap and waits. In a few minutes a handful of little girls troop in, all clad in drab brown smocks like a flock of bedraggled sparrows, led by a poor little thing with a clubfoot who appears to be in charge. They look so alike it takes her a moment to recognize her daughters. Edith is the first to see her – she rushes at Annie with a force that almost knocks the baby out of her arms.

"Mama!"

The child wraps herself around her mother and bursts into tears. Matron, standing guard near the door, frowns in disapproval.

"Now, now Edie, don't cry," Annie says. "Why are you making such a fuss? You'll upset Teddy."

Her daughter wipes her nose with her sleeve and asks if she might kiss the baby.

"*May* you? Of course you may. He's your brother, why would you ask?"

Gently, she presses her lips against the baby's forehead, then asks if she might do it again.

"Edith, for heaven's sake don't be so foolish. Why are you acting like this?"

She kisses him again and strokes his head, gazing at him as if she never expected to see him again.

Annie fully expects Vic to hold back and she does just that. Instead of coming over, she stands just inside the door refusing to approach or even look at her mother. Sulking, Annie thinks. Punishing her for abandoning them to this place. She waves and tries to catch the girl's eye but Vic continues to ignore her until Matron sees what's up and shoves her in Annie's direction.

"Get over there now, what are you waiting for? Go say hello to your ma."

Reluctantly she sidles over, keeping her eyes on the floor. As Annie reaches for her hand she flinches. Feeling a familiar flush of irritation, Annie tries to keep her temper. "Come now, Vic, don't you want to kiss the baby?"

A few more steps, close enough to run a finger along the top of his head. "You still have him, then."

"Of course I still have him, why wouldn't I? What has gotten into you girls?"

Still she won't look up. What, Annie wonders, have they been told? Has someone said she ran out on them? It wasn't *she* who ran away – *she's* not the one who's done the running in this family. If Vic wants to be angry at someone, let her be angry at Bill.

She won't say this of course. She's not about to give her daughter an excuse to dislike her any more than she does. From the beginning Vic has had eyes only for her father. It's so unfair. Having children is such hard work, you expect them to be grateful for all the pain and suffering. Instead they despise you for it. They suffer your presence while they have to and as soon as they can they escape to the arms of someone like their father … someone they can love.

"Have you been behaving yourself, Vicky? You must do as you're told and try to be good while you're here. Are you getting enough to eat?"

Nothing. She simply behaves as if her mother's not there. Annie feels herself getting angry. As if she doesn't have enough to think about without this one conspiring against her. And what have they done to her hair?

"Take off your cap."

Vic stands there looking down at the baby, running a finger along his cheek, saying nothing.

"Victoria Taylor, take off that cap this minute or I'll rip it from your skull myself."

Now she lifts her cap just enough to reveal her poor tattered head, bereft of the only thing about her that was truly beautiful.

"Your hair, Vic. What happened to your hair?"

"They cut it, didn't they? It's what they do, don't you know? Don't you know anything? You should be happy – now I'm as ugly as you."

Without thinking – without meaning to do so – she slaps her. A ruby stain appears on her daughter's cheek and there are tears in her eyes. The baby starts to cry, and Edith looks as if she too wants to cry but is afraid.

"Vicky …"

She turns and runs out of the room leaving Annie with a crying baby and a frightened little girl. Telling Edith to follow her, she gets up and heads to the door.

Matron stops her.

"Where do you think you're going?"

"My daughter – I was just going after her."

"Go back and sit down."

"Her hair's been cut. There was no need for it – my children don't have lice."

"I'm not here to discuss your children. If you wish to forfeit your visiting privileges, keep talking. Otherwise, do as you're told."

Defeated, she leads Edith back to where they were sitting, trying to think of something funny to say – something to take her mind off the slap. "Tell me what you've been doing, Edie. Have you met any nice children to play with?"

"We don't play here. We're not allowed."

"Yes, you are. You can play, you just have to be quiet and not make too much noise."

"No, Mama, we can't play. We has to sit and be quiet and think of God's love."

"You're thinking of church, Edith. You went to chapel this morning, right? When you're in chapel you must sit and be quiet and think about God. The rest of the time you can think other thoughts."

"What other thoughts?"

"Happy thoughts. Ponies and bunnies and things. You drew me a picture of a pony, remember? The pony that pulls the ragman's cart. It had a funny name, do you remember? What was it now?"

A solemn shake of the head. "Don't 'member."

"Yes you do."

"No I don't. I don't 'member nothing."

"*Anything*. You don't remember *anything*. All right, let me think of something you remember – oh, I know! What about the time Gran took you to the market and the organ man was there? He had a little monkey with a red hat that went around with a cup and Gran gave you a penny to put in the cup."

"His name was Billy. He was dressed like a sawjer."

"*Soldier*. That's right. And the organ man let you feed him. Do you remember what you gave the little monkey to eat?"

"A piece of apple."

"Yes. You see? I knew you'd remember. Now it's your turn. Tell me something you remember."

"I guess I 'member the Wax Museum."

"And what do you remember about it? Go ahead, tell me."

"Papa took me and Vicky and we saw the thing they use to cut the heads off."

"The guillotine."

"The giller-teen. And Mary Ann Cotton, we saw her.

'Mary Ann Cotton, she's dead and she's rotten, she lies in her bed with her eyes wide open.' Does she, Mama? Does she lie in bed with her eyes wide open?"

"It's just a skipping song, Edith. Her eyes are closed."

"Your turn, Mama. What do you 'member?"

What *doesn't* she remember?

***

It was on a trip to the Botanic Gardens in Regent's Park that he first called her Ophelia. She thought he was mixing her up with one of the barmaids he knew and he had to explain about it being a character in a play by Shakespeare and a woman in a painting. She was embarrassed not knowing but flattered that he thought she was beautiful.

He *knew* things about people – and places. The parish church on Marylebone Road. She passed it almost every day of her life without giving it a thought and then Bill told her a famous poet had been baptized and another married there. She looked at it differently after that.

They had their first argument at the British Museum, another place he knew about. He couldn't believe she'd never been inside.

"You've never seen the Elgin marbles? You've never seen the Rosetta Stone? You were never curious about it?"

No. No. And, well … no.

Well, that wouldn't do: on her next free afternoon he would treat her to a tour of the museum. And her sister of course. Now that they were courting they couldn't go anywhere without a chaperone.

On their way up to Great Russell Street, Maude grumbled about "playing gooseberry" on what would no doubt be a very dull afternoon. "I don't see why you can't just meet at church like a regular person."

"Mr. Taylor doesn't go to church, he's a Dissenter."

"Dissenters go to church. The cabinet maker next door is a Dissenter and he goes every Sunday."

"Well, Mr. Taylor doesn't. And don't tell Mama. If she thinks he's a heathen she won't let me see him."

"Mama thinks all Englishmen are heathens."

"True. But don't say anything."

He was waiting for them outside the museum stamping his feet with the cold. She apologized for keeping him waiting, but he was happy to see them and ushered them through the large double doors into an expansive courtyard and then into the main building. They deposited their coats in the cloak room and commenced "the tour", beginning with the rooms you might expect of a compositor: those that held cases of rare books. Here he took great pride in pointing out the very first printed book, the Great Bible printed by Gutenberg and Fust.

When they had marveled at this and other dusty tomes, some of which were actually quite beautiful, Bill led them through the Gallery of Antiquities: they began with Ancient Egypt, where he went into great detail about the process of mummification; then Classical Greece through to the Japanese Antiquities, then down to the ground floor to see the Greek and Roman marbles, stopping every few minutes to point out this piece of crockery or that statue of Hadrian until it all became a muddle and she begged to be allowed to sit. Maude went off to get a drink of water and give them a few minutes alone.

They settled on a bench in front of a marble bust of a woman surrounded by leaves. This, Bill said, was Clytie, a nymph who fell in love with the sun god Helios and was turned into a sunflower.

"How do you know all this?"

"How does anyone know anything? I read. I come here and walk around and study the exhibits. I educate myself about the world around me. You don't have to be rich to be educated, Miss Morgan. Knowledge isn't the preserve of the upper classes. Quite the opposite, actually."

Bill was eager to get moving. He wanted to take them through the Zoological exhibits and show them the Reading Room where he first discovered John Stuart Mill. It was too much. She told him she wanted to leave, said she had to get back even though there was still a half hour before the Museum shut for the day. He was disappointed and disappointment always made him angry.

"You'll never get anywhere if you aren't prepared to

learn anything new. I'm trying to help you, don't you see that? Do you want to be a parlour-maid all of your life?"

"What if I do? What's wrong with that?"

"Forgive me for saying this, Miss Morgan, but if you really think there's nothing wrong with that then you're not the person I imagined you to be."

"And excuse *me* for saying *this*, Mr. Taylor – I think you're insufferably rude!"

A good line that – the kind a heroine would say to a cad. Bill didn't see it that way. By the time Maude returned with two paper cups filled with water, they weren't speaking to each other. He walked them back to the cloak room, helped them on with their coats, tipped his hat and left.

On the way home her sister tried to put a good face on it. Maybe it's good you're arguing now, she said, so you don't have to when you get married.

"He's stubborn and opinionated," Annie said. "He thinks there's only one way of thinking and it's his."

Maude gave her a look. "Now, who does that sound like?"

"Oh, shut up." And then, "I've made a mess of it, haven't I?"

Maude linked her arm through Annie's and smiled. "I've seen the way he looks at you. Trust me – it'll take more than that to put him off."

***

The hour is up. Matron rings her bell and the little clubfooted girl begins rounding up the children. Edith gives the baby a final kiss on the cheek and deposits him in Annie's lap. "Will I see you tomorrow, Mama?"

"No, not tomorrow. Visiting hours are on Sunday. That's a week from today. I'll see you then, you and your sister."

"Will Papa be here?"

"No of course he won't – don't be foolish." And then, "I'm sorry, Edie, but Papa is gone away, you know that."

"Gone to Africa to find diamonds."

"Is that what he told you?"

The girl nods. "He's bringing them back – one for me and one for Vicky. And we'll be rich and have nice clothes and everything. I'll buy you something nice with my diamond, Mama. I'll buy you a dress!"

The children are lined up at the door, boys on one side, girls on the other. On an impulse she pulls Edith close and presses her lips to her daughter's forehead. The little girl pulls away and looks up at her mother with some concern.

"Are you all right, Mama?"

"Yes, of course I am. Now run along. And *be good*."

Afterwards Fitz tells her she's lucky Matron didn't see the kiss.

"It's not allowed," she says. "Touching and hugging – they don't like nothing of that here. You want to be careful."

12.

They never had any books at home apart from the Bible and *The Memoirs of Owen Glendower.* Neither was opened on any regular basis. Both her parents could read and write but books were expensive and a penny spent on a newspaper was a penny *not* spent on something more important – like food.

But she was a good reader. At school in Notting Hill Miss Hodge had regularly called on her to read from the Bible: *I will lift up mine eyes onto the hills from whence cometh mine help.* Which hills? What kind of help? They were never told. So while she enjoyed reading aloud well enough, she found the text itself extremely dull.

"Must be able to read." That was one of the qualifications Mrs. Bellwether set out in the beginning, along with being clean and of a "flexible" disposition.

It was because, she explained, she suffered from dyspepsia, a depraved disturbance of the blood which caused, according to the advertisements, "nervousness, constipation and depression of the spirits."

The remedy was two nerve pills followed by a spoonful of Dr. Chase's Patent Nostrum, after which she must lie completely still for an hour until her spirits lifted. During that time she must be read to in order to divert her mind from her discomfort.

"Peter used to read to me," she said, referring to her son, "before he went off to school but now I have no one. The girls are too young and Mr. Bellwether dislikes reading aloud. He doesn't approve of the books I like and won't read them to me. So Annie it must be you."

Mr. Bellwether tolerated his wife's passion for novels only because of her dyspepsia. But his rule was clear: only in the evening after the children were in bed, and only for an hour. In his opinion, romantic novels were detrimental to the mind and temperament of those individuals unable to control their passions. He believed they must particularly be kept out of the hands of young female servants. Servants, like children, were impressionable creatures and the nature of their reading material must be firmly supervised. If Annie must read, then it should be books to improve her mind.

To that end, he gave her one for Christmas: *Little Servant Maids*, published by the Society for Promoting Christian Knowledge. It was a long story of several young servant girls who didn't like to work and were conceited and gossiped about their employers and found other ways to irritate and annoy the good people who paid their wages.

It was a bit of a mystery where Mr. B. obtained that book or who put it into his head that she would like it. Certainly he never read a word of it himself as he took great pride in never having read a novel in his life.

He read the newspaper in the evening to keep abreast of world affairs and to see what "that damned Holland" was up to. Mr. Holland was the Governor of the Bank of England, and her employer frequently disagreed with his decisions. When Mr. Holland had done or said something particularly distressing Mr. B. would leave the table and retire to his dressing-room. Mrs. B. would shake her head and say, "There goes his stomach!" (Her employer had a notoriously weak stomach. Every so often he was confined to his bed on his doctor's orders and made to drink peppermint tea, milk toast, and unthickened broth. A day on such a diet was usually enough to revive him or at least to convince him to get out of bed and go back to work.)

When Mr. Holland had not done anything upsetting, Mr. B. would take the time to browse through other parts of the paper, steering clear of the court cases and criminal reports. Occasionally he found something in the newspaper unfit for any other eyes. When this happened, he asked Annie to fetch the scissors from his desk. He then clipped out several inches of type, leaving a gaping hole in the page and causing his wife no end of frustration as the hole invariably appeared in the middle of something she wanted to read.

"Really, my dear, do you not think you could wait till I've had a chance to see the paper before butchering it like you do?"

Mr. B. argued that it was a husband's duty to protect his wife, not only from physical danger but from what he termed "moral turpitude".

"It is up to me to keep you from polluting your mind

with garbage. If I let you read it first there'd be no point in cutting it out, now, would there?"

***

The readings began on Annie's first night in service. A bell rang shortly before nine, summoning her to the upstairs dressing room. There she found her mistress collapsed on the chaise longue looking like one of the hippopotami in the London Zoo, a beefy arm shielding her eyes from the light.

"Do hurry, won't you? I'm fainting with the pain of it all."

Annie dispensed the medicine as quickly as she could, then fetched a book from the dressing table. *East Lynne*, it was called, by Mrs. Henry Wood. There was nothing about it, at first glance, to hint at the adventure within. The cover was plain brown leather, there were no illustrations, only page after page of words.

But what words! From the first line of the first chapter, Annie was captivated: *In an easy chair of the spacious and handsome library of his town-house, sat William, Earl of Mount Severn.* Here were men and women unlike any she had ever met. The men were handsome, unfailingly polite and wealthy. The women, while often poor, were winsome and genteel. Everything that happened to them was marvelous and tragic and unpredictable – there was nothing in their lives that was even the tiniest bit ordinary. Even the weather was different … more intense: when the sun shone it did so brilliantly and when the wind blew it fairly howled. By the end of that first hour, Annie was converted, wholly and without reservation, to the romance of the novel.

She read tentatively at first, pronouncing the words carefully, nervous about making a mistake. She'd never read anything aloud but Scripture, and that was in front of callow school girls like herself. In succeeding nights she grew more confident; her grasp of the language improved and she dared to evoke different voices for different characters. Her employer was thrilled: "You *do* read well, my girl. As well as anyone I ever heard and that's a fact. I could lie here and listen to you all night."

In the five years that she was with the Bellwethers, Annie and Mrs. B. read their way through *East Lynne* and *Lady Adelaide's Oath*; *The Castle's Heir* and *Lady Audley's Secret*; *Aurora Floyd* and *My Lady Ludlow*; *The Woman in White* and *Armadale*; *The Shadow of Ashlydyat* and *Danesbury House*; *No Name* and *North and South*; *Lord Oakburn's Daughters* and *The Channings*; *Jane Eyre* and *Wuthering Heights*; *Mary Barton* and *Ruth.* They were just beginning *Cranford* when she left.

Books were a luxury, even for Mrs. B.; she would not have been able to afford so many out of her household money. They came to her through her Caritas connections: members had access to a lending library. By pooling their subscription money the women received a new novel every month, each with a distinctive yellow label marking it as property of "Mudie's Circulating Library". They were triple-deckers, these books, meaning they came in three volumes; when a member finished the first volume she passed it on to another and began the second volume, passing that on when she was finished with it. In this way they got through the entire novel.

They each had their favourite books and favourite heroes. Mrs. B. always preferred gentlemen with titles – or gentlemen who became titled – such as Lord Dane in *The Castle's Heir*. Annie liked poor but honourable men, like John Thornton, the hero of Mrs. Gaskell's *North and South*:

> *His heart beat thick at the thought of her coming. He could not forget the touch of her arms around his neck, impatiently felt as it had been at the time; but now the recollection of her clinging defence of him, seemed to thrill him through and through — to melt away every resolution, all power of self-control, as if it were wax before a fire.*

Now *there* was a man! She was sure there was a Mr. Thornton out there – or someone very like him – who awaited her touch to melt his powers of self-control like "wax before a fire". Thoughts of him saving his money to pay his father's debts, hiding his tender-hearted nature behind a curtain of pride – oh, glorious Mr. Thornton! – warmed her at night in those delicious moments between falling into bed and drifting exhausted into sleep.

Occasionally they received a book of a different sort. *The Bride of Lammermoor* came highly recommended, as did *A Tale of Two Cities*. Neither of them was an unqualified success. The first was too tragic – Mrs. B. in particular could not bear the ending – and the second had too many characters to keep track of. They agreed, however, that Mr. Scott and Mr. Dickens were very good writers – almost as good as Mrs. Gaskell – and if either of them were to write something a little less complicated they were sure it would sell very well.

Between books, they read from the illustrated papers, focusing particularly on the criminal court pages which described the most grisly crimes in loving detail. When Frederick Baker was being tried for the murder of little Fanny Adams, Mrs. B. was in a frenzy to hear all about it and had her go out to the shops twice a day in order to buy copies of all the broadsheets. They made for thrilling reading: how he lured the little girl away from her friends and chopped her up so horribly, stuck her head up on a pole and cut out her intestines. There was a diary, too, in which he confessed that he'd killed her. It was a terrible thing, of course, but fascinating nonetheless.

***

Life with the Bellwethers, as tiring as it could be, was also comfortable. Had it not been for the sudden strange behaviour on the part of Mr. B., Annie might have stayed on indefinitely.

It was a Saturday night near the beginning of April in her fifth year of service. There'd been company for dinner and not only had every pot and pan in the kitchen been put into service but Mrs. B. had insisted on the fine crystal, which meant the sink must be lined with a soft cloth and each goblet rinsed in vinegar and water and dried with extra care. Cook had gone to bed and Annie was washing up the cutlery when something made her look up: Mr. B. was standing in the doorway, watching her.

"Yes, sir?" she said. "Can I help you?"

He had never come down to the kitchen before; there

was no need. And besides, it was Cook's domain – she didn't like anyone intruding from upstairs and everyone knew it.

"Is everything all right, Annie?"

"Of course, sir."

After a minute, he said, "Are you well, Annie?"

"Yes, sir. Quite well."

"Oh."

Annie waited for him to leave. It was very late, and she wanted to get to bed.

"I only thought – it seemed to me – that is, I thought you were looking unwell."

This was a most peculiar observation on his part. For one thing, it was beneath him to notice anything at all about the domestic help. The servants were his wife's concern. And for another, between long hours at the bank and an increasingly demanding social schedule, Mr. B. never spent much time in the house at all.

Annie repeated that she was feeling quite well, thank you. He nodded and then, to her relief, he left.

A week later, it happened again. Except this time it was worse because he came up to her bedroom. It was late, almost one in the morning, and he and Mrs. B. had been out for the night. When he knocked on her door, she was asleep. She woke up not sure if there had been a knock or if she had dreamed it. She waited and the knocking came again.

"Annie? May I come in?"

There was no lock on the door; servants were not allowed to lock their doors and besides, there was no need for it. Who would want to creep up four flights of stairs in the middle of the night, just to get to the maid's room? Hitchens might have thought of it if he'd been drinking, but he didn't have a house key. The handle of the bedroom door turned and Mr. B. walked in.

She was too annoyed to be frightened. Surely to God her employers could do without her services at this time of night; they knew she had to be up at six to light the fires and bring Cook her cup of tea.

"I'm sorry to bother you," Mr. B. said. "I was just wondering – did you have a chance to brush my topcoat?"

Annie answered that she had done so, and then, because he seemed to be waiting to hear more, she added, "It's in your wardrobe." Where it always is, she thought, but didn't say it.

Mr. B. received this information as if it were extremely interesting. "My wardrobe. Ah, yes, yes, very good. Excellent, Annie. Thank you for that."

At this point, he should have excused himself and retreated. But he didn't. Instead, he stood and gazed at her for a minute. Annie stared back, which was rude, and something she never would have done normally.

After a minute he said, "Will you be going to the shops tomorrow, I wonder?"

"The shops? Yes, I suppose I might."

"Good. Good. You might pick me up some tobacco, if you will. Egyptian blend. Will you do that?"

"Of course, sir. Is there anything else?"

Sadly, Mr. B. shook his head. "No, I suppose there isn't. Good night, Annie."

"Good night, sir."

And so it began. Every other night Mr. B. tapped on her bedroom door and let himself in. Sometimes he had a request: would she pick him up a new hat brush, one with hard bristles at one end? Had she noticed that he was short of collars? Other times, he simply entered the room and stood at the foot of the bed, saying nothing, looking wistful.

It occurred to her that one of the best things about this position – having a room to herself for the first time in her life – had become a problem. In most households, the servants slept in the kitchen or scullery; if she shared a room with Cook, he wouldn't have been able to bother her this way. She thought of placing a chair under the door handle but that wouldn't keep him from disturbing her sleep. And he didn't appear to want to do anything more than look at her. It was strange and it was annoying but it wasn't actually frightening.

This went on for about three months. She began to think that Mr. B. was perhaps a little dotty. He was, after all, almost forty; people often became weak in the head as they grew older. She had an uncle who developed a fear of starlings in middle age: he took to throwing his boots at them whenever he saw them. After a year of retrieving his shoes from the street, her aunt had him committed to the county asylum. He was declared sane after six months and released, but was never the same after that.

One night, late in June, she woke up to find Mr. B. sitting on her bed. She didn't hear him knock, didn't hear him come in at all, and had no idea how long he'd been sitting there. This was new, and disturbing.

"What is it, sir? What do you want?"

"Oh, Annie."

There was something in the way he said it that made the breath stick in her throat. Had he come to murder her? Only last week she read Mrs. B. a newspaper story about a young servant who was strangled in her sleep. The gardener was charged, but it could just as easily have been her employer.

"Please, sir, you must leave."

Before she could stop him, he took hold of her hand and held it firmly in his own. "Annie. My poor, dear little Annie. What is to become of you?"

There was no doubt of it: Mr. B. was clearly not right in the head. Should she scream for help? Might it not be better to simply report to Mrs. B. in the morning that her husband was entering her room at night uninvited? If that were the case, then why had she not mentioned it earlier? How could she explain that she'd allowed this kind of thing to go on for months without mentioning it to anyone? And would it not be a case of her word against his? During the day, if they happened to meet, Mr. B. treated her as a master should treat anyone in domestic service – as if she were part of the furniture, a necessary part of the household but essentially invisible. It was only at night, when they were alone, that he seemed aware of her as a person. And not only aware, but infatuated with her.

She tried to keep her voice as steady as possible. "Sir, you really must leave. You shouldn't be up here. Please let go of my hand and let me be."

He looked down at her hand gripped in his own, as if he hadn't realized he held it. He released her and she hid her hand under the blanket, in case he changed his mind. Still, he didn't seem inclined to leave.

"Such a sad little face you have, Annie. I never see you smile. Why are you so sad, little one? Has someone hurt you?"

"I'm not sad, sir."

"You're not?"

"No, sir. I'm not sad at all."

"Then smile for me, Annie. Let me see you smile, for once."

Feeling slightly ridiculous, she stretched her lips wide and held them there until he, too, smiled.

"Dear, dear Annie, I fear that is not a real smile. I think you're doing it to please me. Like a child, smiling to please her father. Are you a child, Annie? Do you think of me as your father?"

"No."

To her horror, he reached out and stroked her cheek. "I have so many concerns, little one. Things you wouldn't understand, would you, with your little household chores? Life is so simple for you – dusting, sweeping, busy, busy, all day long. That little head so empty. So sweet. Someday I'll tell you all about the decisions, all the important things your master does all day long, just so little Annie can dust and sweep and keep busy. Would you like that? Would you like to hear about my life?"

She shook her head, conscious of his hand on her face, terrified that his fingers might trace their way downwards to her throat. Again she thought of the murdered servant. That girl was lucky – she was asleep when she was killed. Annie was wide awake and ready to scream.

Or was there something else? Perhaps he had something more evil in mind. The Gloucester clergyman and the girl who'd drowned herself – was that what was in store for her? Was Mr. B. planning to force himself on her, and drive her to suicide? Perhaps he planned to give her chloroform – it happened all the time, if what you read in the papers was true.

To her immense relief, he took his hand from her face and stood up. "Another time, Annie. It's late and I must go to bed so I can get up in the morning and go to the bank and make important decisions, all day long. And you must go to sleep now, and dream your sweet, innocent dreams. Will you do that, Annie? Will you go to sleep and dream of your poor, hard-working master?"

It came out as barely a whisper. "Yes, sir."

He stood for a minute more, smiling down at her. "Poor little Annie. We're a pair, aren't we? Never mind – we'll take care of each other, won't we?"

And with that he departed, having well and truly murdered sleep for her for the rest of the night.

The following day was Thursday and she had the afternoon off. She finished her chores as quickly as she could, and headed west towards Haven Green. It was raining and the green was practically deserted. A few disgruntled nannies pushed their enormous perambulators along the pebble-strewn path while their older charges played hide-and-seek under the bandstand, oblivious to the weather. Annie kept her head down and circled the park, trying to think.

In the five years she'd worked for the Bellwethers she'd learned a great deal and had performed her duties to the best of her abilities. She was certain they were happy with her. Many other girls would have moved on after a year or two, knowing they'd learned enough to be worthy of a paid position. She'd begun to think that way herself but was reluctant to do anything about it as she was so comfortable where she was.

And now, through no fault of her own, she stood to lose it all. The situation with Mr. Bellwether would not improve … in fact, it would likely get worse. If she told Mrs. B. there were two possibilities: either she would not believe her, and would dismiss her for lying. Or she'd believe her and still let her go. No mistress would tolerate a servant under her roof who'd attracted her husband's attentions.

She knew only too well what happened to domestics who were not given a "character" upon dismissal. No respectable lady hired anyone without a letter stating that the servant had done a good job and fulfilled her position as required. Without that you might as well go knocking on the doors of the factories and take whatever work you could get. You'd be lucky to make enough to afford a roof over your head and the clothes on your back. One heard of girls all the time who lost situations and fell very low, almost beyond redemption.

There was only one thing for it: she must find another situation. And she must do so immediately, before things with Mr. B. went further.

She hurried back to the house on Myrtle Street and asked to borrow some notepaper.

"Writing a letter are you, Annie?"

"My sister," Annie said, blushing. She was a terrible liar; her mother always knew immediately when she was fibbing. Luckily, Mrs. B. was more trusting.

In a careful hand, she composed a letter to the *London Daily Telegraph*:

Dear Sir,

I would be grateful if you would place the following under Situations Wanted:

Clean respectable general maid seeks a situation in a respectable London household. Excellent health, early riser. Experienced washing up china and glass, cleaning plate, dusting and polishing furniture, trimming lamps, answering bells and waiting at table. Some needlework and hairdressing. Can give character.

"Cleaning plate" was an exaggeration. Hitchens always cleaned the silver but she'd watched him do it so many times she was sure she could make a proper job of it if she had to. She read the letter over, counted the words, and changed the first "respectable" to "dependable." After a moment she added, "Small family, no washing."

An offer arrived by return post: the advertisement had not even made it into the newspaper. The owner of the paper was offering her a position as under parlour-maid in his house. Her duties would be much the same as before but she'd be working for a grander household, and she would be paid. And the family sent their laundry out once a week; she would not have to do the washing. She accepted immediately.

She didn't like to tell Mrs. B. she was leaving for another position, so she said she was needed at home. Her mother was ill, she said, and had asked her to come back and take care of her father. She blushed and stammered her way through this, yet another falsehood, but Mrs. B. either didn't notice or put it down to her distress over her mother. She told Annie she was a good girl to think of her family this way and said she would write her an excellent character so she could find a paid position once her mother recovered. *If* she recovered, God bless her.

"You've done well, Annie. There's not many girls as good as you, and I shall be finding it very hard to find another one. And I *know* I won't find another who can read to me as you do. I shall miss *that* very much."

She wrote out the letter, praising Annie's hard work, pleasant manner, and cleanliness, and gave her 17*s* out of her household money.

"It's a good deal of money, but I do think you're worth it. You're a good girl, and I've said that in this letter. How I shall manage I don't know."

She was getting tearful, which made Annie feel all the worse. She felt obliged to say there were many young girls out there who'd do as good a job – better, even. Mrs. B. shook her head and refused to be comforted.

"It's not true, Annie. I wish it were, but it ain't." (When she was upset she often slipped back into her Yorkshire way of speaking.) "You hear them saying it all the time, you do, how you can't get good help and the girls aren't to be found who can be trusted to light the stove without setting the kitchen on fire. Oh, Annie, I'll miss you, I will!"

Her mistress went to lie down with a cold cloth on her forehead, and Annie made her a cup of tea. Mrs. B. was a good soul but she enjoyed the dramatics. In spite of her guilt over leaving, Annie did feel it would be a relief to be in a larger house where keeping everything going wouldn't rest entirely on her shoulders.

On her last night there Mr. B. came to her bedroom while she was packing her things. He seemed very sad and she might have felt sorry for him if it weren't for the fact that he was the reason for her departure. He understood, he said, that she was leaving because of him, because he had let her down.

"I showed you my weakness and I shouldn't have done that. It was a mistake, Annie, and I'm sorry."

"Don't be sorry, sir. It's just that my mother needs me."

"Yes, and your father, too, I'll be bound. Could you not think of *me* as your father? Would it be so very difficult?"

"I think it would, sir."

"Very well, then. I'll leave you be. Remember, though, if you ever need anything – ever – you must write and tell me. You can write, can't you, Annie? I know you can read. I've listened to you reading to my wife. Did you know I was listening? Did you sense I was standing just behind the door the whole time?"

"No, sir, I did not."

"Does it make you just a little happy to think of me listening to you that way? In secret?"

It did not make her happy at all but of course she couldn't say it. She looked down at the floor and said nothing.

"And now I will listen no more, my little one. Promise me, Annie, if you ever need me, you will write to me. And promise me also that you will never, ever allow anyone to take advantage of your innocence as I so brutally attempted to do and for which I will never forgive myself."

The following morning as she was stripping the bed and preparing to turn the mattress she heard footsteps on the stairs outside her door. An envelope was slipped between the crack and the footsteps retreated downstairs. Mr. B. had given her a banker's draught for the sum of £10. It was kind of him but it would have been kinder had he given her bank notes instead – he must have known she would never be able to cash such a thing. She tucked it into her copy of *Little Servant Maids* and left it on top of the bed.

13.

Her third night in the casual ward is the coldest yet. The fire in the stove dies during the night and the room is cold enough to freeze the water in the privy. The ventilation holes over the windows don't help. They're meant to keep the air circulating but she would stop them up with rags if she could reach them. She keeps the baby warm by tucking him under her while she sleeps. Better to risk suffocating him than let him die of the cold.

They have a cat now, a big ginger tom brought into the ward to keep the rats at bay. It's a fierce looking animal but surprisingly gentle and loves to be petted and stroked. He prowls the corridor between the beds all night and curls up by the stove during the day. Someone suggests calling him Benjamin, after the Prime Minister; shortened to Ben, the name sticks.

After breakfast the attendant tells her to bring the baby and follow her to the nursery ward, a long, low room at the top of the house. Of all the places in the Union, it is this room that troubles the heart. Here's where young women, most of them unmarried, come to have their babies. And to leave them, in many cases, if they survive. The room is damp, crowded, and cheerless. Forty or fifty pale, miserable-looking waifs lie two and three to a cot, some too sick to cry, all of them wan and listless. One tiny thing in particular is so still and pale it appears lifeless … do they keep dead babies here?

Those few who aren't crying or sleeping stare at the ceiling, having learned already to expect little or nothing from this world. There are no toys. No balls or hoops or even little sticks that might be substituted for dolls the way poor children do. A half dozen women with babies of their own and a couple of elderly paupers tend to the little ones under the supervision of a slack-eyed nurse in a grubby workhouse apron. She takes the child from Annie and deposits him in a nearby cot.

"Will he be all right?"

The woman seems confused by the question. "Why wouldn't he be?"

"Will you bring him to me if he needs to be fed?"

"The very idea! As if we don't have enough to do to be runnin' back and forth all day! You can come back here at dinner if you want. An' you pick him up at six."

* * *

Annie and the other casuals are directed to the oakum-shed, a large cellar with benches placed at intervals along the cold, damp floor. The attendant distributes bundles of nasty old pieces of rope, each about a foot in length, every one matted with dirt and tar.

"Pick it to pieces by dinner-time."

The fibres are so knotted and warped together she can't imagine picking it all apart in a lifetime, let alone four hours.

As luck would have it, she ends up sharing a bench with Maisie. She and Sal had their day out; Maisie returned last night alone but there's still no sign of Sal. For missing curfew Maisie's had her rations cut, although, as she says, she couldn't eat a thing anyway after all the "carrying-on" she'd done. Now she slumps against the wall and waits till the Super leaves, then drops her bundle on the ground, retrieves a small stick from her pocket and begins picking her teeth.

"Don't kill yerself over it, Mrs. Taylor. *I'm* not goin' to, that's for certain."

"Are they really expecting us to finish by noon?"

"They'll give you a good blowin' if you don't get it done, but they can't do nothin' about it."

Mrs. Higgins disagrees. "You're wrong about that, my girl. Wasn't I in Harlech last year and we wouldn't pick 'cause of the state of the place and they give us two nights in the Refractory. *And* they cut our rations."

Another woman offers that you'd best do as much as you can to avoid being "sent away". "They did that with two young girls when I was in St. Giles. One of 'em had a crippled hand but they charged her anyway. Don't take the chance, that's my advice."

Mrs. Hatchett, speaking with the voice of experience, is of the opinion you'd be better off in prison if you had the choice. "The food's better and the cells are cleaner. And they don't feel the need to work you to death for the crime of being poor."

Mrs. Chancer reappears in the doorway.

"Quiet, now, all of you. Yer here to work not talk. I hear one more word and I'll write up the lot of you."

Annie sets to work as best she can, making little progress. It would be easier with a tool of some kind but Pipe Lady says they only give those to elderly paupers and only if they know to ask. The fibres bite into her fingers and refuse to unravel; a half hour's concentrated effort results in broken fingernails and the release of a few wispy strands. The work would be difficult enough but it's made more so by the dust which covers everything and rises in clouds into the air, stinging the eyes and making it difficult to breathe. She's beginning to despair of ever finishing when Pipe Lady, halfway through her own bundle, offers to show her how it's done.

To Annie's astonishment, the woman's fingers practically fly through the rope, unravelling the fibres with a dexterity that seems almost magical. There seems to be a trick to it – untwist the length of rope into as many corkscrew strands as possible, then slide the rope back and forth along the bench to loosen the rest of them. The filthy mesh still needs to be picked apart but at least now there's space to dig your fingers in and tug. In ten minutes she's made more headway than Annie would have done in an hour. Having shown her how to go about it, she hands the rope back to Annie and the two of them go back to picking.

At midday the Super returns and inspects their work. All but Maisie have managed to pick apart their oakum bundle.

"Get in line," the Super says. "You can go in and get your dinner. Where d'you think *you're* going?"

This is directed to Maisie, who is lining up with the others.

"Gettin' my dinner," Maisie says.

"Oh, no you ain't. Yer stayin' right here, my girl. You don't get to eat till you take care of that oakum."

"Go to hell. I'm not touchin' that piece of filth and if you try to make me I'll break your bloody head."

"Very well. Two nights in the hole for swearing. And

another two nights if you don't pick up that oakum and get to it."

Maisie returns to her bench, folds her arms and stares at the Super in defiance.

"I ain't touchin' it and that's that."

"Will I fetch Matron?"

"You can fetch the devil if you like. And you can stuff your rope up your arse."

Telling the others to stay put, Mrs. Chancer marches off. In her absence, some of the women try to coax Maisie into doing as she's told.

"You don't want to get written up, now, do you? Pick up the rope and get to it before she gets back."

"You're keepin' us all waiting, Maisie. We want our dinner even if you don't."

"Come on, girl, behave yourself. Don't be stupid. They'll send you away if you give 'em any more trouble."

Maisie glares at them, unmoved. "You know what you are? You're a bunch of sheep, you lot. You make me sick just lookin' at you. Nobody tells me what to do. To hell with all of you – you can all go to blazes."

The reappearance of the Super with both Matron and the porter in tow seems to trigger something wild in the girl. She starts up and, without warning, throws herself at the officers, striking them with her fists and letting loose a volley of curses. But she's no match for Stoker. He grapples her to the floor, holding her in place with one heavy knee on the small of her back. "Hold still, you cockeyed bitch! What do you want done with her, Ma'am?"

"Take her to the magistrate. A month in a prison cell will cool her down, I'm sure."

"You can't do nothin' to me!" Maisie shrieks. "I know my rights – I'll report you to the Board."

The porter yanks her to her feet. One arm around her waist, the other pinning her arms to her side, he drags her out of the room, kicking and shouting. Her shrieks persist all down the hallway, eventually receding into the depths of the building.

Matron straightens her collar and adjusts her apron. "I believe the midday bell has rung, Mrs. Chancer, isn't that right?"

"Yes, ma'am, it has."

"So shouldn't these women be at dinner?"

"Yes, ma'am. All right, don't stand about gawpin'. Get up to dinner and don't make me tell you again."

Annie heads upstairs to the nursery, fearing the worst, but the baby is fine; when she enters the room she finds him being dandled by the young woman who remembered Calcraft, the hangman.

"He's always smiling, your baby. It's like he never cries. Can I stay while you feed him?"

"I don't want to keep you from getting your dinner."

"It's all right, I have it when the babies are asleep. What do you call him?"

"His name is Edward but we call him Teddy."

"He's ever so sweet. He minds me of Mercy when she was little."

"Is that your sister?"

"One of 'em. I got four – Chastity, Verity, Mercy and Grace. I'm Obedience but everyone calls me Biddie. Pa named all us girls. He said he wanted the Fletcher girls to remember to walk in the way of the Lord all our days and keep to the path of the righteous."

Annie, busy with settling the child to the breast, is only half listening. "He sounds very religious, your father."

"Oh, he is. He says my being here is a punishment for my wicked acts. I pray every night he'll let me come back home."

Wicked acts? The girl has her attention: If a painter wished to depict the Virgin Mary, he couldn't pick a better model. Pale and wide-eyed, she's the picture of youthful innocence. What father of such a girl would wish her in a place like this?

"I can't believe you've done anything wicked."

"Oh, but I have. I was born in sin and fell into sinful ways and being here is my punishment. Pa says we were all born in sin, even Grace, who was a baby when I left. Does it worry you when you think of it?"

"Think of what? Being a sinner? No, I guess it doesn't."

"It don't? Why not?"

"Well – " She has to think for a moment. Does she worry about going to Hell and all that? It's not something she thinks about, for the most part.

"I guess I think it doesn't really make sense. I mean, the idea that God would punish a person just for being – a *person*."

The girls stares at Annie as if she's suddenly sprouted horns and a devil's tail. "Are you sayin' you don't believe in the Bible?"

"I couldn't say. I haven't read enough of it to believe it or not."

Which isn't entirely true. Her time at school provided her with plenty of opportunity to read Scripture. She can still quote a few verses if she has to. But quoting's different from believing or even understanding and she can admit to neither.

"Then I'll pray for you. The Bible says the eyes of the unbelievers are shut to His glory. I'll pray that He opens your eyes."

And she does just that, right there in the nursery. Putting her hands together in prayerful fashion, she closes her eyes, bows her head and prays – in silence, to Annie's relief. When she's done she looks up and smiles.

"I done it. I prayed that God makes you see the light. D'you feel any different?"

"Not yet. But it's early days."

"I reckon it takes a few times to make it work. I'll pray for you regular like and you be sure to let me know when you start believin'."

A tot lying unattended nearby begins to cry. Biddie gets up, fetches him from his cot, and brings him back to where Annie is nursing her son.

"I don't think he's hungry," she says, cuddling him against her chest. "He had porridge an hour ago. Sometimes it turns their stomach if the milk's gone off."

"You seem to have a way with babies."

"I had lots of practice. I took care of Grace and Mercy after Ma died. And I had my own baby once but it died. It was the master of the house where I was working – he was the father. Pa wouldn't have me back home so I went to the Union to have my baby. She was a beautiful little thing – it broke my heart when she died. They said it was a blessing but it wasn't."

"No, I'm sure it wasn't." This she's not sure about at all but the girl's too young to understand. "You mustn't blame yourself, Biddie. Many women have babies who die – you're not a bad person because of it."

"It's not just that. I fell into bad ways – *very* bad ways. If it weren't for Mr. Catlin I don't know where I'd be. Dead, most likely."

The baby is taking a long time to nurse; she'll likely have missed her dinner altogether by the time he's done. And this young girl, Biddie, seems to want to talk.

"Tell me about Mr. Catlin," Annie says. "Is he a friend of your father's?"

"Oh, no," she says. "He's a missionary. He saw me on the street and talked to me and when he found out where I was living he got me out of there. The woman who owned the house, she wanted payment. But Mr. Catlin said he'd call the police so she let me go."

It doesn't take much imagination to picture how Biddie was supporting herself at the time. But it's not the kind of thing one asks.

The missionary found her a place in Highgate, in a home for fallen women. Unfortunately, the home went bankrupt; Biddie, with nowhere else to go, came knocking at the door of the Paddington Union. She's been here, she says, for six months and has no idea how to leave.

"Could you not get work as a servant?"

"Not likely. I got no character 'cause of the way I left. I'm a terrible sinner. Everything as happened to me is because of my sins."

"Sins can be forgiven, Biddie. Remember what the Chaplain said yesterday morning? About the prodigal son? He went back to his father's house and his father forgave him. And so will yours."

Biddie shakes her head. "I don't know about that. He didn't have my Pa."

Part Two: Inside

1.

The New Year arrives with no celebrating, no First Footing, no church bells ringing at midnight. They wake at seven as usual – make their beds, eat breakfast, begin work. No one says, "Happy New Year". No one throws open the door and cries, "Welcome, welcome" to the new year. No one welcomes it, no one looks forward to it, and when it comes there's nothing new about it. There's never anything new inside.

Inside and outside. After a while, that's how you think. Outside is your old life, what you took for granted as the way things are. Inside is the complete opposite. Nothing here is familiar. The rules that work outside don't apply here. Along with your clothes, your dignity, your children, they take away your natural, God-given right to think, to feel – even to laugh. All there is here is work.

There is no calendar, no seeing out of windows or looking forward to any variety to tell one day from the next. But it seems important to keep track of the days. Each morning, right after the bell rings, she retrieves a piece of coal from the night stand and makes a tick on the wall behind her bed.

It's what they do in gaol, isn't it? Make little scratches on the walls of their cells to mark time served. A prisoner knows the length of his sentence, but she has no idea how long she will be here. A few weeks she thought, at first – two or three months at most. Now she understands it will be difficult to leave. There are women here who've been in for five or six years and some who come in every winter with their families because they can't afford to keep warm outside.

She's not a prisoner. She's free to leave any time, if she has somewhere to go. Pipe Lady says no one ever leaves unless a family member takes them in. Who would take her and the children? Her mother said it: she's put them all against her, anyone who might have helped. There are those, she knows, who think Bill's leaving was understandable if not to be commended. Her temper and sudden, volatile moods are common knowledge. Her mother once said the secret to a good marriage was a man who didn't drink and a wife who'd learned to hold her tongue. Likely she thought it was only a matter of time before this marriage fell apart. She certainly didn't seem surprised when Annie told her.

***

Finally, after a week in the casual ward, the women are told to head to the receiving ward: the doctor has arrived and will see them. The room is filled to overflowing with women and girls, babies and small children. Several women are in the family way, for it is here that the poor of the parish come to lie-in, whether or not they are paupers. The pretty young woman who arrived on Boxing Day – the one said to be a deaf mute – sits quietly in a corner off by herself, smiling at nobody in particular. Annie hasn't seen her since that day; perhaps they keep the feeble-minded in a separate ward.

A young girl who can't be more than fourteen writhes about on the floor moaning and holding her belly. An old woman who must be her grandmother tries to comfort her.

"'Ang on, love, 'ang on, it won't be long now, you'll see, it won't be long."

She no sooner says this than an energetic young man

sporting a full beard and moustache bursts into the room with Mrs. Chancer in tow, and makes his way immediately to the young woman huddled on the floor.

Kneeling beside her, he takes a stethoscope out of his bag and places it on her belly. After a moment he turns to the Super who remains a few feet away, regarding the girl with distaste. "This young woman is about to give birth – didn't you realize that?"

Mrs. Chancer mumbles something about it having nothing to do with her, she's not a nurse now, is she, how's she to know of such things?

"Get her to the lying-in ward and be quick about it. And make sure there's a proper nurse on hand to deliver her."

The doctor turns back to the girl who is silent now and very pale. "Can you stand, my dear?"

She nods, eyes closed, and manages with the help of her grandmother and the doctor to get on her feet. Slowly, supported by the reluctant Super, she hobbles out of the room. The older woman waits until the girl is gone then comes back into the room and sits next to Annie.

"Aren't you going with her?"

"With 'er? Why would I go with 'er?"

"Aren't you her grandmother?"

"Oh gracious no! Never met 'er before I got 'ere. Just felt bad for 'er is all."

With the young girl taken care of, the doctor turns his attention to the rest of them, beginning with the elderly and the most frail. He gives no sense of being rushed but stops with each person for as long as it takes, asking his questions in a gentle voice and showing actual interest in the responses. All eyes are on him as he comes to the deaf girl: how will he deal with her, they wonder? He makes several hand gestures; the girl nods and smiles, and moves her fingers rapidly in response.

After a moment, the doctor turns to Mrs. Chancer. "This young woman is deaf but she is perfectly aware of her situation. I'd like you to have her admitted to the lying-in ward without further delay."

In an urgent whisper that can be heard across the room, the Super says, "But she's *simple*, Doctor. She don't belong with the normal ones."

"She is no more simple than you or me. I want her confined with the rest of the women and I hope to find she's being treated as well as any other poor girl in her position."

The baby is awake again and has begun to fret. Annie bounces him on her knee and her neighbour offers to take him off her hands for a bit. She isn't overly clean and stinks of tobacco and sweat but it seems ungracious to refuse.

"He might make strange."

Which is a lie, really. Teddy never makes strange the way the girls did at that age. For some reason this one has come into the world believing every stranger is a friend.

At any rate, it seems he's right about this particular stranger. She cuddles him with the gentle assurance of one who's held many babies and loved them and he settles down immediately.

"He's a lovely baby. Favours his pa, does he?"

"I guess he does."

"They all do at this age. Give him a year – you'll start seeing more of you in him, I promise you."

When it's Annie's turn, the doctor asks that she show him the baby first. She's happy to do so – no sickly pauper's waif this one! As if to prove it the child lets out a happy shriek and reaches for his whiskers.

"Six months?"

"Yes, just."

"Well, he's a bonny bairn, as my Scottish grandmother would say. Now tell me this: are you planning to keep him with you?"

"Oh, yes – yes, I am!"

"Good, good. But you must keep him clean and well fed. Do you feed him pap or is he on the breast?"

The question causes her to blush but she answers as well as she can. "I nurse him, Doctor. But he seems hungry even after I feed him."

He scribbles something on a piece of paper tucks it into his coat pocket. "We'll see that he gets supplemental milk. But keep him on the breast. I'm not in favour of the feeding bottle if it can be avoided. And don't be giving him any of that slop that passes for porridge in this place. Keep doing what you're doing, and he'll be fine."

Turning his attention to Annie, the doctor peers into her eyes, listens to her heart, takes her pulse. After asking her to roll up her sleeves so he might see her forearms, he pronounces himself less than satisfied.

"Too thin," he says. "Are you eating well enough, now that you're here?"

With Mrs. Chancer's beady eyes upon her, she says something about the food being not what she's used to.

"That may be, but we can't have you wasting away now, can we? You won't be much good to your son if you don't keep up your strength. You must eat what's given you and ask for more if you need it. We'll see if we can fatten you up while you're here."

Now he turns to the woman beside her and grins. "You're looking well, Mrs. Geary. Still not in favour of soap and water, I see."

She echoes the bath-house attendant almost word for word: "My Ma never bathed in her life and she lived to be sixty."

"Ah, but she might have lived to seventy if she'd washed."

It's a familiar joke between them; neither seems to be taking offence. After examining her and declaring her "fit as a fritter", he wags a mildly reproving finger.

"I'm scheduling you for a bath tomorrow morning. Don't make a fuss or I'll put you down for two of them in a week."

"You wouldn't!"

The doctor winks at Annie and moves on.

"He's lovely, that man," Mrs. Geary says. "Always makes you feel better when you see him."

"Have you seen him often?"

"Oh, more times than I can count. Last time was in back in July when I come in with my rheumitis. I left in October to care for my sister up in Bristol and I thought I'd be back by Christmas. I didn't want to miss Christmas – they do it up lovely here. But she hung on, didn't she, and I couldn't get away till she was gone."

"She went away?"

"Died, dear. She died last week. And I had to stay to bury her, you see."

"That's – that's a pity."

"Yes, isn't it, though? I hear they had pudding and mince pies and everyone got a cracker. I feel very bad to have missed it. Still and all that's death for you. It can be very inconvenient."

***

Having been pronounced relatively healthy and free of anything "ketching", she is readmitted as a permanent inmate and provided with a new uniform. It's just as dull and just as uncomfortable as her previous outfit, but PROPERTY OF PADDINGTON UNION is now stamped on the inside collar. Which is some kind of improvement. She will no longer be made to pick oakum; instead she, Mrs. Geary and Pipe Lady are assigned to the laundry shed along with twenty-five other "able-bodied females".

Mrs. Dribble isn't one of them. She's not considered able-bodied – in fact, she's been diagnosed as feeble-minded and assigned to the nursery. From now on she will eat and sleep there, helping to keep watch over the babies. Her charges could do worse. She's kind, for one thing, unlike some of the pauper nurses, and she doesn't drink.

Pipe Lady confides to the others she's "pulled some strings" to get laundry duty: the wash-house, she insists, is the best place to work.

"They give you extra beer because of the steam and sweat of it all. Whenever I'm here I try to get in with the washing."

Fitz and Mrs. Knight get kitchen duty and Mrs. Higgins, because of her back, is assigned to darn stockings. Mrs. Hatchett draws the worst task of all – cleaning the privies in the women's wards – but she takes it with good temper.

"Smells don't bother me," she says. "When I was little we lived in Garret Lane, next to the horse-slaughtering yard.

People used to say, How do you stand the stink? But I didn't mind it – never did. You ask me, anything's better than the wash-house."

Annie would agree. From the moment she sets foot in the laundry shed the smells and sounds bring back her time on Silchester Road with sickening familiarity: the hiss of the steam and crash of the mangles … the way the lye stings your nostrils, makes your eyes water … the sweated heat from the fires that keep the great coppers boiling. The equipment, too, is similar: the cumbersome wooden dollies for stirring the clothes in the tub … the metal cones on sticks for "possing" the laundry, punching and pounding it clean, trying not to tear the fabric in the process … the dolly-sticks for lifting the wash from the tubs of boiling water to the cold rinsing tubs … the washboards for scrubbing out the worst of the stains. And the ever-present bags of Reckitt's bluing to be added to the final rinse.

But the boisterous camaraderie of those Notting Hill women – the swearing and name-calling and teasing interspersed with moments of outright hilarity – there's none of that. Here they work in silence, forbidden to speak to each other under penalty of having their rations cut. They are not to acknowledge each other in any way not directly related to the work. The Silchester laundresses brought their troubles and joys to the workplace: a new granddaughter, a drunken husband, a son in trouble with the police. Here they're not women, mothers, grandmothers but working paupers. Stripped of every opportunity to share their stories, they become dull, mute, mechanical beasts of burden.

Twenty thousand articles of clothing and bedding come through here every week, to be washed and rinsed, mangled and dried, pressed and folded. The laundry shed is ancient – the mangles are turned by hand, the washing machines are small and subject to frequent breakdowns, and the soiled linen is counted and sorted in a dark, poorly-ventilated room. The workhouse itself cannot provide enough laundresses – at least half of the women here are out-workers who come in every day and work from eight to six. They get $1s$ $3d$ a day, plus a midday meal. You'd have to be desperate to take on this kind of work.

Almost as desperate as the ones who live here.

***

If asked for her opinion, which she never will be, Annie would admit that the work is difficult and back-breaking, but it's the dreary, unending tedium that wears you down. She thought she knew monotony when she was in service – up before sunrise every morning, sweeping and scraping, dusting and scrubbing all day long. Here she could go mad from the sameness of it all. The never-ending boredom when the work is done – that's what haunts you.

She would give almost anything for something interesting to read. There's no shortage of religious tracts left for them by the Workhouse Visiting Society; they come bound three and four pages together with titles like "What Must I Do to Be Saved?" and "Sickness, God's Chastisement".

The society ladies mean well and, unlike some, Annie looks forward to their visits. For one thing, they improve the temper of the place when they're around. The women, even Sal – who returned, finally, much worse for wear – moderate their language and try to be a little more polite. The visitors usually leave behind small presents – coloured pictures for the walls of the sick room, tea and oranges for the elderly.

When Annie asks for a book, one of the visitors promises to do her best to find something suitable. It's obvious the request unsettles the woman, just a little; pauper inmates are more likely to ask for a plug of tobacco or sugar for their tea. She returns a few days later with *Six Lectures on Repentance, Six Lectures on Sacrifice,* and *Thirty-four Short Sermons for the Sick Room.* Seeing the look on Annie's face, the woman has a suggestion:

"Why don't you tell me what you'd like, Mrs. Taylor, and I'll see if I can find it for you?"

Shyly, Annie confesses her admiration for the works of Elizabeth Gaskell.

The woman's face lights up.

"Oh, isn't she wonderful! Have you read her latest? No? Well, then, you shall have it by the end of the week."

Which is how Annie comes into possession of *Sylvia's Lovers*, the only novel on the premises of Paddington Union Workhouse.

***

News of the outside world comes from the pauper with a recent *Standard* or *Gazette*. Those who can read spread the word to the others: Disraeli is ill and expected to resign. Someone tried to assassinate the King of Spain but failed. Germany and France are sparring again. There are floods on the Rhine.

But it's not politics or foreigners they want to hear about but news that means something to them: What's playing at the Crystal Palace? Is it true there are Zulus on display at the Royal Aquarium? What's happening in the case of the Wandsworth baby farmer? And the Holloway butcher who murdered his wife – will he be hanged?

A woman comes in with a week-old issue of *The Times*. It is only then that they learn of the terrible events that took place on the River Tay a few days after Christmas. A portion of the bridge was blown down in a heavy storm and took with it a train from Edinburgh and all its passengers. Queen Victoria had traveled that very bridge back in June – the man who designed it was given a knighthood. Mrs. Hatchett says he should be stripped of his title.

"Stripped of his title? The man should be hanged." This from Mrs. Higgins, who generally favours hanging when there's any question of wrongdoing.

Pipe Lady scoffs at this. "They don't go 'round hanging titled folk, do they? Slap him with a fine is about it, I think."

There is general consent on this issue: peers of the realm are never hanged.

***

Now that she's an official inmate she's allowed to take her meals in a small room set aside for women with babies. They also allow her a light by her bed in case the child needs feeding in the night. The room where she sleeps is an improvement on the casual ward in that the beds are spaced further apart and there's more than one privy. The beds themselves are better – just as uncomfortable but set on springs with iron bedsteads so they resemble actual beds as opposed to coffins.

Still, she barely sleeps. She turns and tosses half the night, trying to find a place among the lumps and hard places where she might fit long enough to fall asleep and have some respite from the draughts, smells, and noises … the very breathing presence of bodies in every state of distress. What amazes her is how any of them manage to sleep at all. The theory perhaps is that women who have spent long hours scrubbing floors and stairs and baseboards on their hands and knees with or without a kneeling pad – crawling from one room to the next as the pain of standing then kneeling again is too excruciating – women, some of whom are elderly and crippled with rheumatism, who spend the daylight hours in the steamy hell of the laundry shed beating, pounding, and mangling brute cloth into submission – that such women will sleep soundly the whole night long, from sheer exhaustion.

But when the lights dim and the only illumination is a pale flame flickering from the gas jet at the end of the room, another kind of torture begins. Who knew there were so many different kinds of coughs? Who knew the human chest could offer up such a variety of barks, growls and wheezes, more animal-like than anything human? Those who don't cough scratch the sores on their arms and legs or whimper and cry out in their sleep like dogs dreaming of better, kinder masters.

Sometimes, lying awake in the darkness, she remembers the bear.

She must have been four or five. They were still living in Marylebone; her grandfather came to visit and took them to the Zoological Gardens. He was a big burly man and he lifted first Annie and then Maude onto his shoulders that they might see the great white pelicans in their enclosure. But it was the sight of the old bear — a Grizzly they said – that stayed with her. He lay on his platform in the sun, ignoring the crowds, the flies, and the heat. He paid no attention to the bits of fruit and bread thrown into his enclosure, not even when one came within inches of hitting him on the head. Her grandfather said he'd been captured as a young cub somewhere in the mountains of America and transported over the ocean to London. He'd been in that bear-pit for a very long time – almost 30 years – and was blind. Annie asked if the bear was sad to be living there so far away from his family; Granddad said he didn't miss his freedom because he was only an animal.

"Beasts are of a lesser order, Annie. They don't think like us."

When was it he gave up? When his eyes gave out? Or long before that, when it finally came home to him that he would never get back to the mountains?

2.

Annie's new employer was Edward Levy, publisher of
the *Daily Telegraph*. His father had bought the paper and
appointed his son and Thornton Leigh Hunt to run it. Under
their editorship, the *Telegraph* campaigned against capital
punishment and corporal punishment in the armed forces,
and lobbied for reform of the House of Lords. Levy was that
singular kind of reform-minded journalist who knew how to
make friends in high places; the Prince of Wales had been for
dinner, and he might come again. There was every chance that
Annie would see the great man in the flesh, if she were lucky.

There were eight domestics in Mr. Levy's employ,
which was not considered extravagant – many of his friends
wondered how he managed with so few. Annie was hired as the
under-housemaid; besides her in order of seniority there was
a housekeeper, a cook, a footman who served as Mr. L.'s valet
and coachman, a mouse of a governess appropriately called
Brown, a lady's maid, an upper-housemaid, and a kitchen maid.
The family also employed a gardener and charwoman, but they
lived elsewhere.

As was promised in her hiring letter, the drudgery of the
weekly washing was not her responsibility: the washing was
picked up by a professional laundress each Monday morning
and returned – washed, dried, and pressed – the following
week. And the early morning chore of getting the fire started
and the water boiling was up to Mary Ann, the kitchen maid,
who did all the scullery chores as well.

Everything in the Levy household was modern and
grand; it made the Bellwether home look puny in comparison.
The kitchen, in particular, was an enormous improvement
over the damp, windowless room where Mrs. B. cooked her
Sunday dinners. It boasted a modern range with an oven, a
boiler to heat water, and four hotplates to keep soups and
stews simmering. The old stone floors of the kitchen, scullery,
pantry, and larder had been covered with the newly-patented
Linoleum, which was easier to clean and do battle against the
cockroaches, beetles, and fleas that invaded the place every
night. Thanks to a cistern built right in the house, there was a

constant supply of running water. No more trips up the kitchen steps to the outdoor pump, working the handle till your muscles ached, then lugging buckets of freezing water back down to the kitchen with much of it spilling on the way.

A small room off the kitchen, furnished with a long wooden table, was known as the servants' hall. The servant call bells were located here, one for each room of the main house, and a row of hooks for hanging cloaks, aprons and uniforms. A large window overlooking the back garden let in a great deal of light; here is where the servants took their meals and congregated in the evenings, mending stockings, sewing on buttons and polishing the family's shoes.

Being confined to the kitchen and downstairs rooms, Annie seldom saw either of her employers. Relations among the servants were also more formal. The cook was always addressed as Mrs. Earnshaw, and the housekeeper was Mrs. Adams. The lady's maid and governess were Hicks and Brown respectively. The footman was Mr. Bernard to everyone but Mr. and Mrs. L. who simply called him Bernard. Annie, Mary Ann and Kate, the upper-housemaid, were always called by their first names, although Mary Anne's real name was Amelia. In this house, the kitchen maid was always called Mary Anne to avoid confusion for the family. It was considered a more suitable name than Amelia.

With so many servants, there was bound to be a shortage of bedrooms, and after her experience with Mr. Bellwether she considered this not a bad thing. Only Mrs. Earnshaw and the housekeeper had rooms of their own – the cook's was just off the scullery while the housekeeper slept in a room in the attic next to the water tank. Annie shared a room and a bed with Mary Ann on the top floor while Kate and Hicks roomed together across the hall. Directly below them was the school room and next to that the nursery where Brown slept in order to keep watch on the younger children. (The oldest boy, Harry, had his own room although Brown confided that he often came to her in the middle of the night when he'd had a nightmare.) The footman had a room over the coach house at the back – he'd been offered a room in the house, but he preferred to be close to the carriage and horses in case anyone got a notion to steal them.

***

Mrs. Adams had a long list of rules for Annie when she first arrived. The fact that she came with a character extolling her five years in service meant nothing: she might as well not have worked at all seeing as she'd spent those years working in "a *very* different sort of household". In Mrs. Adams's mind the Bellwethers were only slightly higher in the pecking order than the servants they employed. Nothing Annie learned there would be of much use in a household as grand as this.

"You are an under parlour-maid," she said, "and as such you will make yourself invisible to the family. You will never enter the upstairs chambers. If by some chance the master or mistress happen to enter a room where you're cleaning, you will turn your face to the wall until they leave the room. You will not speak to anyone unless you are spoken to and you will keep your answers brief and to the point. You will give room to anyone you meet on the stairs and you will never speak to another servant in your employer's presence. It goes without saying that you are not allowed to smoke and if you break anything, it will come out of your wages. Do you understand?"

"Giving room" meant standing very still and not making eye contact with the other person. It sounded very odd but Annie agreed to do her best to be as invisible as humanly possible.

The housekeeper made it clear as well that there would be no reading of novels under her watch. "Sensational" fiction was proven to corrupt the mind and besides, an under parlour-maid should have no time for such things. If she was caught lolling around with a book in hand, she would be sent packing immediately.

Mrs. Adams was a stiff, desperately unhappy woman; an air of disappointment wrapped itself around her like a shroud. Although she had ultimate authority over the domestic staff and never let them forget that she had the power to recommend their dismissal, one sensed that she'd hoped for better things in life – that she had been meant for so much more.

Annie had not been her choice, that much was clear. Scarcely a day passed when she did not find fault with something or other. If it was up to her – and it *should* have been, there was no question of that – she would never have taken on anyone so young. In her opinion it was always asking for trouble to employ girls under twenty; they weren't moulded yet, they hadn't become permanently fixed in the ways of domestic service. They were like young colts who needed their spirits broken – they needed to be made to see themselves as insignificant cogs in the great household wheel. Once they came to realize that, they could be allowed to feel the importance of their role, albeit small, and take pride in their chores and duties. As long as they kept in mind they could be replaced in the blink of an eye. An employer would lose more sleep over switching his brand of tobacco than hiring or firing a parlour-maid.

Eventually, as Annie got to know the staff better, she understood that Mrs. Adams was universally disliked. The cook said her problem was her singledom – some women just needed to be married. A rule, she hastened to add, that did not apply to her.

"I was never one for walkin' out. It never was something I thought of, especially with what my Ma had to put up with over the years. He was a bugger, my Pa. He never let her alone, and it was no pleasure to her, just a lot of aggravation. 'Stay single, Carrie,' she said. 'Don't let no man come near you.' I took her advice and never regretted it. But someone like our woman there – well, she's like them poor nuns you read about, locked up in them convents and all. It just builds up inside 'em and there's nowhere for it to go, and they comes over all pale and begrumpled."

Mrs. Adams was particularly "begrumpled" over the way the mistress managed the household. Mrs. Levy was a modern woman; she believed in education for girls and property rights for married women and she'd even been known to speak in favour of women getting the vote. In domestic matters she was just as unorthodox and insisted on being involved in running her home. For most women of her station this meant Monday- morning consultations with the cook concerning the weekly menu and letting it be known when she and her husband were going to be out for the evening. Everything else was left in the capable hands of the housekeeper.

Except that in this particular household, much to Mrs. Adams' frustration, things were done differently. For one thing Mrs. L. was inclined to spoil the children, especially the boys. Harry, the oldest, was off to boarding school in September. It would be the making of him, but his mother was practically grief-stricken about it. She'd actually tried to persuade her husband to keep him at home and let him attend a day school in the neighbourhood, but Mr. L., quite rightly, wouldn't hear of it. How would the boy develop character, he asked, if he didn't experience fagging and all the other rituals of the public school? Not to mention the friends he'd make who'd be so useful and important in later years. Mrs. L. sought support from her own mother, but on this issue, Mrs. Webster sided with her son-in-law.

"You'll have Audrey. There's no need for her to be sent away – she'll stay home and keep you company."

Mrs. L. said it wasn't the same – her boys meant the world to her – but she gave in. She took comfort in the thought that James, the younger boy, wasn't as clever as Harry; he was more likely to be commissioned into the army and might be kept at home longer.

At any rate, how the children were raised was none of Mrs. Adams's affair. It was the running of the household that occupied her, and she resented her mistress taking it upon herself to carry out those duties that should rightly be hers. On the few occasions when she tried to allude to this, and suggested to her employer that, for instance, there was no need for her to speak directly to Kate about making up the bed in the guest room for her nephew's visit, Mrs. L. remained firm. She said that as long as the girl was under her roof she wished to maintain good relations with her. Which led Mrs. Adams to complain – privately of course – that if it was relations she was wanting with the staff, why on earth had she hired a housekeeper? Sometimes it seemed that it was her role in this household to set standards of behaviour not just for the other servants but for her employers as well.

Mr. L. was no better when it came down to it. He was Jewish, of course, which might explain his lack of understanding about the need for distance between master and servant. Thankfully, he was a busy man, running a newspaper, and wasn't about much. Still, when he was at home, he had a disconcerting habit of accosting one in the hallway and initiating the oddest conversations. There was the time, for instance, when he stopped Mrs. Adams on the upper landing and asked her whether she thought trades unions should be legalized or not?

"I am not in a position to comment on that, sir."

But he wouldn't leave it at that. Thoughtfully stroking his neatly-clipped moustache he pursued the question. "Are you saying you have no opinion? Or that you don't feel permitted to express it?"

Forced to come up with a response, she replied that, apart from believing them to be the work of anarchists and Bolsheviks, she had never given any thought to trades unions at all, except to hope that she might never have to deal with any of their members in person. Seemingly satisfied, he thanked her and continued down the stairs, leaving her completely flustered by the encounter. Never in all her previous years of service had the head of the household expressed an interest in anything she or any other servant thought about anything. If he had thought to compliment her by questioning her in this way, he had failed miserably.

***

In spite of Mrs. Adams, it didn't take Annie long to settle into her new position and feel almost as comfortable as she had back in Ealing. The cook was by nature an amiable sort of woman; no matter how busy she was, she always greeted her with a smile. If Annie had a few moments to spare, Mrs. Earnshaw had her put the kettle on for "a cup of rosie." And she quickly became friends with Mary Ann, a warm, friendly girl who'd been in service since she was eight. She'd been a workhouse girl originally but you'd never know it. She was lively and well-mannered and had none of the hang-dog look that you often saw in those raised in the Union.

Her other ally in the household was Mr. Bernard, the footman. Apart from Miss Hodge, he was the first truly educated person Annie ever met. He spoke English and French equally well; Hicks had heard him talking with a tradesman in *Italian!* He dressed beautifully whether he was wearing his elegant footman's uniform or the navy blue livery of Mr. L.'s coachman. His manner was always cheerful and polite without being what you would call high-spirited.

Mary Ann said he smelled awful good for a coachman, and he did, which is not something Annie had given much thought to before this. Men generally smelled of the jobs they did. Her father smelled of cows and milk, horse sweat and hay, a mixture she was fond of because it was Papa. Most men smelled of cheap cigarettes and rum, but Mr. Bernard did not drink or smoke. The smell that came from him was of mild peppermint drops and hair oil, which he used sparingly.

The fact is he was different from any other man she knew. He had traveled all over Europe and knew about the politics of those foreign countries. Admittedly he was a foreigner himself but he was so charming and polite most people overlooked it. Once she discovered his first name was René she began to think of him as René in her mind, although of course she never called him that. He was older than her – almost 30 – and was always very proper in his behavior towards her. In short order, Mr. Bernard began to take the place of John Thornton in her nightly imaginings.

Although he never said it directly, she and Mary Ann were convinced the footman was from a noble family. Perhaps he had argued with his father and been disowned. Or – *A Tale of Two Cities* came to mind – might he not be a descendant of royalty who lost his birthright during the Reign of Terror?

It was wonderful to speculate on these things, but when asked for specifics, he always changed the subject. Mrs. Earnshaw said he'd been recommended by a friend of Mr. L.'s, a man who was, like their employer, a Freemason, and kept a livery stable where Mr. Bernard was groom. "Never saw a better man with a horse," the friend said and Mr. L. took him on. But nobody knew much about him.

***

Shortly before Christmas, in her first year of service, Mrs. Adams bustled into the kitchen after luncheon where Annie was helping Mary Ann with the washing up.

"Mrs. Levy is coming downstairs. She has an announcement to make."

Cook was confused. "But she was down this morning. Does she want to change the dinner menu? I've already gutted the ducks."

"It's nothing to do with that, Mrs. Earnshaw. As I said, she has an announcement. Dry your hands, Mary Ann – and for heaven's sake, Annie, straighten your cap. You look like you've been walking in a hurricane."

Mrs. Adams hurried upstairs to gather the rest of the servants. Annie struggled to tuck her hair into place and hoped the juice stain on her apron would go unnoticed.

"What does she want, do you think?"

Mary Ann ducked under the table to scoop up a handful of stray peelings. "Whatever it is, Mrs. Adams ain't half in a state."

Annie wanted to add that that wasn't unusual but knew enough to hold her tongue. In a house that size you learned quickly that the walls had ears.

Presently the other servants made their way down to the kitchen: Brown, with little Audrey in tow, Kate, Hicks, and Mr. Bernard. The housekeeper was the last to arrive, followed by Mrs. Levy and the boys. James was shy and kept behind his mother's skirts, but Harry stood apart in his natty sailor suit, his arms straight at his sides in military manner, his dark, intelligent eyes reflecting the gravity of the situation.

It was a rare occurrence for any of the family to venture down to the kitchen and Harry knew it. When he was younger, Brown used to let him come down and help Cook make little pies and biscuits, but he'd been too old for that for ages.

Besides, the kitchen was for servants and girls. His sister could come down here as much as she liked – she'd be expected to, in fact, when she was older, as even girls from good families were expected to know how a kitchen should be run. And when he came home from school, it would be Audrey who would come down to the kitchen and fetch him his breakfast in the morning; he was the oldest and he was a boy and Brown would expect it of her.

Already, according to the governess, he was the ruler of the nursery – he lorded it over his younger brother and sister like a benevolent despot, exercising authority with brotherly affection. Now and then he tried it on with Brown and was rebuked for it, but in a kindly manner . . . she adored the young heir and secretly admired his imperious manners.

As she confided to Cook, "He's well aware of who he is, Master Harry. I do believe he'll make his mark in this world, there's no doubt about it."

With one hand on her son's shoulder, Mrs. Levy began the little speech she'd rehearsed. "I have a treat for you. Well, to be honest, it's my husband's treat, but it was my idea and I insisted on telling you myself."

It had been her husband's idea originally; he planned to treat his newspaper staff – the compositors, editors, reporters, and apprentices – to a night out as a Christmas bonus. It was his wife who decided the invitation should be extended to the household servants.

"It will be lovely for them. And you're always saying people such as us must try to make life more pleasant for the less fortunate."

Mr. L. claimed he had been speaking of the poor and homeless, not his own well-fed – and tolerably well-paid – domestic servants. But in the end he agreed, although he thought she should leave the announcement to the housekeeper.

She, however, wanted the fun of telling them in person. Now she smiled, hoping to put them at ease. Mrs. Adams gave a quick tight smile in return, but the rest of the staff stood there poker-faced, as if they were attending their own execution.

"You all know, I believe, that my husband's uncle has a little theatre on the Strand. It's called the Gaiety and it's doing rather well."

Everyone knew about the Gaiety – to say it was doing rather well was as much an understatement as describing it as a "little" theatre. The *Times* called it "one of the best built, most convenient, and best decorated theatres of its kind in England".

Mrs. L. continued: "Next Tuesday is the one-year anniversary of the theatre, and we – my husband and I – would like to invite you – all of you – to a performance there. We'll arrange to have a tram pick everyone up here at the house, and bring everyone back when it's done. The men who work on the newspaper will be joining us – I dare say we'll be quite a crowd!"

She laughed nervously, unsure of their reaction. You could see that she had thought it a wonderful idea – very likely she had pictured them clapping their hands in glee. Well, not Mrs. Adams, of course, or the cook, but surely she expected some reaction from the rest. But they were unsure what to do and were waiting for someone else to take the lead.

Mr. Bernard was the first to speak. "It's very kind of you, Madame, I'm sure."

The rest of them nodded and mumbled something similar, and she seemed relieved. "Yes, well, I suppose that's all that needs to be said for now. If you have any questions, I'm sure Mrs. Adams will be able to help you. I do hope you will all come – it will be such a treat."

"And more than you deserve," the housekeeper added once Mrs. L. and the children had retreated upstairs.

It was Hicks who gave voice to what the others were thinking: were they respectable, these music hall places? She'd heard they were frequented by women who were no better than they ought to be. Surely they were vulgar and the entertainment was risqué.

The housekeeper bridled at the suggestion. "I hope you're not implying that Mr. Levy would allow anyone in his employ to take part in immoral behaviour."

Mary Ann, who knew about these things, was quick to assure them that there was nothing objectionable about music halls – unless you were a prude. "When my sister was alive, she and me went all the time – whenever we could get a night off together. 'Course, you have to watch the coster lads, they can get a bit rough when they've been drinking. And Miss Hicks is right, there are girls there you don't want to know, but if you keep yourself to yourself it's just good fun."

Mrs. Adams got very sniffy about this. "I can assure you that Mr. Lawson's theatre is of a very different sort to the gin palaces you and your poor sister frequented. Now get back to work, please, all of you."

"Well, it's very kind of the missus, I'm sure," Cook said, "but you won't catch me going. With everyone out of the house, I'll be putting me feet up and taking it easy."

"Of course, Mrs. Earnshaw, I wouldn't expect you to attend. And you deserve a rest."

The housekeeper always deferred to the cook while ruling over everybody else like a Tartar. Mrs. Earnshaw might not be the most senior servant, or the best paid, but she was in many ways the most important. A good cook could make or break a household, and one like Mrs. Earnshaw who could feed ten people or a hundred at short notice – and who didn't drink – was worth her weight in gold.

Having done her duty, defending her employer and putting paid to any doubts about the respectability of the enterprise, the housekeeper hurried out of the kitchen, leaving the cook, Mary Ann and Annie to exchange knowing looks.

Cook summed it up: "She's not happy about this. Mark my words. All that blather about respectability and all – she thinks she's going to be pulled up on stage to do the Can-Can!"

3.

She's seen her daughters three times since that first visit and has managed to keep her temper with Vicky. The girl was born sulking. They've never got along. And Edith – she's gotten so nervous since coming here … terrified of her own shadow, it seems. She does that ridiculous thing with her hair, twisting it around her fingers till Annie could scream. During the week she thinks of them fondly but when they're together she remembers how much they irritate her. Bill was better with them. You wouldn't call him a patient man but he had more tolerance. He read them funny stories from the paper when he got home from work, and played board games with them like Snakes and Ladders. He was also, if she's going to be completely honest, more affectionate towards them.

She's never been one for petting her children. Mama always said a petted child was a spoiled child. The rich can afford to indulge their children, she said – they have the time to do so and the servants to pick up after them. Children of the poor must learn to take care of themselves.

The boy, though – it's different with him. He's such a happy, trusting wee soul. She can't help fussing over him the way she never did with her daughters. There's something about him that helps to fill the empty place inside her … the one that used to belong to a boisterous, slightly grubby three-year-old who was only just learning to tell time.

***

Today is Edith's birthday, and she has a present for her: *Little Dot*, a children's book given to her by her friend from the Visiting Society. "It's a very moral story," the woman said. "Very uplifting and character-building. I'm sure your little girl will love it."

She hopes that's true. Perhaps Vic will take time to read it to her, if Edie can't manage it herself. Bill was better with them.

Baby in arms, book in pocket, she makes her way to the receiving ward at the usual hour. The room is full of youngsters and their mothers, but she can't see Vic or Edie anywhere. She finds a place to sit and rock the baby and wait. A quarter-hour passes and the girls have still not arrived. There's nothing for it: she'll have to approach the matron.

"Your daughters? They're gone."

"What do you mean? Gone where?"

Have they actually run away? If that's the case why wasn't she told?

Matron smiles. "Well, since you ask, they've been removed."

It takes every resource she can summon to swallow her fury and respond without raising her voice. "I don't understand. Who removed them? Where've they gone?"

"I don't see that it's any of your business."

"They are my children. Of course it's my business!"

The smile that was not really a smile disappears. The woman's mouth tightens into a thin hard line.

"You have forfeited your children, Mrs. Taylor. I am not under any obligation to tell you anything. Those are the rules. If you think those rules are unreasonable you are free to leave. Assuming you have somewhere to go. Do you have somewhere to go?"

"No."

"Then we're done."

"I'm sorry, Matron, but we are *not* done. I demand to know what you've done with my daughters."

"*Demand?*" She spits the word out like a piece of rotten flesh and points to the door. "I caution you to take your child and get back to the day-room. Don't make me tell you twice."

She turns away. Instinctively, without thinking, Annie reaches out to stop her. Matron flinches at the touch.

"How dare you!"

"I'm sorry –"

"Oh, you will be. You'll be very sorry I promise you that."

Stoker, sensing trouble, steps forward.

"Is there a problem?"

"Take this woman to the Refractory Cell."

"What about the baby?"

Her answer is to remove the child from Annie's arms. "I'll take him to the nursery. He's done nothing, there's no need to punish him."

"Give me back my son!"

The porter's hand is on her, gripping her tightly as Matron turns on her heel and limps out of the room, taking the baby with her. Removed so abruptly from his mother's arms he begins to wail – she can hear his cries of distress all the way down the hallway. And Stoker won't let her go. Try as she might to shake him off, he's head and shoulders taller than her and has fists of iron. And he wouldn't hesitate to use them. For all his joking with the casuals, Stoker's hard as nails when he needs to be.

"Now then," he says, "let's have none of that. Behave yourself and come with me."

Keeping his hand on her arm, he steers her down a long corridor, through several doors and finally to a set of stone stairs that curve down to a narrow passage with locked doors on both sides. It might be called a dungeon, it's that cold and damp and badly lit. The dank, stone-flagged floor is uneven under her boots; she trips but manages to steady herself. They pass a door marked "Mortuary" and another half open revealing spades and garden rakes and a wheelbarrow.

Down yet another set of steps to the cellar. They pass three large heavy metal doors secured with strong bolts and iron padlocks. The punishment cells. Collectively known as the hole. Stoker stops in front of one of them, unlocks the door and pulls it open

"All right then, in you go."

Suddenly afraid, she turns to him. "Please –"

"Now don't start. You won't starve. You'll be given bread and water tonight and again in the morning."

"Am I to be kept here all night?"

"You'll be released in time for work tomorrow. That's providing you behave yourself."

He turns to leave and then stops. "You gave her no choice, talking back to her the way you did. Maybe next time you'll think before you speak."

The great iron door clangs shut.

***

It's a prison within a prison. The furnishings are sparse: apart from a chamber pot in one corner, the room contains a makeshift bed attached to one wall and a narrow wooden shelf which serves as a table. A window with an iron grille looks into the cell next to it; it is unoccupied and dark.

She feels a tightening in her chest as if the room is closing in. There's not enough air – there are no windows – what will happen when the air goes? How long does it take to go? She should sit, not waste energy. Lie down perhaps. But lying down is worse – the ceiling's too low, it'll bear down and crush her. All right. Get up and walk. Four paces. Reach a wall. Turn. Five paces. Turn and walk to the next. Four paces. Turn and walk back. Deep breath, do it again. Four, five, four, five. If she has to, if it will keep the terror at bay, she'll walk this cage all night.

There's workhouse time, and there's workhouse black hole time. This is time without clocks, or daylight, or some way of distinguishing between the hours. There are no windows, no sounds from the rest of the building. Not even the workhouse bell penetrates these walls.

A sound of footsteps. The feeding window opens and a tray is handed through: a hunk of bread and a mug of tea.

"Please help me! I can't stay here – I can't breathe!"

"Eat your supper and get some sleep. It'll be morning 'fore you know it."

She recognizes the voice.

"Mrs. Chancer, it's me – Annie Taylor."

"I know who you are. And I ain't all that surprised."

"Have you seen my child? My son, do you know where he is?"

"How should I know? Don't I have enough to be doing? Sending me down here on a Sunday when I should be putting my feet up. Anyway, it's about time you got written up. Serves you right."

"I'm sorry – Mrs. Chancer, please, will you see if my son is in the nursery? Biddie Fletcher might have him. Or Mrs.

Dribble. If you could just …"

The window closes and she's gone.

She carries the plate to the bed and sets it down on the floor. If this is her supper, then it cannot be later than six or seven which means she's been in here for three hours, maybe four. She'll be released in time for work in the morning, that's what Stoker said. Work begins at eight. Twelve more hours … maybe thirteen. She can't think how she can manage it.

The tears, when they come, surprise her. She hasn't cried in so long. She wept over little William when he was laid out on their bed. And again at the gravesite. After that, nothing. There's been no time to cry … not when Bill walked out, not when she had to sell her hair. Bill hated when she cried. He told her once that his mother never cried. She miscarried three times after Bill was born, and buried her youngest daughter at three. Never shed a tear, he said. Good sturdy peasant stock. He said it with a smirk, but he was proud of her – proud of a cold-hearted woman who couldn't cry over her children.

Well, his mother's not here and neither is he. She can weep and wail in the darkness and there'll be no one to judge her for it. For months she's strugged to block it out, fought for self-control. Now she lets it take over – grief permeates every part of her body. All the sorrow of the past six months … all the sadness of death and desertion … the humiliation of being here in this place. What a relief to let it out!

Exhausted, she falls asleep and dreams about her grandfather. She's a little girl and she's visiting him in his tailor shop on Compton Street. He lifts her on to the cutting table and she sits "tailor fashion", watching him cut out the fabric. Do you want to give it a try? he says. Take the scissors and hold them just so. Careful, now. Piece by piece, he says. Follow the pattern. If you fail to do so you must see what is missing, what has been left out, where has the cutting gone awry, the stitching not perfect, so the suit, when it's finally sewn together, won't fit, or hangs tight on the body where it should be loose. You have to tear it apart, he tells her, and start again.

***

Morning announces itself not with any natural light but by the flicker of a lamp in the passageway. "Wake up now – time to get up."

The porter unlocks the door and hands her a mug of tea and a slice of buttered bread.

"Eat this and I'll take you upstairs."

"I'm done then?"

"You're done. Bring your tray and I'll take you back."

She follows him along the corridor and up two flights of stairs, shaking with relief. She survived the night. Whatever else happens to her in this place, nothing will ever be as terrifying. Stoker leaves her at the door of the nursery with a final cautionary word: Behave yourself. You don't want to go there again.

The child is sitting up in his cot, playing with a headless horse donated by the Visiting Society. Seeing her, he drops the toy and pulls himself to standing.

"Hello, Teddy. Have you been good while Mama was gone?"

She picks him up and cuddles him, feeling the dampness through his cotton dress. He would have been lying here wet all night, she knows that. Biddie says the night nurses never change the babies if they don't have to. Still, she's here now. She can take him back to the ward and feed him and change his flannel. She can do that for him. There's little she can do for the girls but this one still needs her.

4.

The night of the outing she stood at the door of the kitchen, a shawl wrapped around her shoulders to protect her from the wind. Her hands and feet tingled, although whether from excitement or the cold she couldn't say. In all the time she'd been in service, she was seldom out of the house at night; never had she ventured into the legendary West End. No matter what she thought of the performance, this evening would be something to remember for the rest of her life.

At half past five, two hackney carriages turned the corner onto Grosvenor Street.

"They're here, Mrs. Earnshaw. I'll tell Kate and Mary-Ann."

The coaches were for the staff; Mr. and Mrs. Levy had already left for the theatre, driven by Mr. Bernard in the landau. Cook had changed her mind and decided to come, and Mrs. L. had found a replacement for Brown so she could come as well.

There had been consternation among the children when they learned they were not to be taken along. Harry was particularly indignant to be left out of the party.

"But I'm seven and I'm the oldest. If I can go away to school by myself I should be allowed. It's not fair."

But Mrs. L., for once, was firm. The theatre burlesque was no place for children.

It was odd to see the staff out of uniform. Cook especially, with her extravagant new bonnet that could have done with fewer artificial flowers. But it was still preferable to Mrs. Adams' ensemble – black crape from head to toe.

"Does she think we're going to a funeral? It's supposed to be a bit of fun."

Hicks wore a demure powder-blue day dress handed down from Mrs. L. It fit her so well it seemed a pity to spoil the effect with a bonnet and wrap. Mary Ann was all in pink, which was not the best colour for her, given her ruddy complexion, but Kate loaned her a serviceable cloak of black-and-white check which toned down the effect somewhat.

Brown's concession to the glamour of the evening was a single strand of pearls and matching drop earrings. She was apologetic about them, explaining they'd belonged to her grandmama and were probably not worth much in today's market.

"It's for sentimental reasons, really, that I keep them."

The others all said they were lovely and Brown blushed under the unaccustomed attention.

But the real star of the evening – in the servants' quarters at least – was Annie. Hicks had approached her the day before and offered to do her hair.

"It's such a beautiful colour. And always hidden away under your cap. Do let me play with it a little tomorrow, won't you? Mr. and Mrs. Levy will be leaving for an early supper – meet me upstairs when they're gone and I'll fix you up."

Annie agreed with alacrity. Hicks was known to be a marvelous hair-dresser; friends of Mrs. L. often came to her to be "done" before an important social event.

"Don't tell anyone," Hicks said. "We'll let it be a surprise."

And so, with their employers out of the house, Annie sat at Mrs. L.'s dressing table and let the lady's maid "play with" her hair.

"There's a lot of very rich ladies would give anything to have your hair," Hicks said. After removing the pins that held Annie's hair in a tight, serviceable bun, she picked up an ivory-backed brush and began to brush it out, first of all assuring her the brush was hers, not her employer's. This was a relief; it was strange enough to be sitting upstairs in her mistress' dressing-room, at her dressing-table, having her hair attended to by her maid. Using Mrs. Levy's hair-brush would be too much.

With long, expert strokes Hicks brushed Annie's hair back from her forehead, then braided the ends and knitted them together with a small tortoiseshell comb. ("Mine," she said, before Annie could object. "Don't worry, I have several.") Using a pair of tongs heated in the fireplace, she created a waterfall of curls that hung around Annie's neck and halfway down her back.

When she was done, she handed Annie a mirror. "Take a look," she said, "what do you think?"

It was as if she was gazing at an illustration in Godey's

Lady's Book. Could this very feminine, very fashionable creature be plain old Annie Morgan?

"It's wonderful – I hardly know it's me."

"It's you all right, and it's *all* you. Most ladies would need three or four hairpieces to get that effect. Aren't you the lucky one?"

She *felt* lucky, right at that moment. She'd had her hair dressed by an expert and she was going to the theatre – two things beyond the reach of any other girl of her station if she lived to be a hundred.

***

Because of the traffic, the trip to the theatre, less than three miles away, took almost an hour. The West End streets were crowded with carriages of every description – grand equipages rubbing shoulders with advertising vans and brewers' drays, hansom cabs and phaetons competing for possession of the right-of-way, stately broughams nose-to-nose with tradesmen's carts. Rival omnibuses advertising Nestle's Milk and Lipton's Tea fought to see who could carry more passengers. Giant advertising vans stopped at random intervals for no apparent reason, blocking the roadway for minutes at a time, ignoring the shouts from other drivers to "Move along, get out the bleedin' way!" Now and then a poor fellow with an advertising board hanging in front and back could be seen trudging along the carriageway, ducking mudballs thrown by street urchins and dodging the kicks of disgruntled ominibus conductors.

The footways were just as crowded: clerks and shop-girls hurrying home; costermongers selling oysters, pickled whelks, sheep's trotters, and ginger beer; young swells on their way to betting shops and gin palaces. And the ubiquitous street arabs: crossing-sweepers, horse-holders, cab whistlers, package carriers.

Those not serving the public were juggling oranges, standing on their heads – anything to earn a penny or two. A homeless woman cradling a baby huddled on the pavement, bringing to mind stories of poor women borrowing babies for the purposes of begging, or maiming or blinding their own children to make people pity them more. Still, it was December and it was cold; a person had to be desperate in some way to sit on the street like that and beg.

And of course there were the women dressed just a little too fashionably who sauntered back and forth, twirling their parasols, stopping at street corners and shop windows longer than was needed. It didn't take much imagination to recognize them for what they were. Mary Ann and Annie nudged each other and giggled, before averting their eyes.

But it was the vast plate-glass windows of the West End shops that captured the lion's share of attention. They were an entertainment in themselves with their displays of books and jewelry, clockwork toys, rich velvet mantles and Oriental carpets. Grocers' windows boasted towering pyramids of fruit: currants and raisins, dates and prunes, candied lemons and preserves. Some of the larger department store windows featured Christmas trees – sapling firs hung with clusters of oranges, lemons and grapes. Even the busiest shoppers were forced to take a moment to stop and admire these windows, the Christmas tree still being somewhat of a novelty.

Annie's family never had a tree. The Bellwethers considered it a German affectation that would soon fade away. The Levy's tree, Mary Ann promised, would be every bit as grand as the one at Windsor Castle.

"They put toys and dolls and candles on every branch, and there'll be gifts for all of us. They set it up in the drawing room on Christmas Eve and they leave it till Twelfth Night so we can all enjoy it. It's ever so lovely, Annie. You wouldn't think they were Jewish."

She and Mary Ann were seated directly behind Mrs. Adams and Brown. By dint of leaning forward to get a better look at the passing scene, Annie could hear every word they said. Or rather, every word Mrs. Adams said, for it was she who was using the relative protection of the pandemonium of the street to air her latest grievance.

"Coming down to the kitchen like that – it's *so* like her. And so inappropriate. I'd never be the one to say it, of course, but I do think it lowers her in the eyes of the staff, don't you agree? It would have been *much* better to have told *me* about the event and had *me* inform the others. I *am* the housekeeper, after all. And now this outing – so different from what one is used to. A picnic in Hyde Park, perhaps, or a day at the zoo, perhaps followed by a little excursion down the Thames. Even a shilling van to Hampton would be more in keeping with the situation. The master in my last place gave us an annual trip down to Greenwich on Easter Monday, weather permitting. He hired a boat to take us to the Isle of Dogs and supplied an excellent picnic lunch. All very good and proper, Miss Brown. If Mrs. Levy had suggested such an outing, I would have been the first to agree. There is no harm in allowing staff the occasional treat. But a trip to a musical theatre! Well, it would not have been *my* choice at all."

When their coach pulled up in front of the Gaiety, the newspaper staff were already arrived. Forty men, all dressed in their best bib and tucker, as her mother would say, waiting to escort the ladies.

Mary Ann was taken aback. "My eyes, Mrs. Adams! are we supposed to pick one of 'em? I never seen so many fellas all in one place. How're we supposed to choose?"

"You will do nothing of the kind, Mary Ann," the housekeeper said. "You haven't been properly introduced to any of these men. You will stay with Mrs. Earnshaw and behave yourself."

As Annie stepped down from the coach, a young man reached out to steady her by putting his hand on her arm. "Careful, now, Miss. You don't want to fall."

She kept her eyes on the pavement, more out of regard for the uneven cobblestones than from modesty, but caught the West Country accent and the scent of hair oil.

"Thank you." Noting that his hand was still on her arm, she added, "You can let me go now. I think I'm safe."

The hand stayed put. "Will I take you in, Miss?"

A quick glance revealed a well-built young man, with bright, restless eyes and short, crinkly hair, like a blacksmith's. He was dressed in a dark brown Ulster and necktie, topped off with a black billycock hat. There was nothing offensive in his appearance but his assumption of familiarity was disturbing.

"Thank you, sir, but I can manage on my own."

"If you'll allow me, Miss, you don't want to be making your way through this mob without a helping hand."

At that moment, like one of Mrs. Gaskell's heroes, Mr. Bernard materialized. Smoothly but firmly he released Annie from her captor and steered her and Mary Ann towards the theatre entrance. The way was blocked by the gallery crowd who'd arrived a good half hour before in order to get a place. Surely all would gain entrance at some point – but the crowd pushed and pulled and elbowed one in the ribs until it seemed it would take a miracle to get through it alive. And the noise! The shrieks of the flower-sellers and pie-men, the young men waving tickets in your face, people calling to each other over the heads of the crowd – she couldn't hear herself think.

None of this bothered their guide. Offering them each an arm, the footman led the way, tunneling efficiently through the mob, as oblivious to the unruly throng as if he were leading a guest to the drawing room. With his help, they reached the entrance without being strangled, smothered, or stepped on. A stout, imposing doorman in red serge and gold braid tipped his hat to them and held the door open until they passed through.

Inside the babble of voices was almost as shrill as it had been out on the pavement. Leading them to a far wall out of the crush, Mr. Bernard suggested they stay and catch their breath while he attended to the others.

This was the notorious Promenade – the den of vice where men-about-town in white gloves and opera hats fraternized with the *demi-monde*. The walls were papered in red velvet flecked with gold and hung with paintings of beautiful women in Greek and Roman dress, many of whom were naked. Smoke from a hundred cigars rose high into the air and floated just below the ceiling. Swells in evening dress greeted each other with boisterous courtesies, accompanied by women whose silk cloaks and sable furs shimmered in the gaslight. It was marvelous.

Mary Ann grabbed her hand and squeezed it in excitement. "It's first-rate, Annie, don't you think? All these ladies and gents – do you think His Highness is here?"

She couldn't tell; to her untrained eye, with their top hats and stomachers bursting at the seams, every other man looked like the Prince of Wales.

Mrs. Adams lunged toward them out of the crowd. Her bonnet was askew and she was clutching her handbag to her chest as if she feared she might be robbed.

"It really is too much! All sorts of people – elbowing one here and there – Madame is waiting by the staircase – must find Mrs. Earnshaw – she's gone missing."

They'd never seen the housekeeper so unsettled. Her forehead was beaded with sweat and her lips were trembling. Annie was afraid she might break down and cry – she certainly looked ready to do so.

"Mr. Bernard's gone to find her, Mrs. Adams. He shouldn't be long."

The housekeeper clutched her shawl tightly around her and shivered in spite of the heat. "All these people – makes one feel unable to breathe."

Where on earth was Mr. Bernard? If the housekeeper chose that moment to collapse, what would they do? Would anyone even notice in all the noise and confusion? She was practically giddy with relief when she saw the footman returning through the crowd with Mrs. Earnshaw in tow and a glass in either hand.

"Sherry," he said, handing one of the glasses to Mrs. Adams. "Drink this, Madame, it will make you feel much better."

He offered Mrs. Earnshaw the other glass but she declined.

"I'll have it then, if you don't want it," Mary Ann said.

Mrs. Adams revived herself enough to sputter, "You will *not*, Mary Ann Graham. Give that back at once."

The sherry appeared to have a steadying effect on the housekeeper. After a few sips she was able to regain her composure; by the time they made their way to where Mrs. L. and the rest of the staff were gathered she was her usual self – for better or for worse.

A most distinguished gentleman had joined the group. Dark hair swept back from his broad forehead, moustache neatly trimmed and waxed to perfection. He greeted them warmly, and introduced himself: John Hollingshead, manager of this establishment. Handing Mr. and Mrs. Levy each a program bound in red leather, he welcomed them to the Gaiety.

"We are honoured to have the nephew of our founder and his household in our audience tonight. I hope and trust you will thoroughly enjoy the performance. Now, ladies and gentlemen, if you will kindly follow me, I will show you to your seats."

Mr. L. was the kind of man who, having decided to do something, goes all out and does it right. His staff had assumed they'd be viewing the entertainment from the amphitheatre or down in the pit. Instead, the manager led them up a wide carpeted staircase to the first landing, where a sign on a velvet rope read "Grand Tier" and several doors were marked "Private". With a flourish, he opened the door nearest them and indicated that they should enter. Mr. and Mrs. Levy went in first, and the servants followed. Occupants of nearby boxes craned their necks to see and Annie heard more than a few whispers: "Edward Levy, the newspaper publisher" ... "friend of the Prince of Wales" … "his wife, isn't she lovely?" This, then, was celebrity. Or as close to it as she was ever likely to be again.

Whether it was by coincidence or not – and she chose to believe it was not – Mr. Bernard ended up sitting beside her.

At first the height made her dizzy; she had to close her eyes for a few minutes until her stomach settled down. When she finally dared to look, she saw they were seated directly above the stage on the right. The balcony containing a tier of private boxes like theirs ran along three sides of the auditorium in the shape of a semi-circle. It seemed to her they were very high up and yet she could see rows of seats continuing almost to the roof. A crimson curtain hung at the front of the stage; Mr. Bernard said this was the "drop" curtain and it would be raised when the performance began.

"Look up, Miss Morgan. Do you see the paintings of women on the ceiling? Those are the Muses of ancient Greece: History, Astronomy, Tragedy, Comedy, Song, Dance, and Poetry."

There were three different Muses of Poetry, he said, because poetry played such an important role in Greek culture.

The Muses were the daughters of Zeus; Mr. Bernard knew their names but only one stayed with her – Calliope. Most likely because of her mother's stories of watching the steam calliope being played in the Crystal Palace. Directing her attention to the long stretch of painting directly above the curtain, he explained that the medieval king and queen painted there were watching something called a masque, a form of courtly entertainment when Elizabeth was Queen.

"Do you go to the theatre often, Mr. Bernard?"

"I live and breathe the theatre, Miss Morgan. It is to me like the air – like water and food. It is essential to my existence."

Now Mr. Levy stood up, cleared his throat, and prepared to give a little speech. Before his father bought the *Telegraph* and put him in charge, he had been the dramatic critic for the *Sunday Times*. If there was one thing he loved – and loved to talk about – it was the theatre. From this very box, he said, he'd seen every new production performed on this stage, beginning with opening night a year ago when Nelly Farren played the title role in *Robert the Devil*. In March, the new Tom Robertson play, *Dreams*, had been most enjoyable, although he felt its charm was marred – and several critics agreed with him – by casting of the great character actor, Alfred Wigan, as the romantic lead – a part which really demanded a much younger man. The Whitsuntide performance of *Columbus*, advertised as a spectacular extravaganza, had lived up to its billing, but a few months later he'd been disappointed with *An Old Score* by W. S. Gilbert.

"Too clever by half. They called it a comedy-drama but I didn't laugh – and neither did the audience. In my opinion, there was too much drama and not enough comedy. Every newspaper man knows the first rule of writing is to understand your public: you don't want to talk down to them, but pitch your writing high above their heads and you lose them in the first paragraph. Or soliloquy, as the case may be."

According to the program, tonight's entertainment would commence at seven with Offenbach's operetta, *The Rose of Auvergne*. Mr. L. assured them it would be "charming – I am most eager to hear it performed in English." After that, they

would be treated to *Uncle Dick's Darling*, a three-act drama by
Henry J. Byron starring Mr. John Toole, the well-known comic
actor. They would also be entertained by a relative newcomer
to the stage, Mr. Henry Irving.

"He is quite good, actually. I saw him last year at
the *Haymarket* and he impressed me as a person one should
watch."

Directly across the auditorium there was a private box,
screened from public scrutiny, which belonged to the Prince of
Wales. They were all desperate to know if he was here tonight
but it was Mary Ann who screwed up her courage to put the
question.

"Difficult to say, really. But if he is, he might drop
by to say hello. He loves the music halls – did you know he
once danced the Can-Can with the Duchess of Manchester?
In private, of course, not in a music hall – that would have
brought down the monarchy."

"Edward!" His wife was shocked – or pretended to be.
"Don't be so disrespectful. And you know that's just a rumour."

"It's nothing of the kind, my dear. His Highness told me
himself. He was quite proud of it, and I think he should be."

Here he was interrupted by a handsome gentleman
with a mop of dark curls. Mr. Bernard, who seemed to know
everyone worth knowing, whispered to her that this was James
Greenwood, "the amateur casual" – the journalist who spent a
night in the casual ward of the Lambeth workhouse disguised
as a tramp. That such a respectable, neatly dressed gentleman
might pass for a vagrant, even for a single night, was difficult
to imagine, but he had done it, along with a stockbroker
companion, and had electrified his readers with his descriptions
of the appalling conditions there. That was four years ago,
but Annie had not forgotten the sensation it caused and Mrs.
Bellwether's response the day the first story appeared. It would
take a harder heart than hers, she said, not to feel for those poor
homeless wretches. She would ask the Women of Caritas to
write a letter to the newspaper, demanding something be done.

The thought of Mrs. B. made her smile, and feel a little
sad at the same time. She'd been good to her – motherly, even
– and Annie had not been honest with her at the end. Should

she have told her what her husband was up to? Might he not try it on with some other young girl, given the opportunity? And, given that the other girl, if she existed, was more pliant, might he not go even further?

Mary Ann squeezed her hand. "Annie, pay attention – it's starting!"

Mr. Hollingshead, the manager, was calling for silence. The din abated a little, just enough to hear him announce a change in the cast of the final performance of the evening, the "operatic extravaganza", *Wat Tyler*. Miss Nelly Farren was indisposed. ("Hit on the head by a piece of falling scenery," according to Mr. L.)

"For this evening and this evening only, the part of Henry Plantaganet will be played by the celebrated male impersonator, Miss Christy Connor. We trust that Miss Farren will be back treading the boards presently."

Mr. Bernard said not to be disappointed; he'd seen Miss Connor perform several times and believed her to be quite gifted.

"She is what they call an *artiste comique*, but I believe she can be serious, too. Some of the women who play men get it wrong but Miss Connor *becomes* a man on stage. I am informed that she has recently become a particular favourite with His Highness."

The manager left the stage, the orchestra began to play the overture, and the curtain rose on *The Rose of Auvergne*. Annie had nothing to compare it with, having never seen anything more elaborate than *Punch and Judy*. But she was entranced from the first song sung by Miss Annie Tremain to the Maypole dance which wrapped up the performance four and a half hours later. Laughter, tears, songs of love and pathos – it was a gargantuan feast of entertainment. To think that all of this was on offer every night for the cost of 10 shillings. Of course, the private boxes, such as this one belonging to Mr. L., cost more than that, but you could sit in the pit or the gallery for sixpence.

The curtain came down, the audience stood for "God Save the Queen" and everyone began filing out of the theatre. But there was more: Mr. Levy announced that the manager had invited them backstage to pay their compliments to the performers.

"Oh, I couldn't," Mary Ann said, and the others agreed.

"I wouldn't know what to say," Mrs. Earnshaw said. "I never spoke to an actor in my life."

"Oh, come now." Mr. Levy tapped his walking stick impatiently. He was annoyed; here he was offering this special treat and nobody was taking him up on it. "They're people like you and me. Surely one of you is brave enough to come back and say hello?"

"Never mind, dear," Mrs. Levy said. "They've had a good time. Don't spoil it."

How she found the courage was a mystery, but Annie put her hand up. "Sir? I'd like to go, if I may."

"Good girl! Come with me – the rest of you can wait downstairs with my wife. We won't be long."

And so she found herself following her employer's top hat and frock coat down three flights of stairs and along a narrow hallway to a basement room marked, "Artistes". Backstage, then, was not so much behind the stage as beneath it. Mr. L. gave the door a couple of sharp raps with his walking stick; in a moment it was opened by a maid in a crisp white apron and cap.

He handed her his card. "Edward Levy of the *Telegraph*. May we come in?"

The room was a study in chaos – costumes were slung carelessly over the backs of chairs … shoes, scarves, and stockings lay jumbled on the bare wooden floor … dressing-table tops were littered with wigs, powder, towels, and jars of lanolin. The air was stifling – there were a half dozen performers in dressing gowns and smoking jackets, and every one of them was inhaling a pipe, cigar or cigarette while removing the traces of face paint and powder.

Upon hearing her employer's name one of the men stood up and crossed the room to greet them. "Levy! Good to see you, old man! Wonderful that you took the time."

It took her a moment to realize that this very ordinary-looking man with a towel around his shoulders was the famous Mr. J. L. Toole whom she'd seen not ten minutes ago in the costume of a medieval peasant. She was overcome with shyness. When the actor asked if she'd enjoyed the performance she nodded and looked down at her boots, unable to think of anything to say.

He seemed not to mind that she was such a dunce. Very kindly, he offered to introduce her to the other "artistes" in the room: Miss Marie Litton, Mr. Charles Lyall, Miss Annie Tremaine, Mr. John Maclean, Mr. Nicholas Marlowe, and Miss Christy Connor, the one who'd filled in for Miss Farren.

Miss Connor looked at her in a peculiar fashion. "What did you say your name was?"

"Annie Morgan." Feeling a little less shy she added, "You were very good, Miss Connor. I shouldn't have known you were a woman at all and neither would the girls I was with."

"Annie Morgan – as I live and breathe! You don't remember me, do you?"

"I beg your pardon, Miss?"

Mr. L. had moved on – he and Mr. Toole were discussing a review that had appeared in the *Telegraph.*

"It's *me*, Annie. Maggie! Maggie Boyle!"

It was then that she saw it – the dark Irish eyes, the pointed chin – the face that had once been as familiar as her own.

"Maggie! I don't believe it."

Laughing, Maggie – that is, Miss Connor – pulled her down onto a chair beside her. "Believe it, because it's me. My God, Annie, I never thought to see you again!"

"Nor did I. Expect to see you, I mean. How did you – I mean, where did …"

"Ever such a long story, dearest. Too long to tell here. We'll have a good chinwag soon and I'll tell you all about it." Impulsively, she took Annie's hands in hers and squeezed them. "It's lovely, don't you think? Finding each other again, after all this time – I swear I'm in shock, I am!"

There was no time to say any more. Mr. L. was finished his conversation and ready to leave. Maggie accompanied her to the doorway and promised to send her a note. "We have so much to talk about, Annie. We'll get together soon."

On the way back up to the lobby, Mr. L. asked how she knew Miss Connor. Annie said they'd been in school together, which sounded reasonable enough, although as far as she knew Maggie Boyle never attended school a day in her life. A "poor, uneducated immigrant" – wait till she told Mama!

5.

It's spring. They will bury the child now if they haven't already.

Will they mark the grave? Bill paid for a stone, she's sure of that. But he didn't stick around to see that it was done. He wasn't happy about the burial ground, the cemetery in Paddington. It wasn't his choice. He wanted the child brought back to Devon, to be buried with the Taylors and Huxtables in the South Molton graveyard. But she put her foot down, for once.

"I want him near me," she said. "I want to be able to go there when I can, and plant a few flowers. I want to be able to visit, the way I do with Papa."

She won that one. One of these days, when she gets out of here, she'll bring the girls there, let the baby play on the grass. They can have a picnic in the shade of that horse chestnut growing nearby. It will be good to do that. To say goodbye.

***

Biddie is still praying for her; she says so one evening in April.

"I just wanted you to know that I ain't forgotten."

"That's kind of you, Biddie. Thank you." Parched with thirst from the steam and sweat of the laundry, she wants only to retrieve her child from the nursery and take the two of them to bed.

With a quick glance to be sure she's not being overheard, Biddie whispers, "I told Mr. Catlin about your girls. How they took them away and won't tell you nothing. I wish you'd let him help you."

"Biddie, I've asked you before – I really wish you wouldn't talk about me with Mr. Catlin."

William Catlin is the London City Missionary who rescued Biddie from the brothel and now visits her here in the Union. Annie's heard all about these missionaries from Bill – his uncle Orlando is one. Bill says he takes every opportunity to preach at you, no matter who or where you are. Mr. Catlin may be a fine man but she has no desire to be preached at. So far she's managed to avoid him.

But Biddie is insistent. "He says he's going to make enquiries. He's going to find out where they are."

Against her better instincts, Annie can't help wondering. "Will they tell him anything, do you think?"

"They have to, don't they? He's a man of God."

***

It's been two months since her night in the hole and she's no closer to finding out what's happened to her daughters. For all she knows they may no longer be in England – shipped away to some god-forsaken country to work as skivvies on a farm. Can they do it without your permission? Is it possible?

Look what happened to Mrs. Hatchett. They knew she couldn't read – was it lawful to do what they did – telling her to make her mark and then shipping her boy off to the Colonies? The paper she signed the day they were admitted – was there anything in it giving them permission to take the girls? It had been such an ordeal – no sleep the night before, waiting for hours in the cold, and then waiting again to be registered. All she wanted was to get it over with. Who knows what she agreed to?

The doctor she saw back in January, the one who was so taken with the baby – he might have helped her but he's left to work with the lunatics in the county asylum. His replacement is a nervous young man who pulls at his moustache, never looks you in the eye, and defers to the Matron at every turn. He would be no help if she wanted an ally.

She writes to her mother asking her to approach the Board of Guardians – explain the situation, beg them to look into the whereabouts of her grandchildren. She doesn't hear back and wonders if someone intercepted the letter. Pipe Lady says Matron's been known to censor things she doesn't like.

"It's against the rules but everyone knows she does it."

She writes a second letter and gives it to Mrs. Knight who's finally being discharged into the care of her daughter. She promises to post it but again Annie hears nothing.

Eventually she swallows her pride and writes to her sister. Maude turns up the following Sunday and spends the first ten minutes waxing indignant about the rudeness of the porter who kept her waiting at the office door for her visiting ticket. Such a vulgar man, and not even a thought of offering a lady a seat. Quite beyond the pale. And the people! If these are the relatives and friends of the inmates here, one can only imagine the class of people actually living inside. Degenerates, most likely.

"Oh, not you, Annie, you know I don't mean *you*. I'm sure you don't mix with these women. Mama said she was afraid you'd be dragged down, consorting with paupers and tramps, and I said, 'Good heavens, Mama, Annie won't be *consorting* with them – she was raised better than that. Just because that awful husband of hers ran out on her doesn't mean Annie's anything like those people.' That's what I told her and she felt ever so much better after that. I'm right, aren't I? You *aren't* anything like the women in here, are you? Of course, I'm awfully sorry for them but if they won't help themselves – well, what can they expect?"

Awfully. Everything is "awfully" and "beastly" and "ra-*ther*" with Maude these days. She didn't use to be like this. She used to be good fun, when they were younger. There was a time they were friends. Before Annie went into service they shared a bed and whispered their secrets to each other, giggling well into the night. Even a few years ago, after the girls were born, Maude used to come to the house and play with them and read them stories while Annie cooked dinner.

It's since she met Christopher. He's an artist, a graduate of the Royal Academy with a studio in Broad Street. Maude is extremely ambitious for him; she hopes to see him exhibited at the annual Salon and eventually become a candidate for membership in the Academy. Her aspirations have turned her into a snob.

Settling herself gingerly on a bench next to her sister, Maude reaches for the baby.

"Can I cuddle him? Will they let me? Do they let other people hold the children here?"

"Why wouldn't they?"

169

"I read a story about someone smuggling a knife in a baby's robe and then stabbing someone with it. The guard or someone."

"That's in *prison*, Maude."

"Well, this feels like prison, don't you think? Anyway, he's lovely, aren't you, Teddy? Yes you are – and you love your auntie don't you? Yes you do. Is he creeping yet?"

"Not yet. He will be soon, I guess."

"Wasn't William creeping at six months?"

"Seven."

"He was such a clever little boy. I remember him telling me he could count to a hundred when he was only two. He was so proud of himself."

Annie says nothing.

"Goodness, I almost forgot." With her free hand Maude fumbles in her pocket and brings out a small brown paper package. "It's just some sugar and salt and a portion of cheese. Are you allowed to have it?"

"It's against the rules, but they don't go after you for it. I'll keep it in my night-stand."

"So, you do have furniture! I *told* Martha you would. *She* said you wouldn't have any furniture at all and only wooden platforms to sleep on. She saw an engraving – by Doré, I think it was … or was it Cruikshank? I'm forever getting them mixed up. Anyway, Martha said it looked awfully uncomfortable."

Martha is Christopher's sister; she and Maude are thick as thieves these days … it's all Martha says this and Martha says that. When the two of them are together you can shut your eyes and not tell one from the other.

"She's thinking of the tramp ward," Annie says. "I'm in the women's dormitory. We sleep in regular beds and they're quite comfortable, actually."

Which isn't true, but Maude isn't to know that.

"What about the food? Do they make you eat gruel and all kinds of horrible stuff? The things you read, Annie – it sounds awful."

"The food's good enough. It's very plain, of course, but there's plenty of it."

What has happened to her? She never used to lie and here she is lying to her sister as if her life depends on it. The food is disgusting and there's never enough to go around. The doctor's promise to fatten her up has not materialized – she's always hungry.

Clearly, Maude is skeptical. "Really? I can't say you look like you're eating all that well. You're awfully thin."

Feeling the need to change the subject, Annie asks about Mama – is she doing well? Maude says she's doing as well as might be expected, considering.

"Considering what?"

"What she's been through. You and the children being in here. It's been terrible for her, you must know that. They moved to another flat, her and Arthur. Well, they had to, didn't they? They couldn't stay where they were. People were simply beastly: 'Why'd you let your daughter go to the workhouse? Why didn't she come to you?' That sort of thing. It was awfully wearing on her nerves, poor thing."

There doesn't seem to be much more to say; they are both relieved when Matron rings her bell signaling the end to the visit. Maude kisses the baby and leaves, promising to inquire about the children. But when she returns the following week she's made no progress – the Guardians have said that as she is not the girls' mother she has no claim to information on their whereabouts.

"Maybe it's just as well. Most likely they're better off, wherever they are."

"Wher*ever* they are? Even if they've been shipped off to Canada?"

"You make it sound terrible. I've heard very good things about these child migration societies. Martha says they're just what's needed to solve our vagrancy problems."

"*Please!* If I hear that woman mentioned one more time I swear I'll do something desperate. She doesn't know what she's talking about and neither do you."

Offended, her sister stands, gathers up her umbrella and handbag, and pulls on her gloves.

"There's a reason no one but me will come to see you. You say whatever's on your mind and you never, ever say 'sorry'. I wasn't surprised when Bill left you – it was that tongue of yours that did it."

6.

In Annie's mind, the night at the Gaiety was a turning point in her relationship with Mr. Bernard. Surely it wasn't her imagination that the footman was more attentive to her after that. Small things, like presenting her with a copy of the *Era* newspaper containing a review of *Uncle Dick's Darling*. And choosing to polish the silver in the servants' hall at night, when the others had gone to bed, knowing she would still be up darning stockings, sewing on buttons and the like.

Aside from Mr. Bellwether's nightly visits – neither invited nor desired – she had never been alone like this with a man who was not her father or brother. This, she thought, was intimacy. If he was to reach out and touch her hand just now, *she* would be the one to melt "like wax before a fire."

Mr. Bernard did not touch her hand. He did, however, ask about her life – her plans for the future. She said she'd never really thought about it, which wasn't true. She did think about the future but was shy about sharing such things.

"But Miss Morgan, you must have a plan. Surely you do not want to spend your whole life scrubbing floors for someone else. You will want your own family, one of these days, and your own household."

"Will I? I don't know, Mr. Bernard. Families seem like a lot of work. I have a good place here – we both do. They treat us well, don't you think?"

"They treat us very well. This is a good place and I am grateful for it. But I don't intend to remain a coachman forever."

She reminded him that he was more than that in this household … that he was footman and valet as well.

"You are right. Indoors there is more – how do you say it? More advancement, *non*? Maybe I will secure a position as a butler, which will pay better and allow me to build my savings. Then in a few years, when I have saved enough – but I am boring you. Sometimes I talk too much, Miss Morgan – forgive me."

"No! I mean, you don't bore me at all, Mr. Bernard. I could listen to you talk for ages. Please, go on. What will you do when you have saved enough money?"

It was late. The room was lit by a single lamp on the table between them; they sat in a pool of gaslight surrounded by shadows. She was aware of the prickle of heat from the fire at her back, the hard, varnished surface of the chair, his long, shapely fingers just inches from her own.

"What I will do, Miss Morgan, is take that money and buy a little shop. A little grocer's shop, with all the usual things – tea, coffee, rice, sugar – but also the kind of things that are difficult to find in this country. *Fromage Gruyère*, and *Dijon* mustard, and the very finest quality vinegar. I will stock all of these things and will price them so they are available to everyone, not just the *bourgeoisie*. What do you think? A good idea? Or do you think I am being foolish?"

"I think it's a wonderful idea, Mr. Bernard. Will you run the shop by yourself or will you take on a partner?"

"Ah, that depends."

"On whether you're married? Oh, excuse me – I shouldn't have said that! I beg your pardon, that was terribly rude of me."

"Do not trouble yourself, Miss Morgan. I don't mind your asking. To be truthful, I do not know if I am the marrying kind. St. Jerome is supposed to have said marriage is good for those who are afraid to sleep alone at night. And I sleep very well, as it happens."

***

It was several months before she heard from Maggie. She did, however, hear from the presumptuous young man who had offered to take her into the Gaiety that night. He turned out to have an acquaintance with the cook, and pressed her for an introduction. Mrs. Earnshaw made a case for him, saying he was a little abrupt at times but a clean, hard-working fellow and one could do worse.

Annie was unimpressed. Her heart belonged to Mr. Bernard; as long as there was the chance he felt the same she was not about to take up with anybody else.

***

When she did finally receive a note from Maggie it was written in a scrawl so illegible she was surprised it had been delivered at all:

> *Annie deerest – Still alive not dead! Been at the palace pier in Brighton w. Arthur Lloyd since xmas and then the music hall in Dublin – Back in London now at the sun – Let me come have Tea and we will have our Chin-Wag – Matinees evry day but sunday – invite me over next sunday & I'll tell you storys about The Famous Mr. Lloyd!*
> *Yr. Old Frend Maggie*

The erratic spelling and odd punctuation was reassuring: she was still Maggie, in spite of her celebrity. They weren't so far apart after all.

Sunday afternoons were free but if she wanted to entertain a guest she must ask permission. And when she brought up the subject with Mrs. Adams, the housekeeper acted as if Annie was planning to open the door to the Whore of Babylon.

"Here? You are asking permission to invite an actress *here* – to the home of your employer?"

It's my home, too, she wanted to say, but didn't. "I don't think Mrs. Levy would mind. After all, it was her and Mr. Levy who brought us together, really. We wouldn't have met up again if it wasn't for them taking us to the theatre that night."

There was not much Mrs. Adams could say to this. This was what came from encouraging young girls to look outside their station. To say anything, however, would be tantamount to criticizing her employer; she might complain to the governess but she'd never do so to a parlour-maid.

"I presume you'll keep your visit to an hour. Two hours at the most. And remain in the servants' hall, of course."

"Of course."

After sending off the invitation, Annie spent the rest of the week worrying that her friend might turn up at the front door. But when she arrived the following Sunday she came downstairs and knocked at the servant's entrance. She obviously hadn't risen so high in the world not to know her place. Or rather, *Annie's* place to be truthful, for it was she who would have been censured for having the temerity to welcome a guest in the upstairs front hall. Servants were fired for less.

The young woman who stepped into the kitchen that afternoon was every inch the artiste. She wore a fabulous cloak – dark green velvet lined with sable – and matching gloves. Her parasol, trimmed in lace, featured a carved bird on the handle, and instead of a bonnet, she wore a pretty cocked cavaliers' hat with a feather to match the cloak. Her dark hair was gathered in ringlets with a fashionable fringe over her forehead, considered very fast at the time. If the housekeeper came down to the kitchen she would be thoroughly shocked.

They were all shy at first. Maggie was so smartly dressed and they were so plain in comparison. But when Cook offered her a cup of tea, Maggie's warm, friendly manner put them at ease completely.

"I won't tell a lie, Mrs. Earnshaw – I would *love* one. It's freezing out there – I haven't been warm in a month of Sundays. I always thought it was the famine that chased Ma and Pa out of Ireland, but I tell you now, it was the rain."

If Annie had wondered what they would talk about, she needn't have. Maggie had come prepared to chat and for the next hour, over tea and Mrs. Earnshaw's biscuits, she did just that. She began by insisting Annie call her Maggie – Christy was her stage name and had been for three years but friends and family still knew her as Maggie.

"My agent said to change it. It was when I started playing the boy parts. He said I needed a name that was more like a bloke's, and I thought of little Christy, my brother who was stillborn, remember? He never had a life and I thought I could give him one, if you know what I mean. But I'll always be Maggie to you."

"And Connor?"

"He was my husband. Well, my former husband, Bert Connor. The first one. I've had three if you count Jack who didn't marry me but stayed long enough to get me in the family

176

way."

So Maggie did have a child?

She shook her head.

"No, couldn't manage it. I lost three babies before they were born, and the one daughter who lived died when she was six weeks old. That was Annie – I said I'd name my daughter after you, do you remember? It was those damn tight corsets. The stays trap you in so tight you can hardly breathe. The customers like a tiny waist, and if you're going to keep them watching, you've got to stay small. That was one of the main reasons I switched to playing a guy – to get out of the damn things. And now they say I can't have any at all."

Annie was sorry and said so, but Maggie said it was just as well. "I've seen performers try to keep working with a babe in arms and no man to help. I'd have had to farm it out and God knows what would have happened to it."

She remembered Maggie talking about the baby-farmers all those years ago – how they took the babies and killed them. Maybe she still believed it, who knew? Sitting with her in the kitchen like that was almost like the old days back in Princess Street. She spoke better, though – a little bit posh, and a little bit racy. Annie said something about that, and Maggie laughed and said it came from hobnobbing with the theatre crowd.

"They're a funny mix, you know. You meet plenty of Good Time Charlies without two pennies to rub together, but you get to know some swells, too. After a while, you find yourself taking on their ways."

Over their second cup of tea Annie screwed up the courage to ask if it was true what she'd heard, that she was a favourite of the Prince of Wales. She smiled and affected an upper-class accent. "I am so awfully sorry, my dee-ah, but I am not at liberty to comment. Let us just say that a certain member of the Royal Household has been attentive of late to a certain theatrical artiste." She laughed. "That's how the illustrated papers put it, and it's good enough for me."

"Imagine! I can hardly believe it. You know, when we were girls I didn't even know you could sing."

"Well, I didn't have much to sing about back then, did

I? It was Bert who put me up to it. He was doing some work at this flash house by Blackfriar's – something outside the law, I'm sure. Bert never did a straight stick of work in his life. Anyway, they had a penny gaff going on there on Monday nights and he heard they were looking for singers. 'You can sing, Maggie,' he says. 'Go 'round there tonight and sing sumpin.' I tell you, Annie, I was terrified – I was shy back then, and I wouldn't have done it but I knew if he meant me to do something it was do it or get a punch in the head."

"He beat you?"

"Only when he was sober. Which wasn't often. Anyway, I went down there that night, dressed in my usual smock. Lord knows I didn't own anything better – I must've looked a fright. The publican looks me up and down. 'What can you do?' he says. I told him, 'I can sing. At least, my husband says I can.' So then he says, 'Who's yer old man?' I told him and I think he felt sorry for me … everyone who knew Bert Connor felt sorry for his wife. So he tells me to go on stage and sing something funny. That's always your best bet, you know, when it's your first time and they don't know you. Make 'em laugh and you'll get on all right."

"I'll keep it in mind."

"Well, the only comic songs I could think of were the Irish ones Pa sang when he was on the ran-tan, so I went to the front and sang 'Rosin the Beau'. And I guess I must've done it well enough because the owner gave me a shilling and told me to come back next week."

"And did you?"

"Bloomin' right I did! Once I got over being shy I liked it. I liked making money, too. I'd never made any money of my own in my life – not that I got to keep it, of course. It went directly into Bert's pocket and from there directly back to the publican. But Bert thought it was great. He went down to the pawn shop and bought me a dress, and set himself up as my manager. Oh, he had big dreams, didn't he? He figured he was going to get rich on me. After that, when he wasn't knocking me about, he was telling me I was going to be a star. Well, not in the penny gaffs, I wasn't – even Bert knew that. So pretty soon he got me into some of the smaller music halls, and they did pay better, even if the audience was just as noisy and just as drunk."

"What happened? I mean, with you and Bert?"

"I walked out. It wasn't the battering – Pa always had a heavy hand – you didn't want to be around his fist when he'd been drinking. So I guess I was used to it. It was the tarts that got to me. Bert thought he was a swell now that I was getting known around the halls. I'd be doing my turn on stage, and he'd be down in the promenade, treating the loafers to drinks and flirting with the barmaids. One night I come home and there he is tipping the velvet with some molly from the pub. In my bed! Well, that was it. I kicked him out and told him I'd sic my brother John on him if he showed his face again. You remember, Johnnie, don't you? He was just a baby when you left."

So one of the Johns had lived after all. Maggie said he was an enormous young man, a loader on the docks. "Nobody wants to mess with our John and that's the truth. Of course Bert didn't stay away for long. After a week he's back with a copper at his side saying I've no right to kick him out of his own home. 'All right,' I says, 'if you want to stay go ahead and stay – I'll leave.' And I did."

Maggie had finished her tea. Annie went to pour her a third cup but she put out her hand to stop her and asked if she had anything stronger.

"I wouldn't be allowed. There's cooking sherry in the pantry – I can ask Mrs. Earnshaw if you like."

"Never mind, pet. I keep a little supply on me for medicinal purposes."

She retrieved a small flask from her handbag, poured a generous amount into her teacup and then offered Annie the bottle. When she declined, Maggie screwed the cap back on and put it back in her purse. "Call it a hazard of the profession. It's what kills most of us in the end. Still, a short happy life beats a long miserable one, right? Here's to friendship."

They clinked their teacups together. Annie couldn't help feeling just a bit envious. Here was her old friend Maggie Boyle living the glamourous life of an artist. And here *she* was, a lowly parlour-maid who'd been to the theatre exactly once in her life and would probably never get there again.

Maggie seemed to guess her thoughts; her dark brown eyes were full of sympathy. "It's not all roses, sweetheart. Whatever you get, you work for it. You might do three, four, even five shows a night, if you want to make any money. Hailing cabs, dashing about from one hall to the next – it wears you down, I'll tell you. And that's six nights a week, every week of the year. It's one reason we all turn to drink."

She laughed but Annie saw she was serious. "It's better now than it was, but it was a knockabout life in the beginning. Like I said, I did my time in the penny gaffs. Have you ever been in one of those? No, I wouldn't think so. They're horrible, those places – rough, beery men trying to see up your skirt, coster boys and girls no more than ten years old getting mullered on gin, growing old before their time. You get very tough, if you weren't already. The way I grew up, you'd think I'd be prepared for anything, but I wasn't. I paid the price, especially after I left Bert and was down on my luck for a while."

Maggie finished the remains of her drink. "Anyhow, that's all behind me now. As Ma always said, 'It don't do to dwell on the past.' I'm my own woman now – or man! I answer to nobody and I like it that way. But here I've gone on about me the whole time and I know almost nothing about you. You must tell me what you've been up to since you left Princess Street. *Princess* Street – good Lord, was ever a street more wrongly named!"

"I haven't been doing much at all," Annie said. "Not like what you've done – I've done nothing compared to you."

On an impulse, Maggie reached out and clasped her by the hand.

"You were my only friend. You know that, don't you? I said I'd never forget you and I didn't. I'm *so* glad we met up. I'll be at the Sun all next week – come see me, will you?"

"Oh, I'd love to, I really would –"

"Then come. Promise me. I'm staying at the Burlington on Cork Street – you can send me a message there and I'll get tickets saved at the door."

There was something about the way she spoke that

touched Annie's heart. She'd never really had a friend since going into service … never had time to make one. She felt like a girl again, the way you do when you're young and silly and your only responsibilities are keeping your brother and sister from falling into the road and getting hit by a bus.

"Oh, excuse me, Miss Morgan. I didn't realize you had company."

Mr. Bernard stood in the doorway, newspaper in hand, in search of a quiet place to read. Annie stood up, delighted to introduce them.

"Maggie – I mean, Miss Connor, this is Mr. Bernard, our footman. Mr. Bernard, may I present my friend, Miss Christy Connor."

She was caught up in the pleasure of the moment, which is why she didn't immediately register the sudden, awkward pause that occurred, a hesitancy on both their parts. It lingered only a moment – a second or two at most – and then it was gone.

"Miss Connor, I am honoured. It is indeed a privilege to be introduced to an artist of such exceptional talent."

"Thank you, sir. The privilege is all mine."

"May I be permitted to say how much I enjoyed your performance at the Gaiety? It was a *tour de force*, in my opinion."

"Oh, so you were there?"

Annie explained that Mr. Levy had treated them to a night at the theatre – all the staff, including the newspapermen. "Mr. Bernard told us you'd be wonderful. He's seen you before and he said we wouldn't be disappointed."

The footman smiled and shook his head. "I think you are mistaken, Miss Morgan. I do not recall seeing Miss Connor on the stage before."

"But – I'm sorry, I thought you said …"

"You must forgive me for intruding. I came in only for a word with Mrs. Earnshaw, but I see she is not here so I will leave you. Again, Miss Connor, a pleasure to meet you."

When he had bowed himself out, Maggie turned to Annie with a smile. "Your friend is charming."

"Oh, isn't he, though? I'll tell you, Maggie – and I

181

wouldn't say this but it's only that now that you've met him, you'll understand, I know you will – I think I'm in love with him!"

"Really? How well do you know him?"

"Well enough, I should think! Why?"

"Has he said anything to you – about his feelings, I mean? Has he said he loves you?"

"Well, no, he hasn't. But he wouldn't – I mean, he's too polite …" She wished she hadn't spoken. Maggie must think her foolish, claiming to be in love with a man who'd said nothing of love himself. "I shouldn't have said anything. I just wanted to tell you because – well, I've been wanting to tell someone for so long!"

Maggie looked down at her empty teacup and fiddled with her bracelets.

"Is everything all right? You seem upset."

It was as if she made up her mind about something. "Annie, I want you to listen to me. I don't know that I should be telling you this but if you truly are in love with that man, then you need to know."

"He's married."

It's what she'd always feared, that Mr. Bernard had a wife hidden away somewhere, maybe back in France, someone he no longer loved but could not divorce. Like Mr. Rochester, who kept his insane wife imprisoned in Thornfield. But how would Maggie know this?

Her friend shook her head. "No, it's not that. At least, I don't think he's married. I doubt it very much."

"Then what?"

Maggie leaned back in her chair with a sigh. "Oh, dear, Annie, I'm afraid you're not going to like this."

"Tell me then – what is it? Is he a criminal? Because if you're going to say he's a criminal I tell you right now, I won't believe it. And how would you know, anyway? You only just met him."

"That's not true. I *have* met him – quite a few times, actually."

"But he said …"

"I know what he said. It's not the truth. Have you ever

heard of the masked balls at Haxell's Hotel in the Strand? There's no reason why you should. They're given by a gentleman who calls himself Gibbings. I've known him for over a year and I still don't know if that's his real name but it's the one he goes by."

"I don't see what this has to do with Mr. Bernard."

"The thing is, these balls are very popular with a certain sort of man. The sort who like to go about in women's clothes. They call it dressing in drag."

"A costume ball, you mean?"

"Well, yes. Sort of."

Annie was mystified. If it was a costume ball, why *wouldn't* they wear women's clothes? What was wrong with that?

"There's nothing wrong with it, except that the men who attend these balls come there to be with other men. *Just* men, Annie. They like to *be* with men."

"You mean …"

"Exactly. The gentlemen buy tickets to attend. Some of them are very genteel and others are just rent-boys and Guardsmen and so on. Your Mr. Bernard is one of the regulars."

"But why would *he* be there? Is he a friend of one of those men?"

"Do I have to spell it out? He *is* one of those men."

Annie was stunned. Maggie waited for her to say something, but she had nothing to say. She could scarcely take it in, what she was hearing.

Maggie sighed again. "Oh well, in for a penny in for a pound. Carlotta – that's the name Mr. Gibbings goes by – he invites a few women to these parties. For decoration, if you like. Anyway, he likes me and he always invites me to come and perform. I've seen your Mr. Bernard there many times. He doesn't go by that name … and he's not French. He puts on that accent for the punters. His real name is Terry something-or-other. He's very popular. I'd know him anywhere. Couldn't you tell when you introduced us? He was terrified I'd blow on him, and I never would have, except when you said you were in love with him – well, I had to warn you. You're wasting your time, Annie – he doesn't go that way."

The horror of what she was implying – the very filth of it! Growing up in the slums, she'd been exposed to all the nasty terms for men who were "womanish". Fop. Puff. Sissy. That anyone would accuse a gentleman like Mr. Bernard of such wickedness was shameful enough, but that it would come from someone she thought was her friend …

"You're wrong. You've mistaken him for someone else."

"No, I haven't. I'm sorry, Annie, but isn't it better to know, before you've given your heart away?"

Annie stood up. Her hands were trembling and she felt faint but she was determined not to let it show. "You're right. You should go."

"Annie –"

"I have to get back to work. Thank you for dropping by, it was very kind of you."

She stood silent while Maggie retrieved her parasol and slowly buttoned her kid gloves. She was determined to say nothing, not even look at her if she could help it. Once she was dressed, Annie held the door open for her, waited for her to pass through and shut it quickly behind her. This was what came from "consorting", her mother's word for spending time with rough, ill-mannered people who would bring you down to their level. This was a person who'd spent time in penny gaffs, mixing with "swells" and coarse men and women. She'd been foolish to think they could be friends.

7.

In spite of Biddie's assurances, Annie doubts the missionary will get very far with his enquiries. The matron's been against her from the beginning. If it's up to her, she'll make it difficult for him to make much progress.

So she's unprepared for the message delivered on a weekday afternoon, when she and Mrs. Geary are feeding sheets into the mangle: "You're to report to the Governors' board room. Mr. Catlin is waiting to see you."

The figure who greets her as she enters the room is far from what you'd expect of a preacher. Short and muscular, with a face ruddy from the outdoors, he looks more like a blacksmith than a man of God. Seeing Annie, he leaps out of his chair, doffs his hat and greets her with great enthusiasm.

"Mrs. Taylor! A pleasure, a pleasure indeed! Do sit down – here –"

He pulls out a chair and waits till she's seated, before settling into another across the table.

"Thank you for meeting with me, Mrs. Taylor. I've been hoping for a chance to introduce myself for a while."

His manner is frank and open – there's nothing judgemental in it. She begins to relax.

"They said you wanted to see me."

"Yes, that's right. I have some information for you about your daughters."

Reaching into his shaggy overcoat, he brings out a folded piece of paper.

"I received this letter this morning, from the secretary of the Board of Guardians. It seems your daughter are in school."

The girls are at school. They're safe. They haven't been sent to the colonies.

"So they're at Ashford? At the District School?"

"I'm afraid it's a little complicated. According to the letter, there's been some confusion concerning your parish. You and your children were admitted to Paddington but you should have been admitted to the workhouse in Hendon."

"I don't understand."

"No, as I say, it's a bit complicated. To do with the settlement laws I believe. As a married woman, you take your husband's settlement parish, which is Hendon. But as you were living in Paddington when you applied for relief, they admitted you here instead. At any rate –"

He picks up the letter and scans it briefly. "Yes, here it is. 'On the 19th of January of this year the above-mentioned children, Victoria Mary Taylor and Edith Anne Taylor, aged seven and five respectively, were removed to the school operated by the Hendon Union, that is, the school at Red Hill.'"

"Red Hill? But there's nothing there."

"It's not overly populated, I grant you. But there's a workhouse there and a school. Quite a large one, I believe."

"When may I see them?"

"Now, you see, this is where things get difficult. Red Hill is a good seven miles west of here. It would be a very long walk and from what I can tell there's no public transport – no trams of any kind. It may not be possible for you to see them. At least, not while you're in here."

"But I must! It's been so long – they'll think I've abandoned them."

"May I make a suggestion? I have a colleague in Hendon, another missionary. If I write to him I'm sure he'd be willing to visit the school and report back on your daughters. With your permission, of course."

"That would be wonderful. Thank you, Mr. Catlin. I'm very grateful."

"Not at all, I'm glad to be of some little help."

He rises, says he must be off.

"I'm due to speak to a group of boxers at seven o'clock tonight. I was one myself when I was a young man so it's like visiting old friends."

It's not difficult to imagine him in the ring; his weather-beaten face bears a few scars and when he clasps her hand in his she feels the strength in that hairy, knuckled fist.

"Wonderful to meet you, Mrs. Taylor. I'll pray for you and your daughters. And I'll be back, I promise. Just as soon as I hear from my colleague in Hendon."

She returns to the Laundry; Mrs. Geary, with a furtive

glance in the direction of the Super, asks if it was good news. Annie nods.

"Very good news," she whispers. "The girls are in school. They haven't been sent away."

"Well, now, that's wonderful, that is. That'll be a comfort to you, knowin' where they are."

"Quiet!" The voice of the superintendent pierces the workplace din. "No talking, you two, or I'll have you written up."

***

Mr. Catlin is as good as his word; he returns two weeks later and finds her with the others out in the women's courtyard. Removing his hat, he takes a handkerchief out of his coat pocket and mops his forehead.

"I hadn't realized how warm the day would be when I set out. You must excuse me while I catch my breath."

"Have you had a long walk?"

"Long enough, I suppose. It's about three miles from my home to here but I've had a touch of the ague and it's left me a little weak in the legs."

"Three miles – and you walked all the way?"

The missionary smiles. "God calls and man must answer. But I have good news. My colleague has visited the school in Red Hill. He says your daughters are both in good health and as far as he can ascertain they're not getting into any trouble. And he sent this."

He hands her a letter, written in a good hand.

"Please go ahead and read it," he says. "I think you'll find it comforting."

Dear Mrs. Taylor,
I am pleased to inform you that your daughters,
Victoria and Edith, have settled into the routine here
at Red Hill and their work is satisfactory. Victoria is
first in her class at reading, writing, and arithmetic,
although her needlework needs improvement. Edith has
recovered from the recent contagion and is working

hard to catch up with the others.
Yours sincerely,
Miss Louisa Tannebaum, Junior Teacher
P.S. Edith has drawn a picture for you and asks me to
include it in this letter. I asked her if the man in the sky
was God, and she said, "No, it's Papa come back from
Africa to get us."

Edie has drawn three stick figures in skirts, one of
them holding something that looks like a pickled whelk but is
most likely meant to be a baby. A man in a beard and top hat
floats above their heads; he's holding a stick – his compositor's
stick no doubt – and what appears to be a rock in the other.
Underneath, she's printed the words, "MY FAMILY".

"She says Edith is recovered. Was she ill?"

"I gather there was an outbreak of scarlet fever in
February. It's quite common in these schools, contagions of
these kinds." Seeing Annie's reaction, he adds, "My colleague
says the school wrote to you – didn't you get the letter?"

"No." Scarlet fever. Little William, and now Edith. And
nobody told her.

"I'm sorry. You should have been told."

She folds the letter and picture and puts them in her
apron pocket. Later, it comes to her – the rock in Edie's picture:
the diamond he promised to bring her.

***

At the end of the day she goes looking for Biddie, eager to
show her the letter. Her bed is empty; one of the women says
she's been discharged – a man came to get her, claiming to be
her father.

"That's wonderful! He's forgiven her then and accepted
her back into the family."

The woman shrugs. "Couldn't say. He didn't look like
the forgivin' sort to me. But she's gone and that's all I can tell
you."

8.

It shocked the entire household when Mr. Bernard gave his notice. There was no need for him to do so, not that anyone could see. He said it was for family reasons but he wasn't known to have any family – not in England at least.

Mr. L. offered him more money; when he turned that down he offered to hold the position for him until his family situation was resolved but the footman politely declined. He asked to be allowed to be given his month's wages and leave immediately, as the family situation was urgent. Mr. L., feeling he had no option, reluctantly agreed.

It happened so quickly none of them had a chance to say good-bye. They simply woke up one morning to find he was gone. He left no forwarding address and had not even asked for a character which could only mean he wasn't planning to stay in England. Cook said he must have gone back to France as they weren't so strict there about letters of character.

"But why?" said Mary Ann. "He had a good place here and we all liked him. It makes no sense."

Annie was too upset to speculate. Cook and Mary Ann both knew her feelings for the footman. Mary Ann made her sit and have a cup of tea; Cook said she'd have a piece of her special plum cake waiting when her chores were done for the day. Tea and cake were never going to ease the pain but it was kind of them all the same.

Later that day, Kate came down to the kitchen with a copy of *The Morning Post*. "Have you seen this story? It's ever so shocking. Here, Annie, read it out to us will you?"

GENTLEMEN IN FEMALE ATTIRE: Two young men, a gentleman and a law student, were on trial at the Court of Queen's Bench, charged with impersonating women. The policeman who made the arrest read out a long list of women's clothes found in their rooms: silk and satin dresses, bodices, petticoats – every kind of thing imaginable that you might find in a woman's wardrobe. Well, not in Annie's, perhaps – she certainly never owned a pair of pink silk stockings or an under-bodice piped in blue satin.

Mary Ann said she never heard of such a thing in all her life: "Were they going to a fancy dress party, like?"

Cook said she once worked for a family in Tunbridge Wells whose youngest son liked to dress up in ladies' clothes; they sent him away to the Colonies and that was the end of it.

Annie would have handed the newspaper back to Kate and thought no more about it had it not been for a name she recognized right near the end: the police were questioning Mr. Amos Westrop Gibbings who hosted masked balls at a hotel in the Strand. This was the "Carlotta" Maggie had talked about. Other witnesses still unnamed were going to be called to testify. The police were promising to prosecute to the full extent of the law all those who had taken part in these "unnatural entertainments".

She refused to read any more. It had nothing to do with her and nothing to do with the footman. Mr. Bernard – *her* Mr. Bernard – was gone. And, as Mrs. Gaskell would put it, a piece of her heart went with him.

***

Cook let a month go by before introducing the subject of Mr. Taylor once more. Annie was young, after all, and opportunities were scarce for housemaids to meet eligible men. It seemed a pity not to at least offer him an opportunity to make his case. Didn't she care to know just a bit about this young man who seemed to be so taken with her, having met her only once?

Determined as she was to nurse her broken heart, Annie was finding it a little boring, playing the tragedienne. She gave in and said he could come as long as Mrs. Adams agreed, assuming that would put an end to it. The housekeeper was known to be very strict about gentlemen followers: with very few exceptions they were not allowed. She adhered to the view that courting should only be done with a view to marriage and as servants were not encouraged to marry, what was the point?

You could argue – and many did – that unless one was permitted to visit with the opposite sex one could hardly know if he or she was suitable marriage material. Mama said it was better in her day when you left it to your mother or your aunt to arrange these things. The first time she met Annie's father was when her mother's sister invited him to tea. Mama sat on one side of the couch, Papa sat on the other, and Great-Aunt Polly planted herself firmly between them. The entire time they were "bundling", as the Welsh put it, they were never alone, not even when Papa proposed.

The cook reported back the following day: Mrs. Adams had given her consent. Annie might have a gentleman caller just this once – in the kitchen, of course, under Cook's supervision. She made it clear this was not to become a regular event; she was granting this enormous concession as a favour to the cook and for no other reason.

It was arranged that Mr. Taylor would come to the house at three o'clock the following Sunday and leave no later than four. Annie would serve him tea and biscuits in the kitchen. They would make stilted conversation while Cook hovered in the background preparing dinner and keeping an eye on them to ensure that nothing improper took place.

She needn't have worried. The hour Annie spent in his company only confirmed what she already thought – she didn't care for him. He had his good points, of course: he was not particularly tall but he was handsome, with clear blue eyes, a sensitive, well-shaped mouth, and thick dark hair with a tendency towards curling. Full beards and long walrus moustaches were in favour at the time, but his whiskers were neatly trimmed and oiled. There was no danger of them dangling in the soup or collecting crumbs, as Papa's often did.

It was his manner that offended her. She found him abrupt and out-spoken – opinionated, she thought, and too self-confident for his own good. He made sure to inform her that he was six years into his apprenticeship and would be a journeyman compositor next year – an aristocrat among working men. Those were his words exactly though he laughed when he said it and added that he didn't care much for aristocrats of any kind. She felt his comment was out of place considering the house he was visiting, and told him so. He took it well enough and apologized, but it rankled. Who did he think he was to be making disparaging remarks about his betters?

She couldn't understand why Mrs. Earnshaw was fond

of him. After he left the cook said it was his being from Devon that made him "rough around the edges" but in her books that was not a bad thing.

"Don't be put off by his northern ways. I've known his family for years and he's a bright young man, he is. Take him home and introduce him to your ma and pa. They'll see what he's made of, and I think they'll be impressed."

Annie had no intention of doing any such thing. She'd agreed to meet him and had done so. As far as she was concerned, the matter was at an end. But Bill was persistent. He wrote to her asking for another meeting. When she refused, he took to sending her comical poems from a weekly magazine called *Fun*. One was called "My Dream", where everything was topsy-turvey:

> *Where vice is virtue — virtue, vice:*
> *Where nice is nasty — nasty, nice*
> *Where right is wrong and wrong is right —*
> *Where white is black and black is white.*

Except for one that made fun of a parson, and was just a little bit shocking, they were harmless bits of fun. She read them aloud to Cook and Mary Ann and had to agree with them that it showed Mr. Taylor had a well-developed sense of humour.

The one that won her over was "The Fairy Curate", simply because of a line in the first verse:

> *Slyly stealing,*
> *She to Ealing*
> *Made a daily journey;*
> *There she found him,*
> *Clients round him*
> *(He was an attorney).*

Did he know she'd worked in Ealing? It seemed like fate, him sending that particular poem. That afternoon she wrote to Mama asking if she might bring a gentleman friend to dinner.

***

The cook was right. Her parents were captivated by his

forthright manner. And he did put himself out to be pleasant. He seemed to know a lot about a great many things – when talking with Mama he askcd intelligent questions about Wales; with Papa, he had some current information about the state of the dairy business. He was charming with her sister without being forward and made a friend for life of her brother by offering to show him around the newspaper building.

She said very little that afternoon, choosing instead to watch how Bill behaved with her family – Papa, especially. She could never care for a man who was disrespectful to her father, but Bill was extremely gracious. The cocksure, even arrogant young man she thought he was disappeared that afternoon, revealing a humbler and far more attractive man. For the first time she saw him as someone she could grow to care for … even love.

Afterwards, the verdict was unanimous: Annie could do worse – much worse – than Mr. Taylor.

But Bill's crowning accomplishment was winning over the housekeeper. Cook might be all in favour of their courtship, and her parents might give their consent, but if Mrs. Adams refused to allow her to have a gentleman follower, there was no point in continuing. As she wrote to Bill after the Sunday visit with her family, "I'm afraid the housekeeper doesn't care for me at all, she's made that clear since I came to work here. I can't imagine she'll allow me any special favours when the other girls are refused."

Bill said to leave it to him. He wrote to Mrs. Adams asking for an interview. The following week he arrived at the kitchen door, asking to speak to the housekeeper. Mary Ann handed him off to Kate who took him upstairs to the morning room. There he spent fifteen minutes in conference with Mrs. Adams and Mrs. L. After he left the housekeeper took her into the pantry and told her she was allowed to meet with Mr. Taylor on her Sunday half-days, provided her sister agreed to act as a chaperone.

Kate and Mary Ann demanded to know what Mr. Taylor had said that had won such a major concession; Annie was unable to tell them. He never told her any more about the interview except to say he'd made a good case and won them over. The next time he came to visit, he had two bunches of flowers: one for her and one for Mrs. Adams.

9.

Mrs. Geary has attached herself to Annie and the child. Assigned to the same section of the laundry shed, they work together in silence, taking turns pounding the linen with their cumbersome possing sticks, beating the dirt from the sheets, shirts, aprons and smocks. There's a rhythm to the work – after a while your mind goes numb, the arms and upper body do all the work – lift, pause, plunge, push, lift, pause, plunge.

Annie, at least four decades years her junior, leaves the shed at the end of the day aching everywhere, her arms heavy as lead, her legs weak from standing. But her friend seems immune to exhaustion. She wipes the sweat from her brow, rolls down her sleeves, and gives Annie a wink: There, we're done now. Wasn't so bad now, was it?

Then one evening as they're leaving the shed, she turns to Annie as if to ask her something and falls heavily to the floor.

Between them, Annie and the super try without success to lift her to her feet. Her eyes are half shut and her face is hot – hotter than it should be even with the heat from the wash house. The super diagnoses fever – "Third one this week" and has her removed to the itch ward. This is the name given to the part of the building set aside for inmates with infectious diseases. (Not to be confused with the foul ward, which is where those afflicted with "the French disease" used to be confined. These days if the poor are afflicted with venereal disease they are carried off to the Lock Hospital where they are treated or die. Or both.)

When Annie goes to check on her the following morning, she finds her friend awake and "raisin' a shindy", as Papa would put it, tossing about and demanding to be removed. Only the fact that she's too ill to stand prevents her from throwing back her blanket and doing just that.

"What is it, Mrs. Geary? Are you in pain? Can I do anything?"

"Her!" She spits out the word like some kind of venomous snake and throws herself back on her pallet. "They've put me next to her, haven't they? The old cow!

They've done it a-purpose to aggervate me."

"I don't understand. Who are you talking about?"

"Her!" A scrawny finger indicates a bundle of rags occupying the bed directly across the room, not more than ten feet away. "The nasty old cat – lyin' right there next to me, makin' me sick just to look at her."

"But there's no one there …"

The older woman refuses to listen. She's carrying on in such a way Annie fears for her safety – she'll do herself harm if she's not careful.

"Mrs. Geary, please, there's no one there. Look …"

In order to prove her point, Annie goes over to the bed and pulls the blanket away. To her shock, the heap of rags sits up, revealing a grey, wizened little face attached to a frame so tiny and skeletal it might be mistaken for a medical student's cadaver.

"Quit your blather, you old boot. Some of us are tryin' to sleep."

"Sleep – is that what you call it? Snufflin' and snortin' like a pig! I can't hardly hear myself think through them noises you make."

"*Leave* then, why don't you? There's none of us cares to listen to you shriekin' and complainin' all day. Get out and be done with you."

It's upsetting and unseemly to hear two elderly women going at each other like this. Whatever their quarrel, they're both at an age where they should know better; Annie's mistake is in telling them so.

"Ladies, please – this is no way to behave. You're not well … you need to lie down and rest. Mrs. Geary, can I get you some water?"

A sharp blow in the small of her back brings her to a stop. The little old woman in the other bed has thrown something at her … a shoe, it seems, delivered with surprising accuracy considering her age and apparent frailty.

"Stay out of this, you. This don't concern you. This is between me and her – the old cow."

The ward nurse approaches, shaking her head in disgust.

"Now, Mrs. Forge, what've I told you about throwin' things around like that? You're going to ruin them shoes and you won't get another pair any time soon, that's a fact. Now lie down and behave yourself. You, too, Mrs. Geary. I've had enough of you two. Any more trouble, I'll send for the doctor and we'll see what *he* has to say about this."

For whatever reason, this appears to work. The two women settle back on their pallets and say no more. It seems a good time to leave. On her way out, Annie thanks the nurse for stepping in.

"It's been like this all morning," she says. "Anything sets them off – if it ain't one thing it's another. They've been at each other as long as I can remember – longer, most likely. I'm told they used to be friends, but one of them said something to the other … or did something … or took something, maybe. Whatever it was, they've been fighting ever since. We try to keep them apart when we can. It's just bad luck them both ending up in here at the same time. Best to keep out of their way, I find. You do yourself no favours getting involved."

"They stopped when you mentioned the doctor."

"He can order them into Hanwell and they know it. So they mind their manners when he's around. Sometimes it's the only thing that works."

Later in the day when she mentions the incident to Pipe Lady her friend says feuds like these are common in the Union.

"There's old gals who been in here so long they can't imagine no other life. They got things against each other going back years. They won't sit beside each other at dinner, won't have a bed in the same ward. And if one of 'em dies or gets discharged and don't come back, they go into a funk. It's the fight that keeps 'em going. It's pretty much what they live for."

***

With Biddie gone, there's really no reason for the missionary to continue to come by each week, but he does, making the round of the sick wards. Time and again his kindness is rejected. The tougher cases laugh in his face while others only pretend to take him seriously. He must know he's waging a losing battle, yet he comes back each week, offering comfort and promises of a better life in the Hereafter.

For her part, Annie looks forward to his visits. There's something about him that reminds him of her father – a kind of gentle nobility in spite of his rough-and-ready manner. He listens without judgment, the way Papa used to. She feels she can tell him anything. And it's rare in this place to be able to talk with someone about things that go beyond the washing of shirts and sheets or whether today's pudding will be suet or rice.

If he truly did nothing but preach, she'd quickly discover a way to avoid him. But he takes off his missionary hat when they're together.

"Tell me about your girls," he says. "Victoria's the oldest, right? Tell me about her."

"I'm not sure what there is to tell. We're not close. To be honest, we don't like each other very much."

It's a terrible thing to admit … she's never said it before, not to anyone. But it's true. If things hadn't happened the way they did, if she hadn't had to leave her job and get married so quickly, she might have made something of her life. She might have stayed in service and saved her money. Maybe she would have set herself up in a shop, like Mr. Bernard talked about – it was better not to think about Mr. Bernard.

"Was it a difficult marriage?"

"It was wrong from the beginning."

"I'm sorry – I didn't mean to upset you."

"No, it's just … There was a time when it was better, after William was born."

"Ah, the little boy who died."

Bill was so happy, having a son after two daughters. And not just a son, but a thriving, healthy child with a smile like the noonday sun. God how he loved that boy! Annie, the girls, even his beloved mother were all chaff in the wind once William was born.

He would burst through the door at night and the first words on his lips were about the boy: Was he walking yet? Was he using a spoon? She was willing to have the boy in bed with them while he was on the breast, but once he was weaned she wanted to lie him down with the girls. Bill wouldn't hear of it.

"He'll sleep with us – he's safe that way."

Safe from what? The girls weren't going to smother him – they adored him almost as much as he did. She tried to explain how she felt, that she missed being close to him, missed the love-making.

"We can't be *together* with little William between us. Let him sleep with the girls. He'll get used to it and we can be close again."

It made no matter; he seemed to feel that now they'd produced a son, their marital relations were at an end. She couldn't understand it. It had been good between them in the past. There was no reason why it shouldn't be so again.

And then he lost his job. Went out every day looking for work, came back angry, shoulders slumped, defeated.

"A skilled compositor," he said. "A journeyman printer. You'll never be out of work – that's what they said, back when I started. Always work for a good man on the press. It's a laugh, isn't it? There's no such thing as a permanent situation any more."

"Can you not get relief?" She'd heard of out-of-work payments for good union men like Bill. "Your friend Brydges, he went on relief, didn't he?"

"Tramp relief is what they gave him. A ticket to go on the tramp and look for work in other places. In the end you're back where you started with nothing to show for it but stories of handouts and hardship. John hated it and so would I."

She said it would be better than starving and he said he'd starve before going on the tramp.

He started coming home late after she was in bed, smelling of beer and other women. Jasmine … honeysuckle … attar of roses … scents she never wore. While he slept she rifled his pockets: a tortoise-shell comb, a musical-theatre ticket stub, a woman's glove. All the classic clues. He seemed to want her to know about the other women. Or didn't care enough to hide them.

She confronted him with the evidence. You're married, she said, or have you forgotten? He would admit to nothing, couldn't even be bothered to lie.

And then, in early January, she was cleaning out the linen cupboard and uncovered a stack of sanitary cloths. She hadn't needed to use them in – what was it, three months? Four? She counted back … December, November, October. The middle of September.

That night she sat up and waited for him. When he came in the door she blurted it out. She didn't mean it to come out that way, she meant to build up to it. But his face was flushed with drink and he swaggered in so full of himself she couldn't help it.

"I'm pregnant."

"You can't be. You're lying."

"I'm not lying. I'm four months gone."

"We haven't done it."

"We have, actually. Four months ago."

He shrugged and went to bed. No business of his, that's what he seemed to be saying.

Things went from bad to worse after that. He was out all day and half the night, and when he was home they argued. About money, usually. A fellow who owed him money paid him back and he used it to buy an insurance policy for William. Two pounds spent on something she thought they'd never use.

Nobody knew how bad things were – Bill wouldn't allow it. Right to the end, almost, he kept up the pretence that he had work, that they were managing to keep their heads above water. When they were down to nothing he swallowed his pride and went to his mother for help. He came home with potatoes, sausages, a bag of flour, dried beans, oatmeal and honey, slammed the lot on the kitchen table. "Make it last," he said. "I won't be doing *that* again."

It didn't help that she had a difficult confinement. She was ill and couldn't keep anything down. Any strong odour affected her badly – she put off doing errands as the smell of sewage, street rubbish and manure made her want to vomit. Instead of gaining weight she lost it. Mama worried she'd lose the baby if she wasn't careful. She went into labour three weeks early; when Mama arrived she brought a small white shroud for the baby, just in case. But the child, when delivered, surprised them both: a ruddy, healthy baby boy, born with a full head of hair.

She called him Edward, after her father, and hoped Bill would come around because it was a boy. But nothing changed. He wouldn't look at the child, wouldn't hold it or pick it up when it cried. And he continued to stay out every night, sometimes not coming home until early morning to wash and put on a fresh collar.

One day her son will ask about his father and she will tell him the truth: he lost his father before he was even born.

10.

She and Bill had only been seeing each other for a month or so when he first spoke about going to South Africa. The union was offering to pay the costs of emigration as there were so many printers out of work.

"There's work in Cape Town, Miss Morgan. They pay more there and it's cheaper to live."

"Not South Africa! You wouldn't want to go live with the Zulus!"

He laughed and said it was unlikely he'd ever meet a Zulu in a lifetime of living in South Africa. "It's very civilized, you know. They speak English there and use knives and forks at table."

She thought it was twaddle. He'd never leave England, any more than she would. They were Londoners, she and Bill, even if he had been born in Devon. People like them didn't run away to the colonies just because times were difficult at home. They weren't Irish, for God's sake.

What she should have realized at the time – especially after the way he'd pursued her – was that once Bill got a thing in his head it stayed there. He showed her a newspaper advertisement he'd clipped and was keeping in his wallet. "Diamond Fields of South Africa," it said. "The Inland Transport Company of Algoa Bay are prepared to convey passengers to the fields, on terms and conditions which may be obtained at the offices of the company."

"Well, which is it, Mr. Taylor? Are you planning to be a compositor or are you going to look for diamonds?"

Maybe he'd do both. His friend Brydges was planning on leaving once his apprenticeship was up. *He* said South Africa was a land of opportunity for men who were willing to take a few risks.

Bill seemed to have a great amount of respect for this Brydges person. When Annie asked about him, he seemed surprised. "Brydges? You've met him – he's a cutter on the paper. He came to the Gaiety with us that night."

"There were so many …"

"Yes, and you seemed to only have eyes for that

footman of yours."

She blushed and said it wasn't true although of course it was. But Bill didn't seem bothered. "I'm not the jealous type, Miss Morgan. My eyes are blue not green. And I'm here and he's not so there's nothing more to say."

He didn't bring it up again, the emigration scheme. But he never forgot about it. Years later, when she was preparing to shorten an old shirt of his for William, she found the advertisement, creased and yellow with age, stuffed into a pocket.

It shouldn't have been a surprise when he left.

***

They chose a small park near his lodgings as their Sunday meeting place. It had a bandstand and there were benches where you could sit and talk and not be heard over the music. Her sister Maude always brought a book; she would sit at the far end of the bench and read – or pretend to – and give them some privacy. On one of those afternoons Bill suggested supper at an eating house a short walk from the park. The menu boasted that it was the "Best Place in Knightsbridge for Cheap Breakfasts, Dinners, Teas & Suppers", and there was no doubt about the cheapness: 6*d* for roast beef and 2½*d* for sausage and mashed potatoes.

He wanted to know what they would have. Maude said she didn't know and Annie didn't like to say, not knowing what he could spend, so he ordered steak puddings and pots of tea all 'round.

Maude finished her meal and excused herself to use the facilities. Once she was away from the table Bill set down his fork and reached for Annie's hand.

"Hear me now, Miss Morgan. I mean to marry you one day. I'll do right by you and if you do the same we'll get along just fine. You won't ever have to worry about me hitting you or meddling with other women or any of that foolishness some men get up to. I'll never give you cause to be sorry you went with me and I'll never go back on my word. That's my promise to you but you can't rush me, hear? Leave me to work things out in my own way, on my own terms. That's what I ask of you. What do you say? Do we have an agreement between us?"

Was it a proposal? She could never say with certainty that Bill asked her to marry him that afternoon. If he had, it was hardly a romantic declaration. Mrs. Gaskell would write it with moonlight and flowers, and she would certainly expect the word "love" to drop from his lips at least once. But he'd made a commitment, that was obvious, and he was looking for one from her.

"Yes, I guess we do."

"Good. Because I have something for you."

He handed her a package wrapped in brown paper, tied loosely with string. Too big for a ring. She tugged at the string and the paper slipped away: *On Liberty*, by John Stuart Mill.

"A book. How lovely."

"I wanted to get you something and you said you like to read. You're disappointed."

"No, not at all." She flipped through a few pages, keeping her face averted. "It was very kind of you. Thank you."

"I owe everything I am today to that man and this book. Everything I think, everything I believe. Read it and you'll know me. All right, then, finish up your tea and we'll get you back before Mrs. Adams sets the dogs on us."

***

The subject of this Essay is not the so-called Liberty of the Will, so unfortunately opposed to the misnamed doctrine of Philosophical Necessity; but Civil, or Social Liberty: the nature and limits of the power which can be legitimately exercised by society over the individual.

She flipped to the back of the book – the words *The End* appeared on page 217. And there were no pictures. She made a quick mental count: if she could manage a page a day – and she was not at all sure she could – it would take her nine months to finish it. As long as it takes to have a baby, she thought, and stifled a giggle.

Mary Ann turned over in bed and opened her eyes.

"Are you still reading? It's almost midnight – go to sleep."

"Sorry. I'll blow out the candle."

She settled back under the coverlet and stared up at the ceiling. After a moment, she gave Mary Ann a nudge.

"What?"

"Do you think it's important to be in love? I mean, if you're planning to marry a man, should you be in love with him?"

"How should I know? I don't know any men, do I?"

"No, I know that, but what do you think?"

Mary Ann turned over so that she, too, was lying on her back. "My sister was in love with her husband and he made her life miserable. I think he killed her in the end, but I can't prove it. So I think maybe it's better to be with a good man you don't love than one you love who kills you."

11.

Sunday, 20ᵗʰ June: her birthday. She's had a package from
Mama – soap and a tin of English Breakfast Tea – and, at long
last, a letter. She writes that she and Arthur are coming to see
her today, and she has something important to tell her.

Annie can only think they've found a way to get her
out. Come into some money maybe, although she can't think
from where. Arthur may have found a position somewhere else,
they may be able to afford a bigger place with room for her
and the children. It wouldn't have to be so very big – one more
room would do it, and a bed.

By the time two o'clock comes around, she's convinced
herself she won't be inside much longer. If she gives her
notice today, she can be discharged tomorrow – mid-week
at the latest. Oh, to be relieved of the constant presence of
workhouse staff … to eat a meal made by her own hands …
to sleep through the night without being kept awake by the
misery of others. She won't forget them, though – not all of
them, anyway. She'll make time to visit the old ladies who've
become her friends. Perhaps, once she's out and settled, she can
make some enquiries … see if she can find a place for Biddie
in a decent household.

She hurries down to the receiving ward and finds Mama
and Arthur waiting for her. She embraces them both; after an
initial moment of surprise, they hug her back. The weather is
perfect: it hasn't rained in a fortnight and there's just enough of
a breeze to keep it from being too hot. Annie suggests they sit
out in the women's courtyard. Arthur unpacks Mama's basket
of goodies: pickled eggs, a flask of tea, a cheese sandwich
for each of them, and, in honour of her birthday, almond cake
dusted with powdered sugar.

Mama dandles the baby on her lap and nuzzles his soft,
blonde curls.

"He looks well," she says. "You both do. It hasn't done
you harm, then, coming here?"

Done them harm? She doesn't know how to answer
that. What harm does it do to a person to take away her
children, her clothes, her freedom? To reduce her to a single

word – pauper – when she'd once been so much more: a school girl, a servant, a mother, a wife. Impossible to explain to anyone outside that it's more than exchanging your clothes for a drab grey uniform … more than going to bed and rising, eating and praying – *especially* praying – to the sound of a bell … more than never choosing what to eat or where to eat it … never having a single thing about your person that says, "This is me. This is who I am."

She shakes her head. No, it's done her no harm. Anyway, it doesn't matter now, does it, now that she's leaving?

"You said you had some news."

"I do indeed. Your sister is getting married. They've set the date – the fifteenth of October in the Church of St. Giles."

"I don't – I'm sorry. That's your news? That's what you came to tell me?"

"Well, yes. The banns have been read out and the church is booked. Maude wasn't going to tell you – she's still upset over that last visit – but I said don't be silly, Annie's your sister, she'll want to know. I said they might let you out for it, if you asked. Would they do that, do you think? I'd like you to be there, Annie. It's important that you show up for your sister."

"Why are you telling me now? October is months away."

"We thought you might need time to arrange things. To get permission and all."

"Are you all right, Annie?" her brother says. "You look upset."

"I'm all right. It's the rich food, I'm not used to it."

"Save it," Mama says. "You can have it later. Teddy will have some, won't he? He has teeth now, don't you, my love? Show Gran your teeth. Oh, what a big boy you are!"

"Hang on," Arthur says, reaching into his vest pocket, "I almost forgot. I saw this in Friday's *Gazette* and clipped it for you. It's that friend of yours, isn't it? The one who went on the stage?"

"PEER AND ACTRESS MARRIED: A Village Wedding. It is reported that Geoffrey Hyde-Winchester, fourth Marquess of Fordingham, aged twenty-six, and Miss Christy Connor, actress, aged thirty-two, were married last Thursday at a registry office at the village of Warnford, Hampshire, before Mr. Thomas Coles, Registrar. The witnesses were George Savage, a villager, and Miss Nelly Farren, the well-known Gaiety actress. The Marquess and Marchioness are spending the honeymoon on the Isle of Wight."

She hands the clipping back to Arthur without comment.
"Don't you want to keep it?"
"Why would I?"
"Well, she was a friend of yours. We saw her onstage that time, remember? In Leicester Square."
"Did we? I don't remember. It was a long time ago."

***

They were living on Park Road, in Kilburn – it was before Edith was born. They'd moved back to London, after a year up north, and Bill landed a job at Hodder & Stoughton, the publisher's; by way of celebrating they left Vicky with her mother and took her sister and brother to the Alhambra to see Arthur Lloyd.

It was only when they were seated and she was reading through the program that she saw another name written there, along with Mr. Lloyd, Fred Finch, Emma Day, and the Sisters Tudor: Miss Christy Connor, "the celebrated and versatile male impersonator". It was too late to do anything about it – she wasn't going to spoil the evening by asking Bill to take her home. It would have meant explaining about Maggie's visit and the terrible things she'd said about Mr. Bernard – and anyway, he'd have refused.

It was well into the programme before she appeared, following an hour of songs and comic sketches by Mr. Lloyd and the others, and several encores of "Not for Joseph" where the audience joined in the chorus:
Not for Joe! Not for Joe!

Not for Joseph, if he knows it!
No, No, No! Not for Joe!
Not for Joseph, oh, dear, no!

A brief intermission, and then a dapper figure strutted onto the stage, so unlike Maggie that had Annie not known it was her, she would have believed she was watching a man. She was dressed very smartly in a pearl-grey frock coat and trousers, a bow tie and shiny top hat. When she got to the front of the stage, she took the cigar from her mouth, raised a monocle to one eye, and called out, "Well now, what do we 'ave 'ere?"

That was her catch phrase and the gallery roared its approval.

"You don't fool me!" She pointed her cigar at the crowd. "You're no better than you should be, you lot, and that's no lie!"

Another wave of shouts and applause, after which Maggie launched into "I'm a Picadilly Swell", sauntering and strutting on the stage like a dandy through and through. Arthur said it was hard to believe she was a woman at all, she was that good, and Annie had to agree, thankful only that they were sitting so far back she couldn't possibly have seen them from the stage.

Maggie sang two more songs – "Seeing Nelly Home" and "Up in a Balloon" – after which she plucked the carnation from her button-hole, tossed it to the audience, bowed and left the stage. Everybody clapped and hollered for more, and so she came back and sang a song about a soldier whose darling girl was back in Ireland. Then it was Mr. Lloyd's turn again dressed as the Emperor Napoleon in exile. He wore a French hat and the livery of a soldier and he looked so handsome it made your heart break. This was so popular that the audience demanded an encore, and he obliged with "I Vowed I Never Would Leave Her".

Afterwards, the four of them linked arms and marched up Picadilly, singing the chorus together:

Tho' I vowed that I never would leave her,
She turned out a cruel deceiver,

Tootle tum, tootle tum, tootle tum, tootle tum,
Tootle tum, tootle tum tay.

***

After Mama and her brother leave, she heads to the women's day room which seems more depressing than usual. Even the arrival of the missionary, whose visits she generally enjoys, does nothing to lift her spirits.

"How do you manage to stay so cheerful?" she says. "You go about day after day meeting with scoffs and ingratitude. I don't know how you can bear it. I know I couldn't."

"If just one poor man or woman comes to Christ because of me I will have done my duty. I didn't choose this, you know, it was chosen for me. I fought it for many years but when I finally gave in to the Lord the submission was sweet."

She envies him, in a way. How fine it would be to believe you were doing something on this earth besides simply getting through the day – trudging from one sunset to the next with no idea of the meaning or purpose behind it.

"We all have a calling, Mrs. Taylor. That is God's great gift to us – the ability to hope that there is something better waiting for us, if not in this life then in the next. As long as you allow yourself to hope, the darkness of the world will not defeat you."

12.

She thought it was influenza at first. She would wake up early and climb out of bed, being careful not to arouse Mary Ann, and reach for the chamber pot. It wasn't until this had gone on for a week that she realized she had not had her monthly sickness for almost two months.

It was the middle of October and she and Bill had been seeing each other for just over a year. Four months earlier Maude had left to take a position as a domestic in Brighton, leaving them without a chaperone. It was understood that they would marry – one day. Not immediately, as Bill made sure to remind her. He'd only just finished his apprenticeship at the Telegraph and was now a journeyman compositor looking for work. Marriage was something that would take place in the future, once he had established himself somewhere, and they'd saved enough money to marry.

"If I'm going to settle down, I want to be able to offer my wife something better, don't you see? There's no need to rush things. We'll do it properly when we can afford it."

She couldn't even fall back on the usual excuse that she'd been seduced. She went willingly that first afternoon to the room he shared with Brydges. Allowed him to kiss her and take the pins out of her hair. Stood with her eyes cast down while he undressed her – with some expertise, she thought later on. And allowed herself to be led by the hand into his bed.

Afterwards, she cried.

What must you think of me?

I think you're lovely, that's what I think.

But to let you – to just do *it like that. And what if something happens?*

He held her, reassured her: *Nothing will happen, Annie. I'm being careful. Nothing will happen.*

Two weeks later, she went there again … and then again. It became their routine – meet in the park, head to his room and spend the next hour and a half in bed. When it was time to leave they got dressed and he walked her as far as the bus stop.

The circumstances were not as she'd imagined: John

Thornton, she was sure, never courted in a third-rate lodging house in Camden Town. The room itself was about what you'd expect of such a place although cleaner than most. When she first began coming here there was a musty-coloured stain in one corner of the wall; it was so ugly Bill complained to the landlord who eventually had it pasted over with flocked paper of such a frantically busy design it hurt your eyes to look at it. And after a while the stain began to show again, working its way through to the surface.

Sometimes, as they approached his lodgings, Bill saw someone he knew – the landlady or one of her daughters. When that happened, he'd leave her on the corner while he went up alone. She would wait until he appeared in the window, waving a handkerchief – *all's clear, you can come up now*.

She never saw his fellow lodger, John Brydges, although there was plenty of evidence of the man himself: shirts in the wardrobe, a pipe on the table by his bed, his work-boots positioned neatly on the floor under the window. Bill said they had an agreement – Brydges would make himself scarce on the days she was there. It bothered her, Brydges knowing. Bill said she was being silly.

"He knows we're going to be married. He's happy to help us out, that's all."

Except for that first time, they never spoke about the consequences. Proper young women were meant to be ignorant of such matters – she would have died before discussing them with Bill. And Bill – well, he was a man. He knew how to take care of such things. Didn't he?

Well, he didn't. And now it was too late. She couldn't tell her mother but she had to tell someone. The time would come when she wouldn't be able to hide it and by then it would be too late. Feeling desperate, she confided in Mrs. Earnshaw. She thought the cook would be upset but it was as though she expected something like this all along.

"It's not the worst thing to happen, Annie. There's many girls stand before the vicar with a baby on the way. You'll just need to hurry things on a bit. Tell him and he'll do right by you, I know he will."

And so she told him.

They met as usual the following Sunday in the park and walked to his lodgings. He was in high spirits. Afterwards, as they lay in bed and shared a cigarette – he was teaching her how to smoke – he shared his good news: he'd found a job in Lancashire with a weekly newspaper. He was lucky to get it, he said, times being what they were. It was a long way to go, just for a job, but he'd have travelled further if he had to.

"Barrow-in-Furness. I've never heard of it. What do they do up there?"

"They make money is what. Timber-yards, saw-mills, blast furnaces – every kind of factory you can imagine. I'm told they mine a half a million tons of iron ore a year. It's a thriving little town is our Barrow."

She said she thought it sounded like a dirty little town, and he laughed. "Muck and money, right? The *Barrow Times* is hiring me and I thank them from the bottom of my heart."

"Will you take me with you? Can we get married and go together?"

"Together? Don't be soft, girl. I'll have barely enough to keep myself let alone a wife."

"Or a child."

"Right."

"Bill, you have to marry me. There's a baby – I mean, there will be. I'm – you know – I'm going to have a baby."

What did she expect? Shock, perhaps. Anger – no, not really. Disappointment, most likely. But he just lay there staring at the wallpaper, saying nothing.

"Bill?"

"I'm trying to think." And then, "You're sure?"

"Yes."

Another long pause while she tried to be hopeful.

When he did speak, it was as though he was coming from somewhere else, like he was trying to put distance between them. "Thirty shillings a week. That's what this job pays. A man can't support a family on 30 shillings a week."

"People *do*, Bill. My father makes less than that and he –"

"I'm not your father!" He still hadn't looked at her. And then he turned to her, and it was as if he came back from wherever it was he'd been. She let herself breathe again.

"I'm sorry. I didn't mean to be unkind. Your father's a good man but I want more out of life. I want to be able to afford a good house in a decent neighbourhood. I want my wife to dress as well as the next woman or better. I want to send my children to school. I want to *be* someone, Annie. I don't want to throw it all away because we were foolish and made a mistake."

He stood up, and began to get dressed. "Give me a week. Have you told anyone yet?"

"Only Mrs. Earnshaw."

"Oh, God. Don't tell anyone else. Give me a week, all right? Can you do that?"

"I think so. Yes, all right."

"Good. Just do as I say and when I see you I'll have a plan. You trust me, don't you?"

"Yes."

"Come along then, I'll walk you to the bus."

She thought how they must look to passers-by: a typical young couple out for an afternoon stroll with nothing more serious to think about than keeping dry under his umbrella. Mrs. Gaskell would describe the flush in her cheeks, rosy from the cold, the drops of moisture on her forehead that might be from the rain or hints of some suppressed excitement. And he, clad in top hat and frock coat, so obviously a young man with a future ahead of him, keeping a protective eye on the traffic, steering her around the horse droppings littering the uneven cobbled streets.

Mrs. Gaskell would describe it much better of course, and it would not be a dull London street in an unfashionable neighbourhood but a quaint northern village set in the shadow of an ancient manor. He would not be off to some bleak mining town that nobody ever heard of but about to set sail for India, perhaps, and she would be going with him. And she would not be in the family way.

They took their places at the end of the queue. He released her, took his watch from his vest pocket, checked it and snapped it shut. He was very proud of that watch. It had belonged to his grandfather and was inscribed with the initials

"WT" for William Taylor, which was his grandfather's name and his own. It was heavy silver and made in Yorkshire at the turn of the century; he had opened the back of it once to show her the movements where it was signed: *Fawcitt, Richmond*.

"Twenty past the hour," he said. "I'll wait with you till it comes."

There were others in the queue, so they couldn't talk. He didn't seem to want to talk anyway, and she said nothing for fear of saying the wrong thing. Just as the omnibus arrived and she moved forward to board, he placed his hand on her shoulder. "It'll be all right, Annie, you'll see."

***

It'll be all right. Those words sustained her until she saw him again. She wasn't alone. She wasn't going to be one of those desperate girls forced to seek shelter in the lying-in ward of the workhouse. She wouldn't have to give up her baby to a wet nurse while she went out to work as a flower-weaver or worse. She could scarcely wait to see him again. For once, she was glad of having her days filled with work so the time passed quickly.

By the time Sunday arrived, she had confided in Mary Ann as well. Bill wouldn't like it if he knew, but Mary Ann had grown up in the workhouse and she knew the signs. She hugged her and said it would be all right. He's a good man, she said. He'll do what's right.

Bill was waiting at their usual place, pacing up and down the footpath. He didn't suggest going back to his lodgings. Instead they found a vacant bench and when they were seated he handed her an envelope.

"There's £10 in there, and information – where to go and all. It'll be all right – Brydges says this man is as good as a doctor. He'll do a proper job and all."

She was confused, so he explained: they couldn't have a baby. It was hard times in the printing trade. Lots of men were out of work. He was lucky to get hired up north, but it wouldn't pay what they paid in London. He couldn't support a family.

"You want me to …"

"It's the only way, Annie. You must get rid of it. Brydges says this fellow is clean and quick. It'll be all over afore tha know it."

When Bill was nervous you could hear it in his West Country accent; he sounded like his father.

"Ten pounds, Bill. It's so much money. How did you get it?"

"I pawned my watch." He saw the look on her face and added, "It's just a watch. I'll keep up the payments and get it back one day."

He had one more thing for her – a wedding band. She was to wear it and tell the man she was a married woman, her story being a familiar one: too many children and a husband who couldn't afford another.

"Do I have to say that?"

"He won't do it if you don't. Brydges says it's part of the game – he knows you're not married, but you have to pretend. That way it's not so bad, do you see?"

Wondering how Brydges knew so much about this, she sat there, the envelope of money in her purse, the ring in her pocket, as Bill outlined the details of this fictitious marriage. Keep to the truth as much as possible, he said. I'm a compositor; you worked as a maid before we married.

He was setting off that night on the evening train for Lancashire. By morning he'd be in Barrow, getting ready to start his new life. There seemed to be nothing more to talk about. She said she might as well be getting back and he walked her to the bus stop.

"Will you write me when you get there?"

"Of course."

"Every day?"

"Annie, I'm going to be working. I'll write when I can, I promise."

She wanted to ask him when she might visit, when she'd see him again. But he hated questions like that. The omnibus arrived, and she climbed up to the top and found a seat at the back so she could get a view of him. He was waiting to cross the street and she called down to him but he didn't respond. And then he stepped into the roadway and a carriage blocked her view and she couldn't see him anymore.

13.

The summons comes out of the blue. Matron wants to see her. Annie can think of nothing she's said or done that could be considered refractory. Since her night in the hole she's done her work as best she can and kept her grievances to herself.

The office door is open. Matron is writing in a ledger and doesn't look up. Knowing the routine, Annie stands just inside the door and waits. If she speaks first she'll be reprimanded. It's like dealing with royalty: you wait upon their condescension.

Setting down her pen, Matron applies a blotter to the page and closes the book. Then and only then does she "see" Annie.

"How long have you been here?"

She means here in the Union, not waiting in her office. And she knows exactly how long it's been. Knows it better than Annie who has stopped marking the days on the wall behind her bed. She could cover the entire wall with coal dust and be no closer to leaving.

"I believe it's just over six months, ma'am."

"Six months, one week and three days. How are you finding it working in the Laundry?"

This is the kind of question that could be a trap. If Annie says she's unhappy, which she is, she'll be punished. If she says all is well, Matron will sense the lie and punish her anyhow.

Fortunately, the woman doesn't wait for a response. "We have a situation. The ward nurse is down with scarlatina leaving only the junior nurse in charge. She has an assistant but she needs help. Your friend Mr. Catlin has suggested you might be put to better use in the Women's Infirmary. What do you say?"

It takes a moment to sink in, but Matron is asking if she would rather do one thing over another. Since coming to this place she's not been offered a choice in anything – what to wear, what to eat – definitely not where to work. It would be a grand thing to say "No" just for the pleasure of hearing herself say it but that would be cutting off her nose to spite her face.

"I'd like that very much, Ma'am."

"Good. Report there immediately."

"Should I go back to the Laundry and tell the Super?"

"Did I *say* to go to the Laundry?"

"No, Ma'am."

"All right then. Get yourself to the sick ward and make yourself useful. That's all."

The nurse is relieved to see her. She's very young, not more than twenty, and newly certified. As she shows Annie through the ward, stopping to point out the most difficult cases, she seems nervous – this is her first placement and the first time she's been given so much responsibility.

"It's so different here," she says. "It's nothing like where we were trained. Everything at St. Thomas's was so clean and orderly and this – well, you can see."

Sickly yellow walls grimy with dirt – square windows in heavy iron frames – low iron bedsteads provided with thin mattresses no better than sacks of chaff. Clean and orderly it isn't. It reeks of unemptied chamber pots and disinfectant and unventilated drains. What's really needed here is a good whiff of fresh air. In the winter the windows are fastened down to keep out the cold and during the summer, because the Infirmary overlooks the women's courtyard where they beat carpets all day, they're kept shut against the dust. One might think they'd be opened late in the day when the outside work is done, but the common dread of night air keeps them permanently shut. The wretched miasma of the sickroom has no place to escape.

The nurse goes on to say it's been a terrible time, everyone sick, not enough staff in the first place, and the doctor run off his feet trying to keep up with it all. He's gone for the day, doing his rounds, and won't be back till morning. "Poor Mrs. Yorke has been ever so helpful," she says, "but we do need more help, don't we?"

Annie has heard a great deal about "poor" Mrs. Yorke. One of several pauper nurses assigned to tend the workhouse patients, she's said to ignore patients she dislikes while secretly helping herself to the brandy and other spirits prescribed by the doctor. At this particular moment she does seem slightly intoxicated.

She eyes Annie with distaste. "Done this before?"

"Nursing? No, I haven't. I worked for a woman once who had nervous headaches. I'd make her a tonic and massage her temples. I guess you could say that's a kind of nursing."

The nurse finds Annie an apron and cap and hands her a list of instructions. "Mrs. Yorke will answer any questions you have. I must run – Number 42 needs a poultice for her bed-sores and Number 8 has been throwing up all morning."

Mrs. Yorke waits for Annie to tie her apron and adjust her cap, then directs her to a figure coiled up in a small alcove at the far end of the room, apart from the others. That, she says, is Number 21 and it's one of the worst cases: syphilis.

Annie has never heard the condition referred to by anything other than *the French disease* – it's shocking to hear it called by its real name. But this is the infirmary and she must get used to such things if she's to be useful here.

"She should be in the foul ward," Mrs. Yorke says, "but they're full up so we're stuck with her."

Gingerly, Annie approaches the bed. She reaches out to lay a hand on her shoulder and the patient turns toward her. It takes her a moment to recognize the haggard, yellow face of this poor, miserable girl: Biddie Fletcher. Or rather, the ghost of someone who used to be Biddie Fletcher.

Judging by the state she's in she's been roughly used … her nose is broken and there are welts and bruises on her arms and chest where someone laid into her with a belt. No one's had the time or inclination to tend to her since she arrived: her hands and feet are caked with dirt, her hair a tangled, filthy mat.

She doesn't recognize Annie; when she tries to wipe the sweat from Biddie's chest and shoulders, the girl shrinks from her touch. Although her eyes are open she doesn't seem to see anyone. She appears to be half dreaming, muttering to herself or some unseen person. Delirium tremens, Mrs. Yorke calls it; she's been like that since they brought her in.

"We get a lot of it in here. They bin drinking and when they go off the drink it hits 'em that way."

Biddie doesn't drink. Annie recalls her quoting

Scripture about the evils of wine and strong drink: *Be not drunk with wine but be filled with the Spirit*. It's possible, though, that someone has been forcing alcohol down her throat – she's certainly been badly treated. The sight of her ribs sticking out is appalling … it's as if she hasn't eaten in weeks. The doctor's given orders that she's to have extra rations along with the usual mercury treatments but Mrs. Yorke says she won't eat. When they tried to force-feed her she threw it all up.

"It's a waste of food anyway. Any fool can see the girl is plainly dying. All right then, you're on your own. Fourteen is on the floor again. Should teach her a lesson and leave her there, that's what I think."

Annie finds a basin and fills it with water from the stove. As gently as she can, she washes Biddie's hands and feet and wipes the traces of dirt and dried blood from her face. What she really needs is her hair washed but that will have to wait. After doing what she can for Biddie, Annie leaves her to her restless dreams, moving on to the other patients in the ward. Some are dying of this dreadful influenza, others of consumption, and there are still others who might be cured if they could only be transferred to a proper medical hospital. Each is assigned a number printed on a small white card and taped to the wall above their beds. Number 12 is a young woman subject to fits; every twenty minutes or so she emits a kind of groan and throws herself out of bed. Another, Number 6, is an hysteric – she gabbles nonsense all day long, eyes shut, hands clasping and unclasping in frantic, meaningless gestures.

Every bed is full. Several must sleep on pallets on the floor until someone dies and a cot becomes available. An obese woman with a leg ulcer says she's not been attended to in three days. When Annie asks Mrs. Yorke about it the woman makes a face and says she can't bear the smell: "It's like rotten eggs and the pus is something dreadful."

"Shall I change her dressing, then, if you won't?"

"Suit yourself. She's always complaining, that one – if it ain't her leg it's something else. But if you can stand the sight of it, go ahead."

Annie unwraps the bandage and is almost knocked off her feet by the smell. In spite of her efforts to be careful, some of the dead, blackened skin comes away from the leg. The woman bites her lip in an effort not to cry out.

"I'm sorry. It must be terribly painful."

She nods, eyes closed. Her forehead is bathed in sweat – the agony must be excruciating. The wound should be cleaned with salt water but Annie can't bring herself to cause any more pain than necessary. She applies a fresh bandage and makes a mental note to ask the doctor to look at her first thing in the morning. As Annie turns to leave the woman puts a hand on her arm.

"You won't let them take it, will you?"

"I'm sorry?"

"Me leg. I heard the doctor say they'd be taking it off if it got any worse. You can't let them – I can't work without me leg. Promise me you won't let them take it."

***

At the end of the day, she asks the young nurse if she might come back after supper in order to keep Biddie company for an hour or so. She's expecting a refusal, but the nurse is pleased – she has no one to take the evening watch and Mrs. Yorke, who sleeps in the ward overnight, cannot be trusted to wake up if anything serious happens.

"That would be wonderful," she says. "I'll clear it with Matron – I'm sure she won't mind, considering."

When she returns to the ward after supper, Biddie's awake and seems more aware of her surroundings. She reaches for Annie's hand. "It's you, Mrs. Taylor. I thought it was you but I wasn't sure. And you brought little Teddy. Ain't he big now! Is he creepin' yet?"

"He scoots around on his bottom, the way Edie did. And he talks to himself all the time."

"He does?"

"Well, it's just baby talk but he said 'Mama' yesterday. And he understands a lot of what you say to him. Don't you, Teddy?"

"He's lovely, Mrs. Taylor. Oh it is good to see a friendly face!"

"It's good to see you, too, Biddie, but you must eat. You won't get better if you don't. I've brought you some soup. Won't you try to eat just a little of it?"

She agrees to try but after a couple of spoonsful she shakes her head and waves the spoon away. "I'm sorry, I can't get it down. Stay with me though, won't you? Tell me about your girls."

"Well, there's not much to tell. I've had a letter from their teacher and she says they're doing well."

"Will you see them?"

"I don't know. The school's a long way from here – it would be hard to get there and back in a day. Anyway, they're better off without me."

"Oh, Mrs. Taylor, don't say that. There's no one in the world a child needs more than its mother. Everything bad that happened to me was after my Ma died. Nothing was ever the same after that."

The baby reaches out and clutches a strand of Biddie's hair, giving it a sharp, gleeful tug. Annie offers to let Biddie hold him.

"I mustn't," she says. "I don't want to make him sick."

"You won't. Here, I'll just set him down beside you and you can have a cuddle if you like. He's a bit smelly – he may need changing."

"He smells lovely. All babies do, don't they? I remember Mercy when she was little, she smelled ever so good."

After a while the girl's eyes close and she slips back into a troubled half-sleep, wrangling with her demons and her ghosts. The ward is quieter now than it was in the daytime, but many of the women are restless and in pain. In the centre of the room Mrs. Yorke is already asleep; her snores continue uninterruped even when one of the patients, struggling to get out of bed to use the commode, falls heavily onto the floor. Annie sets the baby next to Biddie and hurries to help her to her feet. Another woman calls out for water and is admonished by her neighbour: "Don't be a bloody fool! Nobody gives you nothing here but you go and get it yourself."

"I'll get you some water," Annie says, "as soon as I

help this lady."

Why can't they have their names on their cards? It sounds terrible to call them by numbers. The last indignity, really – they take your clothes, your children and, when you get ill, they take your name.

Returning from the sink with a cup of water she hears the workhouse bell toll the eight o'clock curfew. She gathers up the child and prepares to leave, side-stepping two women sleeping on a pallet near the door. As she opens the door, revealing a faint light from the outside corridor, Mrs. Yorke barks at her from the middle of the room:

"Close the bloody door, will you? Some of us are trying to sleep!"

14.

The address Bill gave her was a chemist's shop just off Tottenham Court Road, near the hospital. She caught the bus up Picadilly to Charing Cross Road and then walked the rest of the way. By the time she reached the shop, she was perspiring in spite of the autumn chill.

The boy behind the counter was polite enough till she asked for Mr. Smith.

"*Mr. Smith*, eh? Who is it wants to know?"

"Mrs. Brown."

Too much emphasis on the Mrs.? It was hard to be sure, never having said it before. She removed her gloves, exposing the plain gold wedding band.

"He's expecting me."

"Wait a minute. I'll see if he's around."

As a child she loved the smell of the chemist's – the familiar sweetly rotten smells of chloroform and opium, soap and perfume. Now she thought she might be sick. She was relieved when the smirking shop assistant returned a few minutes later and directed her through a side door.

"Two floors up," he said. "Don't bother knocking."

The door at the top of the stairs was slightly ajar. She pushed it all the way open and found herself in a small room furnished with a modified sofa with one end raised, like Mrs. B's fainting couch, and an armchair. There was also a washstand with a pitcher and a basin of water, and a tea-trolley draped with a checkered cloth.

A short, stocky man in a loose coat and pants was bustling about, clearing away the remains of his lunch.

"Mr. Smith?"

Instead of answering, he drew the blinds and lit a large paraffin oil lamp, hanging from the ceiling. Then, and only then, did he acknowledge her presence.

"You've brought the money?"

"Yes."

"Give it to me then, and be quick about it."

She took the envelope from her purse and handed it to him. He counted it, folded it into his waistcoat pocket and locked the door. Then he removed his coat and proceeded to roll up his shirt sleeves. The cuffs were frayed and dirty – he smelt of whisky and was in need of a shave. All this time he had not asked her name or even looked at her directly. Perhaps that's the way it was done in these situations.

"I'm going to examine you now. I need you to lie down on the couch on your side with your back to me. Are you wearing any undergarments?"

"No. The note – I had a note and it said not to. Do I – should I get undressed?"

"Good Lord, no. Just lie down and be still. You may feel some discomfort but I warn you, if you cry out I will ask you to leave at once. Do you understand?"

She did as she was told. He kneeled beside her and she felt his hands touch her under her chemise. No one but Bill had touched her there ever. She tried not to flinch as his fingers probed inside her. It seemed to go on forever. At one point he said if she wanted his help she'd have to relax. She tried to think of other things – what was Bill doing right now? He would be at work most likely. Perhaps he was writing her a letter this very minute. Maybe there would be one waiting for her when this ordeal was over.

Finally, he stood up and wiped his hand with a bit of rag.

"You can sit up."

Eyes averted, she did so. Could anything be more shameful than what she'd just experienced? And this was only the beginning.

He lit a cigarette and settled himself in the armchair.

"You're married."

It was a statement of fact.

"Yes, I am."

"And you have other children?"

"Two."

They had settled on this number as more than two would be unrealistic given her age, and fewer would make it difficult to argue for a termination.

"You're not more than three months along, maybe a little further. So that's good – I can help you. How old are you?"

"Twenty." This at least was the truth.

"Women younger than you have babies every day. Why not have this one then? You look healthy enough – you could manage it."

"My husband's been out of work and we can't afford another child. He's a compositor and he's just started a new job up north."

Keep to the truth as much as possible. That's what Bill had said. She had other things she could say – they had rehearsed the whole story – but the man seemed to lose interest. He finished his cigarette, flung it into the fireplace and told her to lie down again in the same position.

"Remember what I told you – one word and I'll ask you to leave."

She did as he said and again felt his hands on her. And something else, an instrument of some kind, cold and made of metal with a sharp point like a screw. He began to turn the metal thing inside her. She felt discomfort at first, like the cramping that comes on each month, and then it grew worse. Worse than anything and she had to press her lips together, willing herself not to cry out. Just when she thought she'd have to beg him to stop, he did.

She felt him draw it out of her and the pain began to subside. She tried to sit up but he told her to lie down and be still. Lying there, her faced pressed against the upholstery, she heard him open a window and the sounds of the street came through. Strawberries all ripe all ripe …

"Turn over," he said. "Don't try to sit up."

He poured water in the basin, gave his hands a cursory wash, dried them with the checkered cloth.

"You can lie here for half an hour but no longer. Go down the back stairs and tell no one where you've been. I'll need to see you again this time tomorrow, and then again the day after that."

Bill said nothing about coming back. It'll be quick, he said. He'll do what he must and it will be over.

"I'm sorry – I have to come back?"

"You thought this was it? It takes more than once. Three

227

visits should do it but we might need four. When you return tomorrow come straight up the back stairs. Do *not* ask for me at the chemist's. And remember, if you decide not to return that's your choice but your money will not be refunded."

He rolled down his shirtsleeves, put his coat back on, and blew out the lamp. Once he was gone she waited until she felt she could sit up. The cramping was still there – not as bad as it had been, more of a dull ache. But the pain when he put that thing – when it went inside her … How was it possible that women did this and nobody talked about it? Did it all the time, Bill said. Even though it was against the law. Even though you could bleed to death if it went wrong.

Three visits. Possibly four. She felt the gagging in her throat and crept towards the washstand, held the basin on her lap and retched. Nothing came up and after a minute she set it down again. After a while when she felt she could stand she got to her feet and waited, one hand on the armchair to steady herself.

That woman two doors down in Notting Hill – the one who used to help Mama with the wash. What did she have – six children or was it seven? A long time ago but she still remembers … how the oldest girl found her lying on the floor, vomit everywhere, blood coming out of her – a knitting needle they said. Stuck it up inside her trying to get rid of the baby. A good thing she died, they said. She would have gone to gaol if she lived.

Nobody must know. No one must ever know what happened in this room. Almost happened. She closed her eyes, gripped her hands together: Please. Let me live. Don't let me die. Please.

She made her way down the back stairs, out onto the street. The fog was rolling in. It would soon be dark, in the middle of the afternoon.

***

The next day she wrote to Bill: Send me a ticket or come and get me. I can't do what we talked about and I must leave before I become too heavy.

A telegraph arrived three days later: DO AS AGREED STOP NO OTHER CHOICE STOP WILL WAIT TO HEAR STOP BILL

Telegraphic messages cost a shilling which was more than the cost of a stamp but she was desperate: CANNOT DO AS AGREED STOP COME FOR ME STOP SHALL I TELL YOUR MOTHER STOP ANNIE

She hesitated over the last bit, but she knew him well enough by now to know he would not want her knocking on his mother's door. If nothing else would sway him, the dread of her censure would bring him to his senses.

His response arrived just before five o'clock: GET TRAIN NEXT TUESDAY EUSTON STATION STOP CAN YOU GET MONEY BACK STOP IF NOT WILL SEND MONEY BY POST TOMORROW STOP TELL NOBODY STOP BILL

She wired him back: IMPOSSIBLE GET MONEY BACK STOP ANNIE

His letter came two days later, containing the money for the ticket and directions on which train to get and where to change for the service to Ulverston. There was nothing in the letter about how he felt – no promise of marriage or assurances that he would take care of her. But it was understood, wasn't it? If he didn't plan to marry her once she arrived, he wouldn't have sent the money for the ticket.

She told Mrs. Adams her mother was sick and she was wanted at home. The housekeeper was not Mrs. B. She'd seen a few housemaids in the family way and she was not so easily fooled. With a pointed glance at Annie's stomach, she said she'd tell Mrs. Levy but not to expect a character, given she was leaving without the usual four weeks' notice.

"Actually, Mrs. Adams, I won't need a character. I'm getting married."

"So he's making an honest woman of you, is he? That surprises me. What's the expression they use – why buy the cow when you're getting the milk for free? But you'd know all about that, wouldn't you, being a dairyman's daughter."

Part Three: Hope

1.

The scarlet fever epidemic shows no sign of abating. Just as the ward nurse recovers, Mrs. Yorke comes down with chills and a rash and is removed to the Fever Hospital.

"We need you more than ever," says the junior nurse. "Poor Mrs. Yorke isn't likely to be back with us for a while."

Which is not entirely a bad thing. As the woman with the leg ulcer tells her, "Bein' nursed by Mrs. Yorke is worse than havin' no one at all."

Biddie sleeps much of the time; when she's awake, she wants only for Annie to sit by her and hold her hand. There's little time to do that during the day, run off their feet as they are, but at night Annie comes back and reads a little from Mrs. Gaskell's novel. Biddie manages to follow it, for the most part; however, she tends not to understand that it is just that – a novel. One morning she tells Annie she couldn't sleep the night before for agonizing over the hanging of the heroine's father. It makes no difference when Annie explains that Mr. Robinson, gallant though he is, doesn't exist.

"He was her *father*," Biddie says. "Story or no story, there's no arguin' with that."

Although it's out of his district, Mr. Catlin comes by as often as he can to sit with Biddie and talk. They pray together and she always seems more peaceful after his visits.

With a little prodding, Biddie slowly reveals what happened to her after she was discharged. Mr. Fletcher did indeed come to take her home that day but not to forgive her; he came to carry out the judgment of the righteous. For a week he kept her locked in a room at the top of the house, refusing to let her see her sisters or anybody else while he considered her punishment. At the end of that time he informed her he'd found the answer in the New Testament: "He that committeth sin is of the devil; for the devil sinneth from the beginning." He hammered an iron post into the wall, shackled her to it, and beat her every single day, literally "beating the devil out of her" and forcing her sisters to watch. In all that time she was given nothing to eat; when she was thirsty she was given water from the gutter served in a chamber pot.

It was only when the nature of Biddie's illness became obvious that her father, disgusted and frightened of catching something, agreed to let her go. Mercy, the youngest girl, led her out of the house and brought her back to the Union, rang the bell, and left her on the steps. As far as Biddie knows, her sister hasn't been back: "Pa would never allow it. I have fallen from the path of righteousness. He won't let her come again I know it."

To Annie it's a dreadful story – an evil man using religion to satisfy his brutal, barbaric appetite for violence.

Biddie, however, will not hear a word against him. "He's my Pa, Mrs. Taylor. He wanted what was best for me, and I let him down. The Bible says spare the rod and spoil the child. He had to do what he done. He didn't have no choice."

"He did have a choice, Biddie. He could have forgiven you. Isn't that also what the Bible says? That we should forgive people? Forgive them their trespasses, isn't that right?"

It's no use. She says it's good to hear Annie quote from the Bible. "It means it's working, God is opening your eyes."

When Annie expresses her frustration to the missionary

that Biddie cannot see her father for the monster he is, he disagrees with her.

"The girl isn't capable of that kind of hate, Mrs. Taylor, and she's better off for it."

"Better off? How can you say Biddie is better off? She's been treated badly by the world and tortured by her father and now she's dying before she's really lived."

"You mustn't mourn for Biddie. By continuing to love her father in spite of what he's done, she's found favour with the Lord. Jesus said, 'Blessed are the meek for they shall inherit the Earth.' Biddie's suffering will be rewarded one day, I promise."

It doesn't seem to her that poor Biddie is inheriting anything. And she's getting sicker every day. The ward nurse has given up on her, having seen several such cases over the years.

"Sometimes the ointments and pills do as much damage as the disease," she says, referring to the the cankers and ulcers that have sprouted in Biddie's mouth and throat. "You see her teeth are turning black – she'll be losing some of them. Her resistance is too low for her to make a recovery. They should have taken her directly to the Lock, when they saw what it is. Once it gets to this stage … well, there's not much that can be done."

Turning to leave, she pauses and shakes her head. "It's a hard thing to watch, I know. But we have patients who will recover – they're the ones in need of our attention."

Everyone, it seems, has written her off. Even Mr. Catlin has accepted that Biddie's "reward" will be in the next life rather than this. Night after night Annie steals away from the dormitory to sit beside her bed, occasionally applying cool cloths to the crusted postules afflicting Biddie's chest, arms, and legs. Syphilis, the tertiary stage. So says the doctor, echoing the ward nurse: she should be removed to the Lock.

"They're better prepared to care for her – they have the staff, for one thing, and the wards are clean and airy."

Not like here. He doesn't say that but he could. What amazes Annie is that anyone gets better in this place. Her mother has always said she'll die in the street before going to a workhouse infirmary. After working in one Annie would agree.

***

The August Bank Holiday is memorable for being one of the most grueling days so far in the sick ward: the obese woman has been removed to St. Mary's Hospital to have her leg removed. She doesn't go willingly. It takes several attendants including the porter to manoevre her onto the transportation trolley, hampered as they are by her struggles to get free. Reaching out to Annie, she begs for her help.

"Don't let them take me, Miss – don't let them take my leg!"

The commotion unsettles the others. Number 12 throws herself on the floor and the hysterical young woman begins to sob uncontrollably. By the time they manage to get the woman strapped down and wheeled out the door, the ward is in an uproar. To add to the confusion, a pregnant woman temporarily confined to the infirmary chooses that moment to go into labour.

Annie is mopping the floor and getting ready to leave for the day when the missionary comes looking for her.

"You need to get your dinner," he says. "I won't keep you. I have something for you. I thought you could read it over when you get a minute."

He hands her a pamphlet. Expecting it to be a religious treatise of some sort, she gives a cursory glance at the title: *The Nightingale Home and Training School for Nurses, St. Thomas' Hospital*.

"They're accepting applicants. I hope you won't think it presumptious of me but I spoke to the ward sister and she's willing to have you apply."

"Me? Apply to be a nurse?"

"Yes. I think you'd make an excellent nurse – you *are* an excellent nurse, Mrs. Taylor. Why not be trained properly in it? There's a great need for trained nurses all over London. All over the country, in fact."

It's such an unexpected suggestion – of all the things she thought she might do with her life, she's never considered nursing. It's one thing to care for sick paupers in a workhouse, where they're grateful if you're kind to them and don't drink the brandy, but to work in a proper hospital where there are rules and ward sisters running things and doctors to answer to …

"But I'm thirty. They want young girls for these positions, don't they?"

"Not necessarily. What they want are steady, hard-working women with a disposition for caring. I'd say you have all those qualities. Wouldn't you?"

Would she? She's never given much thought to her "qualities", such as they are. Her mother thought her headstrong and clumsy. Bill, who once thought her smart enough to appreciate the treasures of the British Museum, ended up believing she was only fit for housework and cooking. Mrs. Adams would not have given her even that much credit. Mrs. B. liked her, but she was kind and down-to-earth and her expectations were simple; she probably wasn't in a position to judge.

It was really only Miss Hodge who ever saw anything special in her – and *she* thought she should be a teacher.

"I don't know. I'd have to think it over."

"Do that," William says. "Think about it and let me know. I can arrange the interview once you decide. But don't take too long – these openings come up once or twice a year and they fill up quickly."

***

That night, just before the lights go out, a familiar figure shuffles in and claims the empty bed across from Annie.

"Mrs. Knight – you're back!"

"I am," she says. "And glad of it."

"What happened? Didn't you like living with your daughter?"

"Oh, she was good enough to me in her way. She did expect me to do all the work – cleaning and washing up and all. For my keep, if you know what I mean. And I guess that was fair. No, I didn't have a problem with my daughter."

Mrs. Hatchett has the answer. "It was her old man, wasn't it? He didn't want you around. I told you he wouldn't – they're all like that, don't want to be bothered with the wife's side of the family."

Mrs. Knight shakes her head. "No, that wasn't it. He didn't have much to say to me but he didn't bother me none. No, the problem was me – I was lonely."

Annie can't help saying, "Really? For *this* place?"

"I know. Funny, ain't it? My daughter's boys are grown so they're not around. And she was out all day at the shoe factory. When she come home she just wanted to have her tea and go to bed. There was no one to talk to at night, like. I thought if I'm goin' to skivvy all day I might as well do it with company – and get a meal at the end of the day that I don't have to cook myself. Anyways, I'm back and I'm stayin' put till they carry me out feet first."

2.

Mama gave her a hat for the trip, a high-brimmed spoon bonnet
in dark green velvet. That, then, was her "something new".
Mary Ann's gift was a handkerchief embroidered in blue, and
Cook provided a sixpence to wear in her shoe. Apart from her
service clothes she owned just the one dress so that would
count as "something old" and at the last moment she thought to
ask her sister for the loan of her gloves.

"You can keep them," Maude said. "I know it's
supposed to be something borrowed but I want you to have
them. I do wish you weren't going to be so far away. Will you
be all right?"

Maude, like Mama, knew her secret. It was a woman's
thing, Mama said – something to be kept from the men. Papa
would find out soon enough although, being Papa, he would
make no comment, critical or otherwise.

She reassured her sister that she'd be fine. And it wasn't
for ever – Bill would find work in London and they'd be back
in "civilization" soon enough.

"And you're in love with each other," Maude said.
"That's all that really matters."

He'd sent her £1/10s, more than enough for a single
ticket. Papa was accompanying her to the station, just like
he did all those years ago when she went to work for the
Bellwethers. This time, though, they took a cab – an almost
unheard-of luxury marking the importance of the occasion.

As the cab turned onto Drummond Street, the great
sandstone arch of Euston station came into view, and the reality
of leaving struck both of them at the same time.

"Pansy, are you sure this is what you want? I'm sorry to
be interfering, like, but I want to be sure you know what you're
taking on."

"I do, Papa, I'm sure."

The driver pulled up to the entrance. Papa helped her
down, paid the man, took her case in one hand and offered
her his arm; together they stepped through the wrought iron
gates into the station. A marble statue of a man holding a scroll
dominated the entrance hall: George Stephenson, the plaque

said, founder of the railway system. Papa had met his son, once, Mr. Robert Stephenson.

"My father made him a coat. He was as famous as his father, he was, and he came into Pa's little shop on Compton Street to be measured. He had an office in Westminster, and Pa let me deliver the coat when it was done. I didn't see him myself, but the footman gave me a shilling. That was a lot of money back then. I gave it to Pa and he gave me back tuppence to keep."

The man who took her money said to go to Platform Five for the 10:10 express to Glasgow and Edinburgh.

"Change at Preston for Carnforth, change at Carnforth for Furness, change again at Furness for Barrow. It'll cost you a penny to get to Barrow but you'll get that ticket at the Preston station. Thank you kindly. Next!"

She worried she wouldn't remember all the changes but Papa assured her the guard would let her know when to get off.

"Used to take three days and two nights to get to Cumberland, back in the old coaching days. And you'll be there tonight! It's a wonder, all this modern travel – and we have Mr. Stephenson to thank for it."

"Mr. George or Mr. Robert?"

"Well, both of them, I should say!"

Once they reached the departure gate, the guard took her suitcase and stowed it in the luggage cupboard. After reminding her to be sure to retrieve it in Preston, he led them down the platform to the third-class "Ladies' Only" compartment. There was no sign indicating it as such, but he said they always kept a couple in reserve for women travelling alone. "Especially pretty young ladies such as yourself."

With great courtesy, he opened the carriage door, tipped his hat and left.

Papa looked at the great clock hanging from the roof – the train was due to leave in seven minutes. "I'd best be off. Can't keep the girls waiting, now, can I?"

It was an old joke – he was referring to the cows.

On an impulse, she clutched his arm, not wanting him to leave.

"There, there, girl, don't fret." He kissed her shyly on

the cheek. "I've always been proud of you, Pansy. Still am. Nothing's changed and it never will. You know that, don't you?"

She nodded, not trusting herself to speak. Fortifying herself with the sight of his dear familiar face, she stepped up into the carriage and took a seat between two hefty older ladies, one of whom had fallen asleep and was snoring softly, her head propped up against the window.

The compartment was full now that she was seated, and the train departed right on time. She had brought a book with her – *On Liberty*, by John Stuart Mill. It had been over a year since Bill gave it to her and she was barely a third of the way through. It wasn't that the writing was so terribly difficult – she had after all made her way through *A Tale of Two Cities.* It was that there was no story. And what was the point of a book if it didn't tell a story?

Still, she didn't like to admit to Bill that she hadn't at least made an effort to finish it. As the train pulled out of the station, she opened the book, hoping to make her way through a few more chapters by the time she got to Barrow. Soon, though, she was eavesdropping on her fellow passengers, finding their conversation more interesting than Mr. Mill.

The two girls opposite her were sisters on their way to Keswick to take up teaching positions. The younger girl peppered her sister with questions about the school they were going to and what she knew about where they would live. Between questions, the older girl, who was stuck with the unfortunate name of Dorcas, tried to return to the book she was reading, which was called *The Variation of Animals and Plants under Domestication.* It didn't look very interesting, but she appeared to find it absorbing. Her younger sister had a book as well, *Black's Shilling Guide to the English Lakes,* but she let it lie unread on her lap.

The woman on her right – the one who wasn't asleep – was a friendly Scottish woman who introduced herself to the rest of the passengers as a "regular traveler".

"My daughters live in London and I come down every so often to help with the bairns."

She appeared to be familiar with the route and was

the only one in the carriage who'd thought to hire a couple of foot-warmers – one for her and one for her niece, who was travelling with her back to Perth.

"I've learned. This time of year, you don't know what kind of weather you'll get between here and Scotland. It can be right drcich – be prepared, I say."

A pleasant woman, very old and very deaf, sat across from Annie next to the younger sister. She said nothing, of course, but smiled and nodded regularly, and made herself understood by a series of hand gestures. She had a little notebook with a gold pencil attached and she wrote in it from time to time and showed it to the others. Shortly after leaving London and entering the countryside north of Harrow, she wrote, "The harvest this year has been most satisfactory don't you think?" Twenty minutes later it was, "I have seen three deer running through the farmer's field." In response, the others smiled and nodded with as much enthusiasm as they could muster.

The final inhabitant of the compartment said nothing to anyone. In her way, she was more silent than the old deaf woman, who at least made the effort to communicate. A dark-skinned girl with high cheekbones, she might have been beautiful had she chosen to smile. Annie saw her only in profile as she stared out the window the entire time, never taking her eyes from the passing landscape. She said nothing all the way to Preston, where she disembarked the moment the locomotive pulled to a stop and disappeared into the stream of travellers.

The seats were hard, and there was nowhere to do one's business. There was a dreadful point at the end of the second hour when she knew if she didn't find somewhere to relieve herself she'd be disgraced right there in her seat. She whispered her concerns to the Regular Traveller who said they were close to Rugby station where the train always stopped for five minutes.

"You can use the facilities there, dear – you'll have time if you're quick about it. I always bring a wee chamber pot with me, just in case. It might not be polite, but when the devil drives, well, needs must."

Knowing relief was in sight, she managed to hold on

until the train pulled into the station; with unladylike alacrity she hurried down from the train and was directed to the Ladies' Waiting Room. Men were so much luckier in these matters – from what she'd heard, many didn't bother with waiting to use the facilities, they simply opened the door of their compartments and pissed out into the wind.

It was November, and cold. The swaying of the train made her nausea worse. Somewhere between Crewe and Warrington, the Regular Traveller offered her the use of her chamber pot. Mercifully, it had been emptied and rinsed, although she was in no position to be fussy. She thanked her and took the pot from her hands and was immediately – and noisily – sick into it. None of this could have been pleasant for the other passengers, but Annie was past caring. When she was done, the deaf woman kindly took it from her and dumped the contents out the window, handing it back to her with a smile.

The younger sister watched all of this with undisguised interest. "You're not well."

"No, not terribly well, I'm afraid."

Leaning in towards her she asked, in a whisper that could be heard by everyone except the deaf old lady: "Are you in the family way?"

Her sister was horrified. "Clementine, for heaven's sake – mind your own business! I'm terribly sorry – my sister often speaks before she thinks."

"It's all right. Yes, I am."

Clementine was thrilled. "Oh, how wonderful! I do wish I had a husband. I don't expect it will ever happen now that we're going up north."

The Regular Traveller smiled at her. "There are single gentlemen in Cumberland, my dear. The north of England is not quite beyond the pale."

"Oh, no, I just mean now that we'll be teaching. They don't let you teach if you have a husband. Or have a husband if you teach, I guess I should say. I could hide it, I suppose, but then there'd be a terrific how-do-you-do when they found out. Would they take back my wages, do you think?"

Her sister glared at her. "Clemmie, you do talk the most terrible rot. Do be quiet and leave these people in peace."

"Don't be angry, Dorcas. It's different for you – you don't even like men. But I think it's jolly unfair that I should have to go out and work for a living when all I really want is a lovely man to take care of and lots of adorable children to play with. Oh, you're *so* lucky!"

This last remark was directed at Annie. She didn't feel all that lucky – the exact opposite, actually – but Clemmie didn't appear to need a response.

"Don't you think it's unfair that some of us should be poor and have to work and never have money for nice clothes and others should be rich and live in beautiful houses and ride in carriages every day and have maids to do all the work? *I* do – I think we should all be the same. That's what *I* think."

It occurred to her that Clemmie might be a little simple. She might even be a Radical, but she didn't look like one. Still, she was getting herself in a right stew, as Papa would say. Her sister sighed and patted her hand reassuringly.

"All right, dear, calm down. You've made your point, and now let's just sit quietly and enjoy the journey. Look, we're going over a viaduct – let's see if we can find it in the guidebook, shall we?"

***

When the train pulled into Preston, Annie said goodbye to the Regular Traveller, and to Dorcas and Clementine – what *were* their parents thinking? – and waved farewell to the deaf old lady. Having asked directions of a uniformed gentleman in a top hat whom she took to be the stationmaster, she made her way to the porter's hut, a small shingled building just outside the front entrance, and left her case for dispatch to the platform.

Now she had an hour to kill before the train to Carnforth arrived; the ticket wicket wouldn't open until five minutes before departure. At first she thought she'd get herself a cup of tea – nothing to eat, though … she couldn't bear the thought of food at the moment. There was a refreshment room at the end of the platform, but when she pushed open the door she was assaulted by the smell of frying bacon. She decided to forego the tea and spend the hour in the Ladies Waiting Room instead.

There were, in fact, two Ladies Waiting Rooms, next to each other. The one for First Class passengers was furnished with cushioned benches and an assortment of reading material. It was practically empty, while the other, meant for Second and Third Class, was crowded and bleak. It did have a stove, but no benches near it. After standing by the window for almost a quarter of an hour, feeling faint from not having eaten, she decided to take a chance on passing as a First Class passenger. She was dressed well enough – who, except her conscience, would know the difference?

Entering the room, she found a seat by the fire and closed her eyes. It was lovely here, lovely and warm. The cushioned bench was much more comfortable than the Third Class seats on the train, and she was so tired. She felt as if she'd been tired for weeks now, maybe longer. But soon all would be well. Bill would meet her at the train, take her suitcase, kiss her lightly on the cheek. Welcome to Barrow, he'd say. Welcome to your new home. He'd take her to the room he'd booked for her and she'd stay there while they applied for their marriage license. And after that they'd be married and the nightmare would be over.

"Ticket, Miss."

The waiting room attendant was hovering over her like a vulture, holding out his hand.

"I don't have one. That is – I haven't bought it yet. I'm waiting for the wicket to open."

"This room is for ladies what has First Class tickets. *Not –*" and this last bit was pronounced with heavy sarcasm – "for them as is *waiting to buy* First Class tickets. I'll have to ask you to leave."

Mortified, she got up and scurried out, aware of the "tsk-tsks" of those around her. How dare she? There were rules, after all. She walked as far along the platform from the waiting room as she could, and stood outside the station master's office. The wind had picked up. She put her hood up and wrapped her shawl more tightly. That morning when she set off from London she needed only her velvet bonnet but now she was in Lancashire and it was cold.

It was only then, as she stood staring down the track, waiting for the train to Carnforth, that she suddenly realized she'd left her book – the book Bill gave her – on the London train. Too late to do anything about it – the train had left the station twenty minutes ago. A bad omen, forgetting it like that. Not a good start to her new life.

3.

Even here, in the workhouse, where nothing ever changes
– where life is regulated by rules written a half century ago
– small miracles can happen. But only when you give up on
them entirely. She's on her way to the Infirmary, having just
left Teddy at the nursery, when Matron comes to her with some
news: she's to have the afternoon off – on a weekday! – to visit
her daughters at Red Hill. She'll be picked up at noon, taken to
the school and dropped off, and picked up again at four.

And how did this happen? What angel flapped his
wings and brought this about? Grudgingly, Matron says it's
due to "your missionary friend, Mr. Catlin". He's arranged
with the owner of a tannery to have her picked up in one of the
company's carts and transported to Red Hill. It won't be the
most elegant ride, sitting in the back of an open cart surrounded
by cow-hides and pig-skins, but she'll be provided with several
pelts to sit on and nothing to obstruct the view.

The rest of the morning passes in a kind of daze. Her
mind is only indirectly on her work … which doesn't go
unnoticed by the ward nurse.

"Are you well, Mrs. Taylor? You seem distracted."

"Yes. I'm sorry, I've had some news … I wasn't
thinking."

"That's how mistakes happen – when people aren't
thinking. Pay attention, please."

With the tolling of the twelve o'clock bell, she hurries
out of the sick ward, stopping only long enough at the nursery
to give Teddy a hug and ask them to give him a bottle. Then
she's out the door and down the path to the workhouse gate,
where the tanner and his cart are waiting. He greets her with a
smile and helps her up into the back of the cart, which is piled
high with freshly-tanned leather.

"There you go, Miss. Now you settle back and I'll
try not to make it too rough. Don't usually have nothin' but
pigskins back here so I'll keep in mind there's a lady on
board!"

It's a perfect day for a drive – brilliant sunshine, and
just a hint of a breeze. She feels almost giddy. This is how a

prisoner must feel on being released from gaol. The warmth of the sun on her cheeks. And the sounds! Church bells tolling the hour, costers calling out their wares, the din of cabs and trams and policemen's whistles and street-urchins. She wants to wave to everyone she passes: Look at me, I'm out, I'm free!

The silence of the workhouse has become so familiar she's forgotten the cacophony of the outside world. Everything is new and strange and wonderful: the stink of soot and horse manure fills her nostrils like some exotic plant. She sits ram-rod straight in the cart, head up, determined not to miss a single flower-seller or coster-barrow.

A trio of curly-haired Italian street musicians, all of them boys, perform on a street corner in direct opposition to another, older, group across the street.

A well-dressed quack, determined to appear respectable, waits outside a public house with his open case, ready to pounce on unsuspecting customers.

A few doors down, outside a butcher's shop, an argument between a man in a bloody apron who has to be the owner and an indignant customer has drawn a small crowd.

This is London. It's still here, noisy and oppressive and fascinating. It hasn't disappeared – she's the one who left, the city still stands.

The din abates somewhat by the time they reach the cemetery at Kensal Green. This is as far west along Harrow Road as she's been, and it was only once, ten years ago when she and Bill were courting. Maude was still keeping them company and Bill suggested an outing to the cemetery. She agreed, reluctantly. The visit to the British Museum was still a sore spot – a trip to a graveyard didn't sound much better.

But it was suprisingly pleasant: they took a pleasure boat up the canal from Little Venice and picnicked near the tomb of some royal person … the Duke of Sussex, she thinks. Afterwards Bill led them on a hunt to find some of the more notable graves: the actress Fanny Fitzwilliam and the man who owned Astley's Ampitheatre. He also showed them the tomb of Princess Sophia, Queen Victoria's aunt, leading Annie to remark, "So you don't mind royalty once they're dead, is that it?"

Maude said it surprised her to find she could enjoy a graveyard.

"You don't think about people being dead when you're here," she said. "It's just a nice place to visit."

Bill wanted to visit the catacombs beneath the Dissenters' Chapel but Annie refused.

"I can't," she said. "I wouldn't be able to breathe."

Perhaps remembering their visit to the museum, Bill let it go. Instead they they joined a group of children surrounding an Italian ice-man who'd parked his barrow at the entrance to the chapel.

"What will you have?" Bill said.

The sisters hesitated – Mama never trusted barrow-men, no matter what they were selling. But Bill insisted. Annie chose a lemon ice, Maude opted for a cream.

"What about you?" Annie said.

"I'd rather have a cigarette. Do you mind?"

It was good of him to ask permission before striking a match, but he needn't have done so. In the neighbourhoods of Notting Hill and Marylebone men – and women too – smoked wherever and whenever they liked. It was just one of the many things, Annie was learning, that distiguished the poorer classes from their "betters".

That trip was a decade ago … time has served to populate Harrow Road with bootmakers and confectioners and an endless number of factory warehouses. But the road is still narrow and hilly; it feels unfinished, somehow. It needs a tramway to connect it with the city.

By the time they arrive at the outskirts of Red Hill, there are fewer houses and no trams or buses of any kind. The only building of any size is the Union Workhouse, its stone entrance hidden from the main road by a mammoth, overgrown privet hedge. The driver drops her off at the porter's lodge and says he'll be back for her at three o'clock precisely.

The porter directs her to the school building, just north of the workhouse and set well back from the road. A young girl in a drab grey smock answers the bell, takes her name and tells her to wait in the hallway, she won't be long. Across the hall an open door reveals a classroom of small children, similarly dressed, being taught the parable of the lost sheep. Why must their uniforms always be so dreary? Is it a sin to allow these children anything pleasing to the eye?

The girl is back in a moment. You're expected, she says. If you go out into the play yard "Miss" will bring your daughters out to meet you.

The play yard – a depressing stretch of gravel unencumbered by anything relating to "play" – is deserted, but for a couple of starlings perched on a nearby rain barrel. The only place to sit is a long wooden bench located directly below an open window. From this spot she can hear the drone of pupils reciting a passage from the Bible: "*Let Israel rejoice in him that made him: let the children of Zion be joyful in their King.*" Annie doesn't have to see them – she can clearly picture them sitting in rows, hands folded on their desks, facing the front of the room. They sound very young. At one point the Master interrupts to tell Lazenby to get his finger out of his nose and then, a few minutes later, Smith is instructed to quit pinching his neighbour. Perhaps they aren't sitting quite so obediently after all.

A door at the far end of the play yard opens. A young woman in an immaculate white blouse and dark skirt approaches, followed by Edith and Vic. This is Miss Tannebaum, the Junior Teacher, and she is in almost every way the direct opposite of dear Miss Hodge. For one thing, her shirt has puffed sleeves – puffed! She has a cameo brooch pinned at her throat and her auburn hair is worn up in the newly-fashionable Pompadour style. She reaches out to take Annie's hand, saying how lovely it is to meet her, and Annie catches the scent of apple-blossom perfume.

Emmeline Hodge would have written her off as a "flibbertigibbet" – a worthless, gossiping female. But Miss Hodge would be wrong. It's obvious that Miss Tannebaum, for all her chatter, cares deeply for her charges. She begins by apologizing for Edith's hair: an outbreak of ringworm among the infants, she says.

"Such a shame to cut those lovely curls. But they'll grow back, won't they, Edith?"

"Yes, Miss."

The teacher arranges the girls on the bench on either side of their mother and offers to leave them on their own to have a visit. Annie, suddenly feeling shy, asks her to stay. Now that she's finally here, she's not sure what to say to them after all this time. Edith seems pale and enervated, a shade of the child she used to be.

"She seems very quiet," Annie says. "Is she eating?"

"She is now," the teacher says. "It's taken her some time to recover. And she's working hard to catch up with her schoolwork. Aren't you, Edith?"

"Yes, Miss."

Vicky, on the other hand, looks much better than she did the last time Annie saw her. Her hair is growing out from that awful haircut they gave her and she doesn't appear quite such a ragamuffin. When Annie asks her about school she says she's the best reader in her class and the school mistress confirms it.

"Victoria is an extremely pleasant child," she says, adding in a lower voice that she's really too good to be mingling with these unfortunate children.

"She speaks very fondly of her Gran. Could your mother not take her in, do you think?"

Annie promises to look into it, but without any real hope of it happening. She's heard nothing from Mama since that visit in June. She's sure her mother is waiting to hear if she'll be attending the wedding. She *can* go – she's been told that by the matron – but whether she *wants* to go is another question. Maude sent her a note, most likely at Mama's urging.

"Do come," she wrote. "It's just a small gathering of friends and family. There's no reason for you to feel uncomfortable. And Mother would like you to be there."

Mother! Since when did they call her that?

Remembering her gift for Edith, she retrieves the book from her bag.

"This is for you, Edith. I wanted to give it to you on your birthday but you and Vicky were gone by then so I kept it."

Miss Tannebaum is delighted. "*Little Dot*. How lovely, Edith. You'll like it, it's a very good story. Are you going to thank your Mama?"

"Thank you, Mama." Turning to her teacher, Edith says, "Will you read it to me, Miss?"

"Oh, I think perhaps your mother would like to read it to you. Wouldn't you like that?"

"No. I want *you* to read it to me."

The teacher smiles at Annie over Edith's head. "It happens this way sometimes, when they haven't seen their parents for a while. She's just a little shy."

Vicky wants to know if there's something for her, as well. "It was *my* birthday in April, in case you forgot."

She did forget – she should have brought something for Vic.

"Next time," she says. "I'll bring your present the next time I come, I promise."

Her daughter shrugs – obviously she has little faith in promises from her mother. Miss Tannenbaum changes the subject.

"I have to say, Mrs. Taylor, it's unusual to find children who can read and write as well as your daughters. I have twelve-year-olds who can barely print their names. I'm afraid we're not equipped to take them much further. I don't want to come off sounding like a blue-stocking, but I really believe the best thing this country could do to help the children of the poor is build better schools and *make* them attend. Don't you agree?"

Sitting out in the play yard, where not even a hoop or a swing gives it the right to be called that, Annie can see why the teacher would want something better for the children. A few yards of dirt enclosed by a high wall designed to keep anyone from looking out – or in. Her own schooling was not up to much, but it was never conducted in such bleak surroundings. The children who play here must be reminded every day how little they're thought of when the parish cannot even stump up enough for a skipping rope or a ball.

Still, you can see the school – or this particular teacher, at least – has made an impression on her daughters. The girls seem devoted to "Miss" and when asked to stand and recite something she's learned, Vicky doesn't hesitate. Clasping her hands together in prayerful fashion, she affects a dramatic, almost mournful stance. In a voice profoundly different from her own, she begins:

"She dwelt among the untrodden ways/Beside the springs of Dove,
Maid whom there were none to praise/And very few to love:
A violet by a mossy stone/Half hidden from the eye!
Fair as a star, when only one/Is shining in the sky.
She lived unknown, and few could know/When Lucy ceased to be;
But she is in her grave, and, oh,/The difference to me!"

At the end of the recital, Vicky performs a small, neat curtsy, and sits down on the bench.

Miss Tannenbaum turns to Annie with a smile. "Isn't she wonderful? She has such a presence, don't you think?"

At a loss for words, Annie nods.

"Wordsworth," the teacher says. "It's not on the curriculum."

"No, I'm sure it's not. Do you – do all your students learn verses like these?"

"Oh, no. As I said, Victoria is very advanced. None of the others have the *gravitas* for the Romantics. Now, Edith, it's your turn."

Steeling herself for another round of romantic verse, Annie is relieved when Edith recites a bit of nonsense about an owl and a pussycat.

"You must be a wonderful teacher, Miss Tannenbaum. My girls seem to have blossomed under your teaching."

Miss Tannenbaum thanks her and Vicky says *she's* going to be a teacher when she grows up. "Just like Miss."

"You are, are you? Well, good for you." Realizing it comes out sounding a little sour, which was not what she intended, Annie adds, "I think teaching is a wonderful profession. I might have been a teacher if my mother had let me."

"*You*? You couldn't teach – you don't *know* anything."

"Victoria!" The teacher is aghast. "Apologize immediately. You have been rude and disrespectful. I'm very disappointed in you."

"Sorry, Miss."

"You must apologize to your mother, not to me."

"Sorry, Mama."

The hour passes quickly. When it's time to say good-bye, the teacher thanks her for taking the time to come.

"Many don't, you know. I'm afraid some of the girls feel quite forgotten."

"I would have come sooner. And I'll come again, once I'm … free to do so."

Edith has gotten over her shyness and wants to know when that will be? Vicky, too, is looking at her – waiting for an answer. When will she be free to come and see them?

"I can't say exactly, but I can tell you this – I'm applying to train as a nurse. A friend has referred me to the Nightingale Home at St. Thomas' Hospital."

"Really?" This from Vic, skeptical as always.

"That's wonderful," the teacher says. "We are in such need of good, well-trained nurses. I do wish you all the best of luck. Girls, you may kiss your Mama."

Dutifully, they do so, then turn to follow the teacher back into the building. At the last minute, Vic comes running back to give her a hug.

"I'm glad you came, Mama. I'm glad you're going to be a nurse."

"Me too, Vicky. I'll see you soon, I promise."

Would she have said it if it weren't for Vic, looking at her like that – daring her to actually *do* something? But she *has* said it and now that she has it seems so sensible – so absolutely right – she can't imagine why she hesitated. Mr. Catlin would say she has found her calling. And he'd be right.

4.

At Carnforth they were told the train to Furness was running late, leaving at 6:10 instead of 5:40 and arriving at Barrow at 7:40. Would Bill know that? The telegraph office was open – she could send him a message but there was little point as he wouldn't receive it in time. The refreshment room was shut and the waiting room door was locked, despite a notice declaring it open from 8 a.m. till 9 p.m. weekdays. Her fellow travelers were thoroughly disgruntled by the delay, although, as one said and they all agreed, it was the way it was with the service in these parts: the time-table "bain't worth the paper it be writ on".

Being the only woman in the group, she felt shy about taking part in the conversation. She left her suitcase in the care of the guard and walked along the platform to the far end, away from the others.

The sky was overcast and even the stars were hidden from view. The night seemed to permeate everything – it was as though the world had fallen into a great dark pit. The only light came from the distant blast furnaces, their chimneys spewing flames into the western sky. They called this the Black Country and it was well-named. They'd been making iron here since the days of the Romans – she remembered that from school, although why she should remember that and so little else she couldn't say. Something Miss Hodge taught them about the Scots invading during the reign of Edward II and carrying off all the manufactured iron they could find, preferring it to other forms of plunder.

Henderson!

Yes, Miss!

Who were the invaders?

The Scots, Miss.

And what did they plunder?

Iron, Miss. All that they could carry.

Standing here at the edge of civilization, she feared what might lie beyond the horizon. She longed to go back, to return to London, throw herself on the mercy of whoever would take her in. Noisy, filthy, crowded London with its coal-fires and gas lamps, its streets surging with pick-pockets and prostitutes, its gutters overflowing with dirt and debris. Cab drivers and street sellers, paper boys calling out the news, dustmen's carts rattling the cobblestones, shoeblacks and penny-ice men and drunks reeling home at every hour of the morning.

Strawberries all ripe all ripe … Mussels a penny a quart … Repent! Repent! The day of reckoning is nigh … Salmon alive sixpence a pound …That was *her* London – not the clubs and supper-houses of Covent Garden and the Haymarket – not the fashionable promenades of Mayfair and Hyde Park – not the quaint, old-fashioned houses of Cheyne Walk or the stately homes of St. James. She'd never seen Buckingham Palace, visited the Tower of London or sat on the steps of St. Paul's Cathedral – never sailed past Traitor's Gate or been inside Westminster Abbey. In twenty years she'd done none of the things a visitor to the city might do in a week. And yet she knew it through and through.

Her London was small and evil-smelling and dirty, and at that moment it seemed to her a kind of Paradise. She would give the world to be there rather than where she was, alone and pregnant in the middle of nowhere.

She could go back. Mama would take her in. She wouldn't be happy about it but she would. She was a realist, after all. She knew that young women sometimes found themselves with babies on the way and no husband – she would make the best of a bad situation. She always had.

Out of the darkness the screech of a whistle announced the approach of the train.

"Miss?"

The guard has come down the platform to fetch her, suitcase in hand.

"The train to Furness, Miss. You'll wanting to get on."

"Yes, of course. Thank you."

"All aboard – all aboard now."

5.

> *When I am dead, my dearest, Sing no sad songs for me;*
> *Plant thou no roses at my head, Nor shady cypress tree:*
> *Be the green grass above me With showers and dew drops wet;*
> *And if thou wilt, remember, And if thou wilt, forget.*

Christina Georgina Rossetti (1862)

Biddie lapsed into a coma and was transferred to the Lock Hospital on Harrow Road. She died a few days later. They notified her family, but no one came to claim her so she was given a pauper's burial in the large communal cemetery at Woking. There were no mourners present.

They learn this a week after the burial, when it's too late for any of them to be present, if they wanted to do so. In any case, the distance from London to Woking and the cost of taking a train to get there make it impossible to attend.

That day she asks permission to be excused to use the facilities. She leaves the sick ward and walks down the corridor to the stairs that lead down to the basement. There's a room, next to the Laundry, where they keep discarded clothes and bits of cloth that might be useful for cleaning rags and such. It takes a little digging but she eventually finds what she's looking for: a scrap of black crape about eighteen inches long and a foot wide.

Very carefully, she tears off a strip and returns the rest to the box. She unties the top of her smock, unbuttons her dress and wraps the band around her bare upper arm, knotting it firmly against her skin. She wants to be able to feel it – she wants to know it's there, even if no one else does.

Satisfied that it's in place, she buttons up her dress, re-ties her smock, and goes back to work.

Manufactured by Amazon.ca
Acheson, AB

11195067R00142